C is for Courting

Also by Shelley Shepard Gray

The Amish ABCs series

A Is for Amish

B Is for Bonnet

C Is for Courting

The Amish of Apple Creek series

An Amish Cinderella

Once Upon a Buggy

Happily Ever Amish

C is for Courting

Shelley Shepard Gray

KENSINGTON
PUBLISHING CORP.
kensingtonbooks.com

KENSINGTON BOOKS are published by

Kensington Publishing Corp.
900 Third Ave.
New York, NY 10022

All Kensington titles, imprints, and distributed lines are available at special quantity discounts for bulk purchases for sales promotion, premiums, fundraising, educational, or institutional use. Special book excerpts or customized printings can also be created to fit specific needs. For details, write or phone the office of the Kensington Special Sales Manager, Attn. Special Sales Department, Kensington Publishing Corp., 900 Third Avenue, New York, NY 10022. Phone: 1-800-221-2647.

Library of Congress Card Catalogue Number: 2025937904

KENSINGTON and the K with book logo Reg. US Pat. & TM. Off.

ISBN: 978-1-4967-4890-4
First Kensington Hardcover Edition: November 2025

ISBN: 978-1-4967-4891-1 (trade)

ISBN: 978-1-4967-4892-8 (ebook)

10 9 8 7 6 5 4 3 2 1

Printed in the United States of America

The authorized representative in the EU for product safety and compliance is eucomply OU, Parnu mnt 139b-14, Apt 123
Tallinn, Berlin 11317, hello@eucompliancepartner.com

For August and Sloane

You belong to God's family.
—Ephesians 2:19

*Things turn out the best for those who make the best
of the way things turn out.*
—Amish proverb

CHAPTER 1

October 18
Walden, Ohio

The weather was miserable, especially for the middle of October. Wrapping her grandmother's thick black cloak around her more tightly, Beth Schrock carefully made her way over to Patti Coblentz's house. The first time she'd visited, the weather had been warm, the well-worn path leading from the Schrocks' old barn to the neatly tended path in front of Patti's door was easy to find, and Beth had nothing but time on her hands.

Today, with the wind blowing specks of sleet onto her face, was another story. She couldn't wait to get to her destination and then return to her grandparents' farm next door.

That wasn't going to happen very quickly, however. Her arms were filled with loaves of bread, and her body felt heavy and sluggish.

She was uncomfortable, cold, and worried about her future. She was also feeling guilty because her grandmother was getting over a cold and still felt a little under the weather and she hadn't done half the things she'd promised she would. Which was why she was walking to Patti's house in the rain and sleet instead of watching it from the other side of the living room window.

As another blast of wind threatened to turn her eyelashes into mini-icicles, she grimaced. "Are you happy now, Beth?" she chided herself. "Was this what you dreamed about when you imagined leaving your 'real' life behind?"

Of course, her subconscious didn't have an answer for that, and thank goodness.

Of course, that wasn't a surprise, either. She didn't seem to ever have a clue about how to live her life. Not anymore.

Almost two years ago, when she'd imagined living Amish on her grandparents' farm, she had thought all her troubles would miraculously fade away. She'd been such a fool.

Today, it felt like every one of her troubles had doubled in size, but she had less of an idea about how she was ever going to solve them. What had happened to her? How could she have gone from being the most levelheaded of her family to being pregnant, unwed, and unsettled?

Patti's door opened just as Beth reached the front steps.

"Beth, what in the world are you doing here?" Patti asked as she stepped out to lend a hand.

She held up two mittened hands. "Obviously, I'm delivering Mommi's bread."

But instead of looking pleased, Patti's scowl deepened. "I canna believe you!" she scolded as she reached for her arm. "You should not be outside. It's sleeting."

"I know. I didn't melt, though." She smirked, hoping to make Patti smile.

She did not.

After allowing Patti to pull the loaves of bread out of her arms, she attempted to defend herself. "I didn't think it was that bad out when I started."

"Did you also not think to look out the window?" Patti asked as they climbed the three steps.

Since she'd already realized that much of her life didn't make sense, she responded with a barb of her own. "Ouch. That's kind of harsh."

Immediately, Patti looked shamefaced as they entered her warm house. "You're right. I'm sorry." Closing the door behind them, she continued. "I just hate the thought of you slipping and falling."

She would hate that, too. "I was careful," she said, as she toed off her boots and pulled off her mittens.

Patti collected all of it and set them on the welcome mat. "Come into the living room. I've got a fire going. We'll take off your cloak in there. It needs to dry before you put it on again. Then you can stand in front of the flames and warm up while I get you some tea."

Hot tea sounded wonderful, but making Patti fuss over her like that was not. "I came over to give you bread, not make more work for you."

"Making tea isn't work."

"Okay, but I can just turn around. You don't have to go to the trouble."

"You are not going to do anything but come in here. Now, don't worry about the tea. I know some of it is loaded with caffeine, but not this one. I made sure to buy some decaf last time I went shopping."

Beth knew Patti well enough to realize that continuing to argue wouldn't make either of them happy. Patti would simply dig in her heels. *"Danke."*

"Of course, dear." She clapped her hands together. "Now, you get warm, then take a seat. Put your feet up and rest a bit, okay."

"Okay."

"Gut. I'll be back in a jiffy."

And with that, Patti hurried to the kitchen. Realizing that

she had no choice but to take her new neighbor's advice, she stood directly in front of the fireplace and held out her hands. And then, before she could stop herself, she moaned in contentment. The heat coming off the grate felt heavenly. Continuing to face the fire, she called out over her shoulder, "I'm so glad you had a fire going. It feels heavenly."

"I thought the same thing when I sat down in front of it with my devotional early this morning. Stormy days are for inside reflection, ain't so?"

"Yes." Much better than giving herself a hard time while walking through the sleet.

"Now, don't even think about leaving until you have a rest and warm up."

"I'll stay for a few, but please don't worry. I'll be fine. It's a short walk." Unhooking the cloak, she shook the few drops of precipitation that clung to the fine wool before tossing it on the magazine holder on the ground. She'd hang the garment up properly as soon as she could feel her hands.

"Would you like some strudel with your tea? It's cherry."

"Thanks, but I better not. The doctor already told me that I shouldn't be gaining so much weight so fast." Looking down, she rubbed a protective hand across her belly. Within the last two weeks, she'd gone from looking a little chubby to definitely having a baby bump. "Honestly, it's probably good that I'm walking every day, even in bad weather."

"You aren't walking back," Patti called out from the kitchen. "Junior can drive you. Right, Junior?"

Wait. What? They weren't alone?

"Of course," a deep, masculine voice replied from the hallway. "I don't mind at all. Besides, we finished our work quickly today. I've got more than a little bit of extra time."

"*Danke*, Junior. Please, go into the living room and join my friend Beth."

Feeling her cheeks heat, this time having nothing to do with the temperature of the fireplace and everything to do with pure embarrassment, Beth turned to face the new-comer. Junior-whoever-he-was.

The man walking into the room was a complete surprise. Looking at least five years older than her own age, Junior looked to be in his midthirties. That wasn't the shock. It was his looks. The man was so handsome: clean-shaven, clear hazel eyes, and thick blond hair. He also had muscles on top of muscles. Honestly, he was massive. He kind of looked like a Viking in one of her favorite television series.

What he didn't look like was a "Junior."

She also couldn't figure out why he was sitting with a con-tented expression in Patti's kitchen. She'd thought Patti and her brother Martin had something special between them.

When she realized he was taking in everything about her as well, she found her cheeks heating. Nothing like being a twenty-eight-year-old, unwed, un-Amish mother dressed almost-Amishy to give off a first impression.

A bad first impression.

Just as quickly, Beth shook off those feelings of discom-fort. First of all, her personal life was none of his concern. Secondly, she might be contemplating a life in Walden, but that didn't mean she still wasn't the same woman she'd al-ways been. A little too assertive, and tough enough to stand on her own two feet.

"Hi," she said.

He got to his feet. "Hiya. You must be Beth Schrock. I'm John Lambright, but everyone calls me Junior."

If she'd been at work, she'd step forward and hold out her hand. Since she was in Patti's kitchen, she stuffed her hands in her dress's pockets. "It's nice to meet you."

"Junior is one of my bookkeeping clients," Patti said as she carefully slid a healthy portion of strudel on a plate. "Beth here is living with her grandparents next door."

"It's nice to meet you," he said with a slight nod. "I've heard a lot about you and your family."

"Oh?" She glanced at Patti.

"Don't worry, Beth. It weren't nothing bad. Just normal news."

"I see." Though, she kind of didn't.

"Pretty much everyone in the area has been following the adventures of you and your siblings," Junior said with a smile. "What with your sister marrying a preacher and your brother marrying Treva Kramer soon after."

"Yes, I can imagine there would be talk."

"Please sit down, Beth," Patti said with a kind look. "You need to get off your feet for a spell."

And . . . there was the reminder of her pregnancy. Out there in the open. "I'm all right." Suddenly noticing the ledgers and pair of manila folders open on the other end of the dining room table, she mentally groaned.

Once again, Beth realized she had a lot to learn about living Amish—and disregarding stereotypes. Just because Patti was Amish didn't mean she did nothing but cook, clean, quilt, and wait for visitors to come knocking on her door. She was a busy woman with her own business.

"Patti, this pastry looks so good. I'll enjoy it while you two finish your meeting."

"Are you sure you don't mind? I don't want to be rude, but Junior and I do have a few more things to discuss."

"Would you like me to go into the kitchen? It might give you some more privacy."

Patti turned to Junior. "What would make you feel most comfortable?"

"There's nothing too secretive about taxes or savings plans. Beth can stay put. I don't mind finishing our work here."

"Very well." After shooting a quick look at Beth, Patti sat down at the head of the table, put on reading glasses, and picked up a pencil. "Here's where I think we could make some changes."

After reading her notes, he asked, "What about when the quarterlies are due?"

Patti pointed to an open calendar. "We could either agree to meet here or I could give you a call and remind you to mail that check."

"You wouldn't mind?"

"Of course not. It's my job."

Beth tucked her head as she pretended not to notice how deep Junior's voice was. It sounded a little husky, and like it was touched with sandpaper. She liked it.

And then there was his grin. That smile tugged at her insides. Made her think about things she didn't want to think about. Such as Kiran and the night she couldn't wait to forget.

Or the way her brother Martin's eyes always sought out Patti when she was near. How his yearning for her was almost palpable. And how she, herself, had never felt anything close to that.

You're being a fool, she reminded herself. Junior Lambright was at Patti's house for work. She'd come over uninvited.

She was eating cherry strudel while they worked. Not only did that feel rude, but she was pretty sure that staring at the guy while he talked about his personal finances was rude, too.

So how come she kept stealing glances at him?

Shouldn't a man's smile be the last thing on earth she should be thinking about? Hadn't the last two months taught her anything?

Stabbing a wayward cherry on her plate, she frowned.

"Ah, Beth? Beth?"

She started. Lifted her head. "Yes?"

"Are you all right?"

"Of course. Why?"

"You were stabbing that pastry like it had personally offended you."

Beth dropped her fork. "Sorry about that."

Patti continued to look concerned. "Does it not taste good to you?"

"It tastes fine, Beth," Junior blurted.

"*Nee.* I mean, um, I've heard that sometimes foods taste different when one . . ." Obviously embarrassed, she cut herself off.

She might wish she had done things differently in her life, but Beth knew she was long past the point of pretending that her pregnancy didn't exist. "When one is pregnant?"

"*Jah.*"

"I suppose that might be true, but my attitude has nothing to do with the baby." Standing up, she collected her plate and undrunk tea. "I don't think I'm the best company today. I'm sorry to not have your tea, but I think it's best if I head on home."

Patti's brown eyes filled with worry. "But your cloak is still wet and it's still raining."

"I'll be fine. Our houses are close."

Junior's chair scraped against Patti's wooden floor, no doubt scuffing it. "I'll take you."

"There's no need."

"I think differently." His voice was firm. It was obvious he wasn't going to accept her pushing him away. Or, perhaps, burdening Patti.

There was only one way to respond. With as much grace as she could muster. "Thank you."

Ten minutes later, she had her grandmother's cloak back on and was sitting next to Junior in his buggy. His horse was a sturdy gelding named Arthur, of all things. He'd glanced at Beth when Junior had helped her into the buggy and then seemed to stomp a hoof. She wondered if he was anxious to go or wasn't real pleased to have yet another person to cart around.

"Ready?" he asked.

"Sure."

"All right, then." He clicked. Arthur, obviously eager to be on his way, pulled the buggy forward with a lurch and then off they went.

Needing to break the silence, she said, "How long has Patti been your bookkeeper?"

"Not long."

"My brother said she's very good at accounting."

"Is he a client, too?"

"No, he's more of a friend to her." She bit her bottom lip so she wouldn't add that Martin was a special friend.

"How are you settling in at your grandparents?"

"Well enough."

"That's *gut*."

"I think so, too."

Still looking straight in front of him, he blurted, "What about your man?"

Her man? "Who might that be?" she asked sarcastically. Junior might be giving her a ride home, but her personal business wasn't his.

"The father of your unborn baby."

Well, she supposed one couldn't get much more specific than that. But did she appreciate the question? No. No, she did not. Though it was tempting to say that the father was none of his business, Beth knew that he was going to be one of many folks who would either ask outright or reach out to someone in her family for more information. Her grandparents did not deserve that. "I don't have a man. This baby is a product of a foolish night."

"Wow. That must have been some night."

She was about to be offended . . . until she saw the hint of a smile on his lips. "Are you joking?"

"I am."

Beth didn't know whether she should be mad or not. De-

ciding that keeping her mouth shut was the better idea, she
grunted.

"Are you upset? I'm sorry. I suppose my joke was in poor
taste." Before she could respond, he added, "It's just that my
cousin and her husband had to try for months for their first
baby. Here, you got pregnant in one night." Twin splotches
of color appeared on his cheeks. "And, I've just become very
aware that my teasing was not only rude, but I've gone on
about it far too long. I'm sorry."

"No . . . I mean, it's okay." She shook her head, not sure
what to say but needing to say something. "I . . . well, this
pregnancy caught me off guard, too. And the guy I was with."

About a dozen thoughts seemed to roll around in his head,
but he remained silent.

And then he was setting the parking brake. "Stay put. I'll
come around and help you down."

"I can get myself out."

"I'd prefer to help you." Those eyes that seemed to see far
too much settled on her. "If you wouldn't mind, that is."

Beth didn't reply. She also didn't move until he opened
the buggy's door and held out a hand. Accepting his help,
she pretended she didn't notice the way his left hand curved
around her waist and his right hand's fingers were slightly
rough. Or that he smelled faintly of oranges, like he'd eaten
one that morning.

"Thank you for the ride," she said.

"Anytime." Glancing behind her, he nodded his head
before climbing into the buggy, clicking the reins, and driving off.

Wondering who he'd seen, she turned to see Martin in the
doorway.

Immediately, her heart lifted. Her brother was here. Now,
at the very least, she wouldn't feel quite so alone and out of
place.

CHAPTER 2

Martin felt guilty for not being all that happy to see his sister walk through the door. No, that wasn't quite right. He did want to see Beth. He wanted to see his grandparents, too.

All of them had a lot of things to catch up about. But ever since he'd arrived in Walden an hour ago, he'd been stuck doing everything but what he wanted to do, which was see Patti.

He really missed Patti.

Though they'd talked on the phone almost every night, it wasn't the same. He wanted to see her smile, to watch the way her nose wrinkled when she was mentioning something distasteful or see how her expression lit up when she laughed.

He'd been starting to think that he lived for those moments when she laughed. The tight control she had on her emotions seemed to release in a rush whenever she burst into laughter. Happiness would infuse every feature. The sight never failed to lift his spirits.

Or maybe it was just the sight of her that did.

Yeah, it had been way too long since he'd seen Patti.

But it looked like their reunion was going to have to wait a little bit longer.

"Martin!" Beth called out as she rushed toward him after pulling off her cloak.

He took advantage of that second to look her over. Though she now sported a definite baby bump, the rest of her looked smaller. That seemed odd. Had she been sick?

Grasping her arms, he pulled her close. "Hey, Bethy. It's good to see you."

"Same. I've missed you."

Realizing her cheeks were cold and damp, he said, "Where've you been?"

"Over at Patti's."

"Why?" he asked, hoping that he didn't sound envious. "Just to pay her a visit?"

"Yes, and to give her some loaves of bread."

"She walked over there," Mommi said as she joined them in the living room. "Though exercise is good for her, I thought she should've worn a better hat."

Focusing on his sister again, he said, "It's sleeting outside. The ground is no doubt slick. You could have slipped and fallen."

"I didn't."

"Still, you shouldn't have walked."

"I needed to get out of here, and it was no big deal. I was fine. Plus, a friend of Patti's gave me a ride home in his buggy. I only walked there, not back."

His? Jealousy, his unwelcome new best friend, roared to life. "Patti had a man over?"

"She did, but he was a client, not a suitor. Settle down."

"I'm settled." And he was, kind of. "What's his story? Is he married?" Ignoring the amused glances his sister and grandmother were exchanging, he added, "Was he English or Amish? And how old was he?"

"He was Amish. He drove a buggy, remember? As far as his status and age, I'm not sure about either. If I had to guess, I'd say he wasn't married and is older than Patti."

"By how much?"

"Oh, for heaven's sakes!" Mommi exclaimed. "Bethy, how about you tell me this man's name and I'll fill in your *bruder*."

"Junior Lambright," Beth replied. "Do you know him?"

Their grandmother leaned back with a pleased expression. "Ah, to be sure. He's a nice man. A good one."

"I thought the same thing," Beth commented. "I mean, at first I thought it was strange that he was named Junior, but it suits him."

"I reckon it does. But with a name like John, it's better that he goes by Junior, ain't so?" Eyes sparkling, she added, "Some days, it feels like every fifth man I meet is named John."

"Just like there are lots of Katies and Marys around," Beth mused.

"*Jah*. Just like."

Martin couldn't care less about popular Amish names, though he figured the women had a point. A lot of folks in Walden had the same last names and popular Bible names. It could get confusing from time to time. He cleared his throat. "Circling back to Junior. Are you sure he was at Patti's because he was a client?"

Beth's eyes lit up in a knowing way. "Yes, brother."

Little by little, Martin relaxed. Picturing a man in his late fifties or sixties, he added, "That's good for Patti. Sometimes older men don't want to trust young women to manage their books."

"I sat at the table while they finished up their work. Junior seemed to trust her just fine."

"Good. That's good." Feeling more comfortable about

Patti's client, he added, "Hopefully he got home safely in the bad weather."

Mommi tilted her head to one side. "You're acting as if he's a doddering old man. That ain't the case."

"Of course not, Mommi," Martin said quickly. He didn't want her to think he considered her and Dawdi to be anywhere near doddering.

Beth folded her arms over her chest. "You sure seem to have a lot to say about someone you've never met. Why all the questions, Martin?"

"No reason. I was just curious." And jealous. Which didn't make a bit of sense, given the fact that Patti had a successful business and she probably had quite a few clients. And . . . he'd yet to figure himself out, so of course she had every right to date other people.

Mommi studied him for a long moment before she rearranged two books that were on the coffee table. "Well, if you ever get the chance to get to know Junior better, you should do it. He's a nice young man with a bright future ahead of him. He started his own business from scratch, you know."

"What kind of business is that?"

"He makes candles."

"Candles?" Beth asked. "Really?"

"Oh, *jah*. Junior is a candlemaker. They're real nice ones. They smell *gut*, too."

"Good for him," Martin murmured. And, good for *him*, too. He figured every person had the right to choose what they wanted to do for a living, but obviously Junior wasn't doing that great if the best he could do was make candles in his kitchen. Then, there was the fact that he couldn't even manage his own books. "That's kind of Patti to give him a helping hand."

"*Nee*, he pays for her work."

"I'm sure he pays what he can." Sure, he sounded full of himself and probably not a little bit stuck-up, but he was relieved that Junior, the candle-making Amish guy, was no threat to him. Martin made a great living. He could take care of Patti very well. If she ever chose him to be her guy, he'd make sure she had every comfort she might want.

"How long are you here for, Martin?" Beth asked.

"Through the weekend. I want to spend time with all of you." And Patti.

"Oh, good," she replied, looking visibly relieved. "I was worried you were just coming down for the day."

"No. I want to see Kelsey and Richard and Jonny and Treva and Mommi and Dawdi and you, of course." And Patti . . . ASAP.

"That's a lot of people." Beth smiled. "We should all meet at the Trailside Café. Then you won't be running all over town."

"That would be great."

"Or, we could have everyone here, Beth," Mommi offered. "That way Treva wouldn't feel obligated to serve everyone *kaffi*. What do you think?"

"If everyone brings something, I think it will be perfect. I don't want you and me to have to make all the snacks. Looking at their grandmother's kitchen phone, Beth said, "I'll reach out to Treva and Kelsey now. Say, for ten a.m. on Sunday?"

"There's no church, so that works for me." Mommi turned to Martin. "Now that that's settled, let's take care of you, child. Are you hungry? If so, I can heat you up some potato soup. We have some left over from last night."

"Thanks, but I've got something to do first," he said, as he grabbed his coat and pulled it on. "I'll be back in a little while."

"Take your time. We'll be here," Mommi said.

She wasn't asking where he was going.

Neither was Bethy.

Surprised by their silence, Martin paused, but didn't trust himself to look at either Beth or his grandmother. If he did, he was afraid that he'd see exactly what they were thinking on their faces.

And he had no idea how he was going to explain his need to see Patti right that minute.

He walked out the door and quickened his step. In less than ten minutes he'd be seeing her. In person. He couldn't wait.

Patti knew she'd spent far too long cleaning up the kitchen and dining room after Beth and Junior left, but she couldn't help herself. Her house was too quiet, and the only activity she had left in her day was tending to the chickens. Since the henhouse was clean, that chore wouldn't take long at all. After that, she'd have to find something else to occupy her brain. Perhaps she could finish the somewhat boring book she'd gotten at the library. Or work.

Neither was appealing.

Though the rain and sleet had finally stopped, it was still cold out. The skies were gray. None of those things made her feel like doing laundry or even mending.

She also refused to do her new secret favorite hobby, which was count down the hours until Martin called. She wasn't proud of this new activity, especially since she had a very good feeling that his calls were going to end sooner than later. They were too different, and she was also very sure that he was not going to become baptized in her faith, after all. It was disappointing, but she knew that the Lord was in charge of their future and Martin's faith. If He didn't think that Martin should become Amish, then that was what Martin needed to do.

She would just have to find a way to accept it. And she

would. She just didn't know if she was going to be able to re-
cover from the disappointment.

When she heard the knocking on the front door, she let
out a sigh of relief. She had another visitor. Maybe Kelsey
was stopping by or even Sylvia.

Throwing open the door, she started to smile. Then froze,
because it felt as if she'd been struck by lightning. She was
that shocked. "Martin."

His blue eyes seemed to scan her body before meeting her
gaze. Only then did he slowly begin to smile. "Patti. You
look beautiful."

If there was ever a man who could make her heart beat
double time all while making her mouth go dry, it was Martin Schrock. What was even more amazing was that she
knew he wasn't just saying the words. He really did find her
to be pretty. Even with the port-wine stain that marked her
neck and had made her the focus of jokes and teasing and
even suspicion all her life.

"Martin, the things you say."

"May I come in?"

Only then did she realize that she'd been letting in the
cold and making the poor man stand there in the freezing
weather. "I'm sorry, of course." She stepped back so he could
come inside.

After he shut the door, he chuckled softly.

"What?"

"Nothing. Only that you look so surprised to see me."

"That's because I am. Last night when we talked, you gave
no indication that I'd be seeing you today." If she'd known,
she would have put on a newer dress. Or maybe even made
snickerdoodles, his favorite cookie.

Or maybe she wouldn't be acting so jumpy and skittish.

"I didn't tell you for a reason."

"What is that?"

As a smile played on his lips, he unbuttoned his coat and hung it on one of the hooks by the door. "Because . . . I didn't know I was coming down."

"This is a spur-of-the-moment thing?"

"Very much so. One moment I was thinking about ordering a pizza for supper, and the next I was packing a bag and tossing it in my car."

That was very much unlike Martin. He was a steady sort of man. Beginning to worry, her mind began to toss out possibilities. "What happened? Is someone sick? Has your grandmother's cold taken a turn for the worse? Is she worse than I thought?"

"She's fine." Stepping closer, he lowered his voice. "It's more of an I-can't-wait-to-see-Patti-in-person thing."

She blinked. And then stared at him like a lovestruck fool. "Martin."

"Now, are you going to hug me hello? It's been weeks since I've been to Walden."

"Um . . ." Truth be told, she was eager to give him a hug. She was eager to chat with him, hug him, hold his hand . . . kiss him sweetly.

But she had no idea how to make the first move. Not with Martin still staring at her with a mixture of amusement and affection in his eyes. What was she supposed to do now, just throw herself into his arms?

"You make me smile, Patti." Reaching for her hand, he curved his own around it and tugged. "Come here."

And then, there she was, wrapped in his warm arms. Her face pressed against his shoulder. Surrounded by his scent.

It was almost too perfect a moment.

It was also something she probably shouldn't be doing. She'd missed him so much that she didn't want to leave the embrace. Honestly, if she was just a little bit braver, she would do what she wanted to do and raise her head, gaze into his eyes, and part her lips.

Giving him an open invitation to kiss her again. For the first time in months.

Although it was wrong to want such things. After all, they were unmarried and there wasn't a chaperone in sight.

She couldn't care less.

CHAPTER 3

Junior's father had been one of the smartest people he'd ever known. Though he, like most Amish, had finished his formal education in the eighth grade, he'd continued to be a lifelong learner. His father could chat knowledgeably about most everything. He'd been a voracious reader and one of their library's best patrons. In addition, his *daed* had possessed a common sense that surpassed most everyone else's.

That wasn't just Junior's opinion, either. People all over Walden used to ask his father's opinion on approaching storms, the political climate, and on business plans. Even their bishop would stop by from time to time to ask Levi Lambright for his thoughts on a problem he was wrestling with.

In addition, his father had been kind and generous. Junior didn't know of a better man to dispense advice or offer suggestions whenever he had a problem. Unfortunately, both of his parents had gone to heaven many years ago.

That was why he'd decided to call on his Aunt Rhoda that afternoon. He needed information without a well-meaning, informative lecture. She was mighty skilled at that . . . and so different than her brother, his father. If Levi Lambright had a fault, it was that he'd been unable to dispense advice in a quick way.

After unhitching Arthur and leading him into the fenced field by the barn so he could graze for a spell, Junior opened his aunt and uncle's back door after a brief knock.

"Hiya, Rhoda. It's me!" he called out.

When there was no answer, Junior frowned. It was quiet in the mudroom and the kitchen, too. After spying his aunt's newest kitten playing alone in living room, he headed down to the basement. "Aunt Rhoda? Hello?"

Nothing.

Heading back upstairs, he began to get worried. All sorts of worst-case scenarios entered his head. Maybe she was sick and had fallen and hit her head? Or she was deathly ill and in bed?

"Rhoda?" he called out. "Aunt Rhoda, are ya here?" Still not hearing a word, he ventured into the living room and the three-season room in the back of the house before climbing stairs to the second floor.

When he heard the comforting sounds of her treadle sewing machine, he felt like sagging against the wall in relief. Instead of doing that, he marched into his aunt's favorite spot in the house—his old bedroom, which was now her sewing room.

"Hiya, Junior," she called out in a sunny voice.

"Aunt Rhoda, didn't you hear me calling for you?"

She didn't stop her feet. "I did."

"Well, why didn't you answer me? I was starting to get worried about you."

"Sorry. Hold on, though."

He took a seat on the edge of his old twin bed and watched her finish a seam on what looked like a tablecloth.

After another four minutes passed, she turned to him with

a bright smile. "At last, the tablecloth I've been working on for the mudsale is done." Holding up the pale-pink fabric with embroidered daisies on the edge, she said, "What do you think?"

He was still a little irritated that she'd made him worry for no reason. Of course, she would say that was his problem and not hers. "I think it's pretty, but I'm more concerned with how you are doing."

"Me?" She carefully folded the finished product. "I'm fine, dear. Better than fine, since you've decided to pay your old aunt a visit."

"Don't act as if I never come over. I just saw you on Sunday." He checked in with her often, too. Unlike his brother, Sam, who seemed to have forgotten that he still had a pair of relatives who loved him dearly.

"That was days ago." Standing up, she added, "You rarely step away from your candle shop during the week, ain't so?"

"That's true. I am there a lot." When she cast him a knowing look, he laughed. "I guess you aren't the only person in the family who gets so preoccupied with a project that they forget about other things."

"I am sorry for worrying you, Son. More importantly, I'm mighty pleased to see ya." She reached out to give him a hug.

"Do you have time to talk?" he asked after they parted.

"For you? Always. Are you hungry?"

"*Nee.*"

"Are you sure?" She glanced at the clock on the wall. "It's heading toward suppertime."

He wanted advice in a timely manner. If she started getting out dishes, he'd be there for another hour. "A cup of *kaffi* would do me fine for now. I really only wanted to talk for a bit before I headed on home."

A little bit of her smile faded. "All right, then. Let's go downstairs and visit."

Following her down the hall toward the stairs, he said, "I saw your new kitten."

"Did you? She's a sweetheart, ain't so?"

"Indeed. Are you going to name her?" Rhoda loved her cats, but she didn't seem to like to name them. She only ever called each one "cat" or "sweetheart." He'd always found it maddening.

"Maybe. I haven't decided yet." She brightened. "Sit down and I'll bring you a cup of *kaffi* and a couple of cookies."

He sat, thinking that some habits were so ingrained in their history that deviating from them wasn't an option. This was one of those moments.

"Where's Uncle Eli?" he asked as he watched her fill the percolator on the gas range.

"I'm not sure. He mentioned something about visiting the new bicycle shop on the trail."

"Jonny Schrock's?"

She paused with her hand literally in the cookie jar. "Maybe?"

"Jonny Schrock sells the electric bicycles. Is Eli interested in them?"

She chuckled as she arranged the cookies on a plate. "Your uncle is interested in most everything."

While that was true, Junior felt obligated to give his opinion on the matter. "Uncle Eli is a little old to tackle a new-fangled bike."

"I agree, though I don't believe he aims to get one. Most likely Eli wanted to learn more about 'em." She winked. "Let's hope and pray that Jonny has time to answer all his questions."

"I will. Uncle Eli's curiosity seems to know no bounds."

"Perhaps. Though I'm sure Jonny will be able to handle him well." She opened a cabinet and pulled out a pair of cups.

"If your uncle was here right now, he'd say you need to have more faith in him."

"I have lots of faith in Eli. I just don't want him to decide to try out an electric bike. It's his reflexes that I'm not too sure about," he joked.

When Rhoda approached the table, she held a tray filled with two cups of coffee, the plate of cookies, and a dish of peanuts. "Here you are."

"This is a feast."

"Hardly that," she scoffed, though her cheeks were pink. "Now, enough of this small talk. What information are you looking for?"

"Information about Elizabeth Schrock."

"Elizabeth?" She frowned. "That name . . . oh, do you mean Beth?"

"*Jah.*"

"I see." Looking lost in thought, she remained quiet for a moment. Then she added, "Beth is Sylvia and Josiah Schrock's granddaughter. One of them. They have two granddaughters."

"I know that."

"You do? Well, let's see. Beth has an older *bruder* named Martin and a younger sister named Kelsey. Kelsey married Richard Miller and recently had a baby girl. He's a preacher in another church district, you know." She paused. "Oh! And of course, there's Jonny, who married Treva Kramer."

"I know who Elizabeth's siblings are and I know about their grandparents, too."

"Then I'm not sure what you need to know. Though, I am curious as to why you're referring to Beth as 'Elizabeth' and not 'Beth'."

"I think it suits her better."

His aunt studied him closely. "Hmm," she said with a hint of a smile.

"Rhoda, I want to know what you *know* about Beth."

"Such as?"

He waved a hand. "You know . . . I was hoping for some specifics. Like, did she go to college? Does she have a job?" He lowered his voice. "What is the story about her being pregnant and unmarried?"

She leaned back in her chair. "I don't have those answers."

"Come on. Please? You're the friendliest person I've ever met. You always know stuff about people."

"That doesn't mean I gather information in order to gossip with my nephew."

"I don't want to hear gossip about her. I only want to try to get to know her better."

Her eyes narrowed as she picked up a cookie and took a bite. "I think it's time you gave me more information, too, Junior. I'm curious about why you need to know such personal things about Beth."

"Fine. When I stopped by Patti's, we got to talking. I ended up giving her a buggy ride home. There's something about her that I really liked. Since she's not Amish, I feel like she and I are on uneven ground. I just want to know a little bit more about her."

"I believe she finished high school, went to college, and does something in real estate."

"She's a real-estate agent?"

"Perhaps? Or, maybe she does something with mortgages or loan applications?" She shrugged. "All that I know for certain was that she is successful."

"I see."

She stared hard at him, then added slowly, "I've also heard she's far more closed off than either Kelsey or Jonny. She's got her guard up."

"I've noticed."

"Tell me, what about Beth sparked your interest?"

Everything. But no way was he admitting that to Rhoda. "I don't know."

"Junior, do you hear yourself?"

"Yes, I know I sound confused. But that's because I am. I'm really confused about why I'm so taken with Elizabeth."

Her eyes narrowed. "Perhaps she led you to believe she was interested, too?"

"She didn't." Remembering their conversation—what there was of it—he frowned. "She was kind of prickly."

"I have no doubt she was prickly, if you were asking her a bunch of personal questions."

"I wasn't."

After taking a bite of a cookie, she said, "John, the things you want to know about Beth are personal. You should be asking her these questions, not me."

"All I wanted to know were some basics."

"Which you already knew. Are you sure you don't want to tell me the real reason you're so interested in Beth Schrock?"

"What I told you was the truth."

"If that is the case, then I suggest you start asking yourself some questions, Junior. Maybe you should do a bit of soul searching, followed by a prayer?"

He couldn't deny that she had a point. Plus, prayer always helped. "I'll do that."

"I hope so . . . and I hope you find the answers you are looking for, too."

"*Danke*, Aunt." After draining his cup of coffee, he leaned over and kissed her cheek. "I love you."

"I love you, too. Now get on with ya, before I decide to ask you some personal questions . . . or tell Uncle Eli to get involved."

"Please, no. If Eli was here, we'd talk about this for another two hours."

"Will I see you on Sunday?"

Meeting her gaze, Junior knew that she was thinking about Samuel. Ever since he'd jumped the fence, he hardly ever stopped by. Then, sometimes even when he did promise their aunt and uncle that he'd visit, he wouldn't show up.

It was yet another reason Junior wanted to shake some sense into him from time to time.

"I'll be here," he promised.

After giving her a quick hug, he scurried out the door. He had a lot to think about. He not only needed more information about beautiful, secretive Elizabeth Schrock, he had to figure out why he couldn't stop thinking about her.

He hoped he'd be able to find some answers in the near future.

CHAPTER 4

A full week had passed since Martin came over. During that time, Patti had met with four of her clients, completed another client's quarterly taxes, cleaned and organized some shelves in the basement, and read a book. She had been busy doing a lot of things—except going to the grocery store.

Now, as she stared at the contents of her cabinets, Patti frowned. She had lots of food but nothing to eat.

Well, nothing that she wanted. She really wished she'd picked up more at the market when she'd gone on Saturday. Or, perhaps gone when the weather was drizzling on Monday. Now that the wind had picked up—making it far too dangerous to go anywhere on her bike or in the buggy—she was stuck at home.

She was going to have to make meals out of what was on hand, which was noodles, rice, canned veggies, and some thawed-out chicken and hamburger, for the next couple of days.

There was nothing wrong with that—except for the fact that lasagna sounded really good. So did chocolate cake.

"What is wrong with you, Patti?" she muttered to herself. "Mamm would be ashamed of how spoiled you have become. You should be giving thanks for what you have—not wishing for things that aren't necessary."

When someone started knocking at the door, she exhaled in relief. No matter who had stopped by, it would be a welcome break from staring at her kitchen cupboards. She was glad for the break.

But she sure didn't expect to see *him.* "Martin!"

He was standing out in the cold and wind, looking as if the elements didn't affect him in the slightest. Instead, he was staring at her intently. "Hiya, Patti."

"What are you doing here?"

"Seeing you, obviously."

"I know, but you came last week."

"I know."

When his lips turned up at the corners, she realized she'd been standing there like a lovestruck fool. Pulling open the door with a bit too much force, she gestured toward the entryway. "It's mighty cold out. I'm sure you're freezing. Come in, come in."

"I hope I wasn't interrupting anything?"

"You weren't." She could barely form any other words, especially since all she wanted to do was stare at him. He was in a thick tan canvas coat lined with flannel, boots, an undershirt, and a V-neck black sweater over that. His hair was messy, like he'd just run his fingers through it. He was freshly shaved, too.

As always, he looked good. Maybe too good for her heart. Irreverently, she wondered why he couldn't be a little more homely. Maybe have a bad nose or squinty eyes or narrow shoulders. Or a paunch in his midsection. Instead, he looked exactly the way he appeared in her daydreams. He seemed to play a starring role in them far too often.

Everything she imagined him looking like when they talked on the phone. "I'm so surprised you're still in town. I thought you were going back last night."

Closing the door behind him, he said, "It was kind of a spur-of-the-moment thing. One minute I was telling myself that it was time to pack and head back, and then next I asked Dawdi if I could stay here for a couple of more days."

"I'm so glad." Patti beamed at him another few seconds— before she came to her senses. "Goodness." She held out her hands. "Here. Let me take your coat. And may I get you a cup of coffee?"

"I can take my own coat off, but yes to the coffee," he said with a grin. "Thanks."

"Hang it up on the hook then and come join me in the kitchen. I'll make a fresh pot right now."

She turned away, needing the brief break to settle herself. Martin didn't need her staring at him like he was a dish of frozen custard in the middle of July.

Or worse.

Plus, she needed to gather her thoughts. This was the second time he'd come over to see her in a week. What if he asked how she felt about him? What if he wanted to talk about their future once again? What would she tell him now? Her circumstances hadn't changed, but she was beginning to believe that her heart had a mind of its own.

"I went ahead and took my boots off, too. Your floor looks spotless."

Glancing down at his thick wool socks that had blond dogs stitched all over them, she grinned. "I never pictured you with dog socks."

He grinned. "This is what all the guys at my office wear. Fun socks. I guess they do look pretty silly in an Amish home."

The things he thought about! "They suit you." She turned

to fuss with the percolator some more. "I'm sorry, I don't have much to offer you in the way of treats. When you knocked, I was just lamenting the fact that I should've bought more at the market on Saturday."

"Do you need to go to the grocery? I can take you."

"You can? I mean, you came over in your truck?"

"I walked, but it's at my grandparents' place."

"I'll be fine. It's probably best if I eat the food I have." Lasagna and chocolate cake weren't very good for her, anyway.

"Whatever you want."

"*Danke.*" Pulling out two stoneware mugs, she said, "The *kaffi* is ready. Milk or sugar?" He usually took it black, but she wanted him to be happy.

"Black is fine."

"Would you like to sit in the kitchen? I haven't had time to get the fireplace going yet."

A line formed in between his brows. "You have gas heat, yes?"

"*Jah*, but it's expensive. Plus, the fireplace is nice. I like to watch the flames dance around."

"I do, too. Let's sit down and catch up, and then I'll help you with the fireplace. And then I'm taking you out to dinner and to the grocery store."

Even though her insides were jumping up and down, she tried to sound a little less excited. "Martin, that's very bossy."

"It is, but I'm beginning to think you need someone to boss you around a bit."

"Certainly not."

To her shock, instead of arguing some more, he started laughing as he took both mugs and led the way to the living room. "Sit down with me and stop fussing."

Since she didn't have a choice, she followed Martin into her own living room and sat down on the sofa by his side.

He took a sip of his coffee and grinned. "You make the best coffee. I'm not sure how that is, but you do."

"It's the percolator."

"Maybe it is. Or . . . maybe it's you," he added in a quiet tone.

Martin was also staring at her so sweetly. "I hardly know what to think about you right now." That was the truth, too. He was acting both flirty and familiar. How could that be when it had been weeks and weeks since they'd seen each other in person?

His expression turned more serious. "Patti, I know we're in a hard place and I don't know what the Lord intends for us to do in the future. But that said, I don't want to pretend that we haven't gotten close. Do you?"

"*Nee.*" When he looked at her steadily, she realized that she was going to explain herself. She was going to need to be honest and even a little bit vulnerable. "One of my favorite parts of the day is when we talk on the phone at night."

"Me, too. I've blown off dinner with friends in order to make sure I was around for those phone calls."

"You didn't have to—"

"What I'm trying to say is that I enjoy hearing about your day. And how you listen to me and give me advice. I really enjoy that." He lowered his voice. "I've come to believe that I need your perspective in my life. It helps center me."

She sipped her coffee. "Tell me a story, then," she teased. "What's been going on in the marketing department between Jenny and Marissa and Ted from accounting?"

He laughed. "Are you sure you want to hear about their shenanigans? The latest event might shock you."

"I'm very sure." Hoping to make him laugh, she winked. "The shocking stories are the best ones."

"They're certainly the most memorable." Putting his mug down, he crossed one ankle over the opposite knee and started talking.

His story had something to do with secret lunches and emails falling into the wrong hands. If someone asked Patti to repeat the story, complete with all the specifics, she wouldn't have been able to do that. It was too tempting to study his features while he spoke. His eyes lit up when he told a joke, and a faint wash of color appeared on his cheeks whenever he relayed something rather racy.

She loved every single one.

Just like the way he held up his hands to illustrate his words. Or the way he kicked out his feet whenever she giggled. She wished she could take every little thing he did and hold it tight. Pocket it for safekeeping.

But as much as she wanted for her daydreams to become her reality, for the two of them to have a future together, she knew it wasn't possible. Martin Schrock was not meant to be Amish.

And she? Well, she'd already become Amish. She'd spoken vows during her baptism. Vows that she never intended to break.

That meant these conversations weren't going to continue for very long. Eventually he would find a woman to marry. Then all she would have left of him would be memories.

Which made a lump form in her throat.

Stay in the moment, a little voice whispered in her ear. *You won't get it back.*

That was good advice . . . especially since there was a very good chance that she might not get too many more of these moments in the future.

Which, she admitted to herself, would just about break her heart.

CHAPTER 5

"Martin, you mustn't push the buggy up and down the grocery store aisles for me," Patti said as they meandered near the canned food aisle of Walnut Creek Cheese.

As usual, Martin thought her soft tone of voice combined with her independent streak was adorable. So was her serious expression. If he had spied her from across the way, he would have imagined that she was talking about something very important.

Though, he was starting to get the idea that Patti believed they actually were speaking about something very important. He would've never imagined that his pushing a grocery cart could create such a stir.

It would've been even better if he'd had any idea why Patti was acting so flustered. They were friends now. Very good friends. Plus, he'd seen Kelsey and Richard help with several tasks around her house. She'd always accepted their assistance rather easily.

Since it was obvious she was expecting him to react, he said, "All I'm doing is pushing the buggy so you don't have to. It's a guy thing."

"No, it ain't."

Oh, brother. "Patti, if you'd stop fussing and start shopping, we could get done a lot faster."

"That isn't the point." She propped both of her hands on her hips.

"What is it, then? I don't know what you need, so I'd rather push the cart than simply stand around and not do anything." When she looked even more mutinous, Martin felt his temper rise. "I think I'm doing a pretty good job with the grocery cart, Patti. I haven't knocked into anyone or anything yet."

"Oh, stop. Don't you understand the problem?" She lowered her voice. "People will talk."

"About what?"

"You know." Her pretty brown eyes stared at him intently.

"I promise, I do not. All we're doing is walking around the store."

"If we're together like this, folks are gonna think that I'm buying groceries to cook for you. Or that maybe you are going to pay for them."

Since he was going to offer to do just that, he didn't see the problem. They were talking about food, not diamonds. Besides, it wasn't all that different from if he was taking her out to eat. "If people think that you'll be cooking meals for me, then they would be right. Don't you remember that you promised me lasagna if I drove you here?"

"That isn't what I meant and you know it."

He was a blockhead, but at long last Martin was finally understanding that she was really upset. Ignoring the two sets of people nearby, Martin stepped closer. "Patti, honey. Settle down and listen to me. If someone says something about us shopping together, I'll tell them the truth."

Her eyes widened. "But—"

"I'll tell them that I would feel like a jerk if I wandered

around the store and watched you do everything." He'd also probably tell those busybodies that Patti's shopping cart was none of their business, but he reckoned it would be best to keep that to himself. "I promise, everything is going to be just fine."

She took a deep breath. Exhaled. Then, at last, seemed to find her voice. "I wouldn't quite describe pushing a grocery cart as a job, Martin."

"Well, I wouldn't describe pushing your groceries around the store as gossip-worthy, so there you go."

"Fine."

Pleased that she was calming down and that he'd gotten his way, they continued. Without a word, he followed her up and down the aisles, stopping whenever she looked at a box or container and then moving when she was ready.

Sure, they got a few strange looks, but not as much from the Amish as the Englishers in the store. He was actually kind of surprised no one tried to start up a conversation to get more information. Some folks had no fear of overstepping boundaries.

"Martin, did ya hear me?"

"Sorry, I was thinking about something else. What did you say?"

"Do you prefer ricotta cheese or cottage cheese in your lasagna?"

"I'm not sure."

"Truly?"

"I've never made a lasagna, Patti."

"You're in a for a treat, then," she declared as she picked up the carton of cottage cheese and popped it into the buggy. "I have found the cottage cheese makes for a lighter lasagna. I think you will like it better than some of the others you might have tried in the past."

"I can't wait to try it." Though, honestly, Martin knew he

would likely not be able to tell the difference. And, more importantly, all he cared about was sharing a meal with her. Anything she made would taste good.

Just as they went down the last aisle, they ran into a couple who looked maybe five years older than him. Both were wearing thick boots, dark colors, and inquisitive expressions.

After looking him over, the woman smiled at Patti. "What a nice surprise to see you here."

Though Martin felt like raising his eyebrows—after all, visiting the grocery store wasn't an unusual undertaking—he did his best to keep his expression neutral.

As usual, Patti responded graciously. "I'm certainly here too often, and that's for sure and for certain. I can't seem to stay away," Patti joked.

The woman's expression eased, but not into a smile.

"Martin, this here is Steve and Mary Rose Troyer. They are in my church district. Steve and Mary Rose, please meet my friend Martin Shrock."

He held out his hand. "It's good to meet you."

"You as well." Steve asked, "I believe you're Sylvia and Josiah's grandson and Jonny's brother?"

"I am, indeed. I'm also Kelsey and Beth's brother. There are four of us."

"I've gotten to know Kelsey," Mary Rose said as the ice in her expression slowly chipped away. "Kelsey is a lovely girl and already such a helpmate to Richard."

"She's happy," he said simply.

"So, what are you two doing?"

"We are grocery shopping," Patti said.

"Together?" Steve asked.

"Yes." There were a thousand questions shining in the other man's eyes, but Martin was in no hurry to answer them.

After a slight pause, Mary Rose said, "That's kind of you

to help our Patti out. I've always thought cold and windy days made shopping on one's own difficult." She shivered dramatically. "It's too chilly by half, ain't so?"

"It is. I don't know what's going on, but I'll look forward to when things are more seasonable."

"The weather reports say that's not likely for another couple of days," Steve said. "Patti is blessed to have your help today."

"Indeed," Patti murmured, looking down at her feet.

"I told Patti I'd lug all her grocery bags inside her house without a single complaint," he teased.

"Martin is a prince among men," Patti added with a laugh.

"We'll leave you to it, then," Steve said. After a few more parting words, he and Mary Rose were on their way.

Glancing at Patti's profile, he searched for a sign of how she was feeling. "Hey, are you okay?"

"Of course. Why?" Her expression was closed off, though.

"No reason."

After peeking to see that the older couple was out of sight, she said, "It did feel as if they were aching to ask a bunch more questions than they did."

"I thought the same thing."

"I don't suppose I blame them."

"I do. What we are doing is no one's business."

Patti nodded. "I agree, but it's human nature for people to be curious about the two of us, I think."

"Maybe, but that doesn't mean they need to ask you a bunch of nosy questions in the middle of a crowded store."

"It wasn't so bad." She chuckled. "Martin, I guess we're going to have to stop worrying about what everyone thinks about our relationship, aren't we?"

"I think so." Especially since he wasn't quite sure what God had in store for them.

After walking a few more steps, she turned back to face

him. "I'm starting to think that no matter what happens, it will feel right."

He was humbled by her words—and by her insight. For the past two years he'd been attempting to figure out what the Lord wanted him to do. As he'd watched Kelsey and Jonny fall in love so easily, he'd wondered why he was having such a difficult time.

When he was with Patti, he didn't want to be anywhere else. And when he was home in Cleveland, their conversations on the phone were usually the highlights of his week.

Realizing Patti was still waiting for him to respond, he said, "That would be a good thing for both of us to remember, wouldn't it?"

"*Jah.*" As they continued on, Martin was surprised to realize that he didn't feel better. Instead, his chest felt a little tight, like he was almost out of breath.

No, it was more like he was on the verge of something amazing, but it lay just outside his grasp. Was it Patti or the life he couldn't quite embrace?

Disgust filled him. It was the same question, different day.

"I'm looking forward to making lasagna with you, Patti."

Her smile didn't reach her eyes. "I hope you will find all this effort to be worthwhile."

Martin had a feeling she wasn't just talking about the lasagna. If that was the case, he could say the same thing.

CHAPTER 6

Being pregnant was harder than it looked. Sitting at her grandmother's kitchen table and sipping tea, Beth was trying her very best not to throw up. But as her grandmother kept talking about hens and eggs and Sunday suppers, all while washing the fronts of all the kitchen cabinets and doors with vinegar, she was starting to think it was inevitable. Why her Mommi thought that discussing the possibility of butchering a hen was a suitable topic, Beth had no idea.

Happily oblivious to Beth's gurgling tummy, Mommi continued. "That's why I told your Dawdi this Sunday might be the day to do it. What do you think?"

She was thinking that she would happily hand over her last real-estate commission if her grandmother would speak about anything else. Flowers, perhaps. The weather. World peace?

Mommi put her washrag down. "Well?"

She had no idea what she was supposed to say. Taking a deep breath, she said, "I'm sorry, I seemed to have zoned out for a minute. What do I think about what, again?"

Her grandmother sighed as she propped both of her hands on her hips. "Roasting Anna."

Roasting. Anna. It took a second to put the two words together . . . and then it all made sense. In absolutely the worst way possible. "Are you referring to the hen that vexed Kelsey so much?"

"Well, *jah*, Beth."

She was beginning to feel queasy. And hot. And possibly hormonal, because all she could seem to think about at the moment was her younger sister confiding in a chicken. "I don't think—"

"Come now, you haven't gotten attached to that hen as well, have ya? Dawdi and I have told you from the beginning that it wasn't wise to grow attached to livestock."

"I know, but Anna is special."

"No, she isn't. What do you think? Does roast chicken sound good for Sunday supper?"

Her stomach groaned in protest as saliva pooled in her mouth. Panic set in, thanks to her new friend—tears. Yep, she was about to burst into hot, horrible, noisy tears, and there wasn't a thing she could do about it. "No, Grandma. You can't cook her!"

Her grandmother looked alarmed, but after a brief pause, her expression turned more serious. "Child, I know you think animals should be coddled and such, but that ain't our way. You need to remember that if you aim to become Amish."

"Surely one can be Amish and not enjoy killing pets with names." She swiped off a pair of tears.

"Anna never had a name until you all got involved."

"You know Kelsey named her. Kelsey needed a friend when she first got here. She's special."

"You might think so, but she's also a chicken." Her

grandmother shrugged. "Beth, dear, you know what I mean. Anna was never meant to live to a ripe old age."

She knew they needed to switch topics fast. But first, she had to say the right thing. "I think you need to rethink your plan. Hurting that hen will make Kelsey upset. Really upset."

Her grandmother frowned as she dipped her washrag into the sink and wiped down the front of a cabinet. "To be sure. That's why I don't think we should tell her until after supper."

No. Way. First of all, she wasn't going to be able to handle the stress of knowing that her grandmother was about to make her sister cry. And secondly? Secondly, she honestly couldn't handle two conversations about killing chickens in one day.

"You're going to tell Kelsey while we're doing the dishes?" she joked.

"*Nee*, child. I thought I'd bring it up during dessert."

"Dessert? No. No way."

She paused. "Whyever not? We're having baked custard. All those eggs in that dish are a perfect reason to bring up a useless hen."

Her stomach gurgled. Loudly.

Beth's armpits were getting damp, too. Now feeling queasy and a little gross, she frowned. When was the last time she'd broken out in a sweat without exercising? Ugh. "Mommi, if you bring up anything about Anna's demise, Kelsey will start to cry." Just like she was doing.

Her grandmother's back was still facing her. "If such a thing brings on tears, then she's going to have to get thicker skin," she announced as she scrubbed. "She's an Amish wife now, ain't so? She needs to stop thinking that all food comes in plastic containers."

Beth didn't think there was anything wrong with that. Desperate to move on the conversation, she blurted, "If you make Kelsey cry over egg custard, then Richard is going to get upset with you."

Her grandmother chuckled. "Surely not. He was raised on a farm, Bethy. He's used to such things."

"That might be, but he's also very smitten with his newly-wed wife. He likes her happy."

"To be sure, but—"

"*Nee*, Mommi. Richard *really* likes my sister to be happy. He's extremely protective over Kelsey. Why, I've seen our mild-mannered preacher cast more than one dark look when someone corrects her Pennsylvania Dutch."

Tossing the rag in her wash bucket, Mommi sighed. "This is true."

"Mommi, I don't know much about raising chickens, but I have spent a lifetime doing my best to take care of Kelsey. She might have a husband now, but I still hate seeing her upset. For everyone's sakes, don't bring up killing Anna again. As in Don't Do It."

"Don't kill Anna?"

"Yep. That bird might be a royal pain, but you'll be glad you didn't hurt her in the long run. Kelsey comes over to visit the hen."

Dipping the washrag into the soapy water again, Mommi grunted. "You might be right."

"I know I am. I think you should wait." A really long time. Months.

"Wait to tell Kelsey, or wait to wring that chicken's neck?"

That question! The vision it produced in her head!

And just like that, she couldn't handle it. Feeling her stomach churn and the muscles clenching, she ran to the bathroom as fast as she could.

She barely had time to get on her hands and knees before she lost everything in her stomach.

When the episode was over, Beth collapsed against the wall with a moan. Attempted to catch her breath. She felt so bad. And she'd felt so bad for days and days now, too.

She wished it would end. No, she wished she had some control over her body. That would be a wonderful thing.

Had her mother gone through this very same thing? She couldn't remember her mom ever mentioning it. If she had, she had no idea how she'd gone through this four times.

"I am sorry, Bethy," Mommi said from right outside the door. "I keep forgetting that your stomach is still giving you fits. I shouldn't have brought up butchering Anna."

As another wave of dizziness riled up, she lost her temper. "For heaven's sakes, Mommi. Stop! Don't talk about hens or eggs or chicken for the next six months. Please."

"That won't be necessary. Before you know it, you'll be feeling right as rain again. This is just a fleeting sort of thing."

"I don't know. It feels more like an entire pregnancy thing. Like a nine-month penance thing."

"A penance? For what?"

Beth was so glad that her grandmother was standing on the other side of the door. "You know. For being stupid and careless one night."

"The Lord don't hand out punishments for imagined bad behavior, child," Mommi replied in a chiding tone. "He especially don't dole out babies for imagined wrongs." In a softer tone, she added, "They are a blessing. All babies are."

"I know." Wiping her eyes—because why wouldn't she now be crying ugly tears?—she murmured, "I'm sorry. I'm just so tired of not feeling well."

Her grandmother opened the door, studied Beth sitting on the floor. No doubt looking like she was at death's door. "Oh, Beth."

"I know. I feel so miserable. Like, really bad."

Instead of giving her a sympathetic hug or offering a cold soda, her grandmother leaned against the wall and folded her arms across her chest. "Beth, dear, you've hardly left this house from the time you got here."

"I know."

"You're used to being busy. I think sitting on this farm ain't helping your mood much."

"Maybe. I don't know."

"I think you need a change of scenery."

She agreed. "Maybe I'll visit the bike trail and see if Jonny needs any help."

"I doubt he will, child. It ain't like you are going to start washing bicycles or repairing gear shifts. Besides, I think you forgot that he and Treva just went down to Pinecraft for two weeks."

"Oh. I had forgotten." She got to her feet, went to the sink, cupped some water in her hands and took a sip, swished it around, and spit.

Her grandmother wrinkled her nose.

"Sorry. I'll clean the sink in a minute."

Mommi's voice softened. "Maybe you should visit the library. Or the coffee shop and visit with one of the girls working there. That will do you some good."

"Thanks for the suggestions, but I already have a book to read. And, sorry, but I don't want to sit in a coffee shop for an hour. I can't drink much coffee," she added, as she washed her hands and dampened the towel and pressed it to her cheeks.

Reaching out to another towel rack, her grandmother pulled off a towel and handed it to her. "I guess not," she said. "We need to do something for you, though."

"Don't worry. I'm fine."

"Bethy, you just got sick in the powder room."

"I feel better now." Gazing at herself in the mirror, she saw that there were now twin spots of color on her cheeks. Whether it was from getting sick or not, she had to admit that she did look a little better. Not quite so pale and ghostly. Pleased, she walked into the hall. "I'm sorry I ran in there like that."

Mommi waved a hand. "You couldn't help it, child."

"After I brush my teeth, I'll go help with some dusting."

"*Nee.* Wait a moment." Looking delighted, Mommi snapped her fingers. "I have an idea. I think you should reach out to Junior to see if you can be of some help to him."

Junior, Patti's client? "Doing what?"

"Doing any number of things. He has a booming candle-making business, you know."

"Booming?" That sounded a bit generous. Not to be mean, but it was an Amish-run company. Didn't that mean that there wasn't much to it?

"Very much so. Junior's company sells candles all around the country."

"I didn't realize he made that many."

"How would you know? You barely spoke to him when he was kind enough to drop you home in the sleet storm."

"I guess I was kind of rude."

"I'd say more than that, Elizabeth. Perhaps it is time to make amends, *jah*?"

"Yes, Mommi," she replied meekly. Because, what else could she say?

"That's what I wanted to hear, dear." Smiling at her, she said, "Go stop by and take a peek."

"You don't think he'd mind?"

"Beth, why would you think he would?" Looking slightly impatient, she waved her hands. "Go over, child, and say hello. Take a tour and see if you might be of use. He had to work fifty and sixty hours a week last fall to keep up with the demand. If there's anything I know about you, it's that you're a hard worker."

"I'm beginning to think that you're trying to get rid of me."

"Never that, but I do think that you need to do something besides sit around here and worry and hold on to misplaced guilt, dear," she said in a soft tone.

"I'm trying to move on."

"You are pregnant, child. Soon you will be holding a baby

in your arms, and he or she will become your whole world. You'll move on even if you aren't ready."

"I suppose that's true." To her surprise, the idea of working a little bit made her feel much better. It might not be real estate, but she was good on the computer, on the phone, and could even box candles or something. It all sounded better than sitting all day long.

She took a deep breath. "I think I'll go see Junior's candle company. What is it called?"

"Walden Wax Works. It's a big metal barn two blocks off of Maple. You can't miss it."

"Okay. I'll head out in a couple of minutes."

"*Gut.*"

"Hey, Mommi?" When she turned, Beth said, "Thanks."

Walking over, she enfolded Beth in a warm hug. Running a hand down her hair, she whispered, "I know you're scared, but everything will be good soon, Bethy. The Lord doesn't make mistakes."

Beth realized that she was counting on that.

It turned out that Walden Wax Works was not only easy to find, it was really big. She thought that two or three of the Schrock's family home could fit inside the structure. There were also about twelve cars in the parking lot and at least a dozen bicycles parked near the door.

This was a real business. If she was going to apply for a job, she should have dressed more professionally.

Looking down at herself, Beth was pretty sure that she'd chosen the wrong clothing to wear. She was still wearing the dark yellow Amish dress that she'd been wearing when she'd gotten sick.

All she'd done to spruce herself up was wash her face, brush her teeth, and slip on her favorite butter-colored V-neck cashmere sweater over the dress. Since it wasn't too cold, she'd elected not to wear a coat.

She had thick black stockings on her legs and black suede pull-on tennis shoes on her feet. She wasn't wearing a *kapp*, but she had pulled her hair into a ponytail. She was actually very comfortable.

Compared to her power suits, four-inch heels, and expensive accessories that filled her regular life, she felt frumpy and wrinkled. And, compared to the young-looking Amish receptionist who looked like she should be on the cover of a book—she was so neat and pretty in her lavender dress, apron, and simple black cardigan—Beth didn't feel like she looked Amish enough, either.

She supposed she looked exactly like she was—a woman who seemed to be constantly tired, nauseous, and two or three steps away from having a mental breakdown. Way to go, Beth, she chided herself. Now you can give Junior yet another reason to think you're a loser.

"May I help ya?" the perfect-looking Amish woman said when Beth walked through the door.

"Yes, I came to see Junior Lambright."

"You want to see Junior?"

It might have been her imagination, but Beth was pretty sure that the girl's dark brown eyebrows lifted an inch.

Unease filled her. Was she not supposed to call him Junior? Her mind had gone blank. Beth had completely forgotten what his given name was.

Deciding to bluff her way through the exchange, she raised her chin a bit. "Yes. Is he in?"

"He's here." She frowned as she looked at the calendar on the desk. "But I didn't see that he had any appointments this afternoon." The girl eyed her more carefully. "What is your name?"

"Beth Schrock."

"Hmm." Looking up at Beth again, she wrinkled her nose. "Did he forget to tell me about ya?"

"No. I don't have an appointment, I just thought I'd stop by to say hello."

"I see." The girl was now looking at Beth as if she couldn't imagine Junior would want to interrupt his very important day to speak to her.

And, based on the way she'd treated him when he'd driven her home, the girl was probably right.

And now Beth felt officially embarrassed. Even though it had been her grandmother's idea for her to stop by, she'd been part of the business world for a long time. She knew that no one appreciated anyone who stopped by out of the blue. "If he's busy, maybe I could leave a note?"

"What's your name again?"

"Beth. Beth Schrock," she said slowly. Because she was pretty sure the receptionist was messing with her.

"You're one of Sylvia Schrock's grandchildren, aren't you?"

"Yes, I am."

"I met Jonny." Finally, she seemed to thaw and looked a whole lot more approachable. "My cousin bought a bicycle from him. He's nice."

Beth smiled at her. "Jonny sure is." He was easily the most outgoing of the four of them. Everyone liked her younger brother.

"Have a seat and I'll go tell Junior that you are here to say hello." Just before she reached a glass door, she paused. "It might be a minute."

"I understand. I'll be fine right here."

The girl smiled at her before she opened the door and walked inside.

Leaving Beth completely alone—and with plenty of time to worry, berate herself, and overthink things.

She hoped the woman returned soon.

CHAPTER 7

After spending two hours helping three of his employees painstakingly pour wax into their new special edition glass containers, Junior had returned to his office to answer emails.

When he turned on his computer, he mentally groaned. He'd received thirty emails since he'd left his desk. Some were orders, other folks wanted status updates on orders placed. Finally, about six of the notes were inquiries about his company's products and were requesting phone calls instead of brochures.

He couldn't help but shake his head in wonder. Walden Wax Works had sure come a long way over the last decade.

But he was also starting to feel like he was drowning in work.

Each one of the emails was important and Junior valued them. Answering those thirty alone would likely take much of the rest of the afternoon . . . especially since he would likely receive at least another thirty emails before the end of the day.

Just thinking about the amount of work that was piling up

was overwhelming. He was either going to have to work late or return at six tomorrow morning.

He really should've brought the dogs with him today.

"Junior!" she called out in a singsong voice. "Junior, I need to tell you something."

He grimaced. Cherry's interruptions always took time, and he wasn't in the mood to deal with her at the moment. *"Jah?"* he asked, barely looking up.

"How are you?"

"I'm busy, Cherry. What do you need?"

"Oh. Well . . . sorry to bother ya, but there's someone here to see you."

"Who is it?" Hopefully it was somebody whom Cherry could deal with.

She grinned. "A stranger."

Most of the time he was amused by the way Cherry attempted to make a game out of most anything. This was not one of those times.

Still staring at both his computer screen and the stack of papers on his desk, he fought to keep his voice even. "Who is it then? A salesman?"

"Nope. And it ain't a saleswoman, either. Guess again."

Her singsong tone forced him to lift his chin and meet her gaze. His receptionist's eyes were lit up like it was Christmas, her birthday, and her anniversary all rolled up into one. Obviously, she was amused by something.

Very amused.

This was never a good sign.

"What's going on?" He held out a hand. "And just to warn you, don't make me listen to another clue. I've got too much paperwork to play games, and my mood ain't the best right now."

She exhaled dramatically. "Oh, fine. Your visitor's name is . . . Beth Schrock."

Suddenly nothing in his computer's inbox mattered. He turned to stare at Cherry. Beth. Schrock. The woman whom he'd verbally sparred with for ten minutes before dropping her at her grandmother's house. The woman who was currently the focus of most every gossip's fodder in Walden.

The woman who was not only English, but pregnant with another man's child . . . and a man—rumor had it—whom she'd barely known.

She was also the prettiest thing he'd ever seen. And maybe the bravest.

And she'd also been rather snippy with him.

Getting to his feet, he said, "What does she want?"

Cherry shrugged. "I don't know. All she said was that she wanted to see you." She bit her lip. "No, that ain't the truth. She said she came over to say hello."

"She showed up here just to say hello?"

Cherry shrugged. "That's what she said. What do you want me to tell her?" She popped a hand on her hip. "Beth Schrock is sitting on the sofa out front, probably drinking the last of my coffee. Do you want to see her?" Brightening a bit, she added, "Or, I could just tell her that you're far too busy to chat and that she should make an appointment in the future."

"Did she just get here?"

"Oh, no. I couldn't come back right away because I had things to do. She's been here five or ten minutes."

Beth had already been sitting out in the lobby. Waiting on him. "She's been here that long?"

Some of Cherry's smile dimmed. "*Jah.* Maybe longer. It took me a second to figure out her purpose, you see. No way was I going to let her just wander about without an appointment."

He doubted Cherry had given Beth a chance to speak a word. "Cherry, you shouldn't have left her there."

"Sorry, but what could I do?" She deftly stepped to her

left while he strode out the door. "I knew you wouldn't an-swer your phone if I called."

Cherry had a point, but still. He didn't like the idea of Beth being told to wait in the lobby like she was some ran-dom salesperson.

Walking into the cavernous area where his twenty em-ployees were melting wax, setting wicks, and mixing fra-grances and colors, he headed toward the front of the shop.

"Junior, you got a second?"

He turned to see Edmund walking toward him. "Only a second. What do you need?"

"We just received an order for three hundred candles for a wedding reception in Iowa."

"Okay . . ."

"The kicker is they need them by next week. Can we do it?"

"I'm not sure." He hadn't yet gotten around to looking at the orders, timetables, or current delivery times.

"I need to know right now. They're waiting on the line. What should I tell 'em?"

"That you'll get back to them within a couple of hours."

Edmund crossed his arms across his chest. "They ain't going to like that. They really want these candles soon. If we canna give them to them, they're going to go find someone else."

And . . . that was Edmund to a T. He didn't like waiting and he didn't like gray answers.

"They can't expect for you to have an immediate answer, Edmund. Ask them for two hours."

"But—"

"Sorry, but your second is up, Ed," Cherry interrupted. "Our boss has someone waiting on him." Sounding even more important, she raised her chin. "It's a woman, too."

All traces of impatience on Edmund's expression trans-formed into a new, almost mischievous one. "Junior's get-ting female visitors?"

"He is."

"Who is it?"

Cherry waggled her eyebrows. "She's a stranger to me . . . but not our boss here."

Junior gritted his teeth. Of course, Cherry had brought out her singsong voice again.

As if all his concerns about the waiting Iowans had vanished, Edmund grinned. "Hey now. I better go sneak a peek."

Junior crossed his arms over his chest. They were talking about him like he wasn't in the room. "Excuse me, but I'm standing here."

Edmund looked his way again. "I see ya, boss."

Cherry's lips twitched. "Don't be mad at us for being interested in your life, Junior."

"*Jah.* We've all be wondering when you were going to ever think about something other than candles."

"I think about other things," he blurted before he remembered that he absolutely did not need to go down this slippery conversational slope.

"Like what? Wicks and wax?"

"Start walking, Cherry," he grumbled.

"I'm walking." She passed him, opened the reception door, and said, "I found him."

Junior's heart started beating faster as he followed.

And then practically ran into Cherry, who was gaping at Beth Schrock.

Beth was sitting in Cherry's chair, talking to Jimmy, one of his salesmen, glancing at the computer, and then writing something down. "Does this make sense to you?" she asked Jimmy.

Leaning close to her, Jimmy nodded. "Well, I think so . . . if you believe it could work."

Junior was taken aback. And, dare he say it? Confused? "Hey," he said. His voice squeaked a bit. Yep, he probably sounded like his voice was changing, but he couldn't help it. He was pretty sure his mind had just gone on vacation.

"Hi, Junior," Beth said in a calm and cool tone. Standing up, she looked apologetically at Cherry. "I'm sorry I took your place, but you were gone for a while and things started heating up around here."

Cherry folded her arms over her chest. "Heating up how?"

"I'd be interested in hearing this, too," Edmund announced.

Looking increasingly guilty—but somehow also defensive—Beth pointed to the desk. "First, about a minute after Cherry left, everything started going crazy. Two of the office lines started ringing, and the FedEx guy came in with a delivery. I couldn't have just ignored it."

"Why not?" Edmund asked.

"Well . . . it's not my way."

Cherry appeared torn. Like she couldn't decide whether to thank Beth for meddling or chew her out. "FedEx should've gone to the back," she muttered.

"Perhaps, but he needed a signature."

"So you signed?" Junior asked.

Beth's blue eyes fastened on his. "Well, yes. He was in a hurry. His truck was blocking parking places. Anyway, it's right there." She pointed to a flat envelope on the corner of the desk. "After I signed for the delivery, I decided I might as well help Cherry out and answer the phones. This is a business, after all. It wouldn't do for customers to have to leave messages. No one likes to do that."

"Hmm," Cherry said.

"So, I started answering phones."

"On your own," Edmund said.

"Well, yes." Beth shrugged. "I thought I'd take messages if nothing else. And then Jimmy here came in."

Now Jimmy got into the fray. "I was just going to say hi, but when I heard Beth here was talking to someone about candle sizes and the new spring catalog, I walked over to show her where that was on Cherry's computer. She was doing her best, but she needed a helping hand."

Beth held up a catalog. "I found one of these, too." After smiling at Jimmy, she continued. "Between the two of us, we were able to answer the caller's questions."

"No, she did one better. She placed an order for seven hundred sets of our new line." Jimmy grinned. "Ain't that something?"

"You sold seven hundred sets of the Daylight line?" The Daylight line was their most expensive line of candles. Selling seven hundred sets was a minor miracle.

Glancing down at the form on the desk, Beth nodded. "Yes. Now, I took down all the information and did warn Emerson that someone might be calling back because I was new."

"You're new all right," Edmund said with a chuckle.

Jimmy fist-bumped Beth. "She might be new, but no doubt about it. She's a natural."

Beth chuckled, but abruptly stopped when she glanced at Cherry.

Only then did Junior notice that Cherry had slowly looked less and less amused about Beth taking over her desk. She was now glaring at Beth with her hands on her hips.

"Sorry," Beth said as she stepped farther back from the desk. "I didn't mean to overstep."

"Really? You just couldn't help yourself?" Junior asked.

Obviously stung by his sarcastic tone, Beth lifted her chin. "I was only trying to help. Like I said, it was crazy in here for a few minutes and no one was around."

"That's true. No one was here," Jimmy said.

"That's because Junior was taking his time about coming out to the front," Cherry blurted.

Edmund cleared his throat. "I don't think it's right to blame Junior for everything. . . ."

"And she *was* helping, Cherry," Jimmy added. "I've heard you say more than once that you wish you had more help up here."

"She's said that?" Junior asked.

"Of course she has," Edmund said. "This ain't no sleepy company any longer, Junior."

"Hmm," he said.

"All I know is that when you left your desk, she signed for important documents, took a message, and helped a customer. If she hadn't, you would've come back here to two messages and a note from FedEx saying that they couldn't deliver something important," Edmund said. "As far as I'm concerned, Beth Schrock saved your hide. What's your problem?"

"Well—" Cherry said.

Beth interrupted. "Her problem is that I stepped in where I didn't belong," Beth said quickly. "I shouldn't have done anything."

When Jimmy looked ready to argue that point and Edmund appeared determined to spout off his opinions to anyone who listened, Junior knew it was time to get Beth out of there. "Want to come back to my office to talk?"

"Do you have time?"

"Of course I do. Come on."

"Don't forget all the work you said you have piling up, Junior," Cherry called out. "It won't get done on its own."

"I won't forget. Jimmy, do you need something as well?"

Looking slightly amused, Jimmy nodded. "I did come in to discuss some things with ya, but I can wait. Cherry here can help me for now, seeing as she has nothing but time on her hands."

"Jimmy, for the record, I do not."

"Come on, Beth," Junior said. Without thinking, he pressed his hand to the small of her back, happy to carefully lead her out of the reception area and into the warehouse. "It's time I got you out of here."

Beth glanced up at him in surprise but didn't move away.

He wondered if she appreciated his touch, or if she was so used to mannerisms like that in her regular life that she didn't think anything of it.

As they walked back through the cavernous space, he felt the eyes of nearly every employee on the two of them. When they got to his office without being interrupted, he counted that as a win. "It's warm in here," he said. "You're welcome to take off your coat and get comfortable. Would you like a water?"

"Sure. Thanks."

He walked to his small refrigerator and pulled out two bottles.

When Junior faced Beth again, her sweater was off and Beth was staring at him with her big blue eyes. Her soft-looking lips were parted.

She looked pretty. So pretty.

All of a sudden, he couldn't care less about anything else. Deadlines didn't seem that urgent. Neither did Edmund's mood nor Cherry's demeanor.

Oh, who was he kidding? At the moment, he couldn't care less about candles, the weather, or pretty much the state of the world.

All he wanted to think about was standing in front of him and looking far too pretty and vulnerable.

It was all he could do not to pull her into his arms and promise to do whatever it took to make her smile again. He didn't even care that she was sporting a small baby bump.

Which showed him that there was no doubt about it . . . he was in over his head. He needed to get a grip on himself. Fast.

CHAPTER 8

It was cool and comfortable inside Junior Lambright's office. It was also spacious and surprisingly modern looking. Exposed red brick rested beside painted drywall. The concrete floor somehow looked perfect underneath a comfortable beige area rug and the industrial-looking ceiling.

In the middle of it all was a gorgeous Amish-crafted desk, shelving unit, and chairs. A cozy-looking couch upholstered in dark charcoal fabric looked both masculine and inviting.

Beth was drawn to every inch of the space.

Oh, who was she kidding? She was drawn to the man standing in front of her.

Everything about Junior Lambright was a surprise. No, everything about him was intriguing, Beth decided.

His name, which seemed to suit him even though he was a grown man.

His looks, which were unusual and striking.

His modest-sounding candle business, which didn't seem to be very modest at all.

The way he handled nearly everyone in his surroundings.

He acted like everyone around him were both his best friends and the company's valued employees. It shouldn't have worked, but it did. Everyone seemed comfortable around Junior yet respected him.

In less than an hour, Beth was reevaluating everything she'd ever known about running a business. Actually, Junior was taking everything she'd ever imagined about an Amish-owned business and an Amish bachelor and tossed it on its ear.

Or, perhaps, showed that she'd been a narrow-minded fool where a lot of things were concerned.

"Hey, are you feeling all right?" he asked after she continued to stand silently for several moments.

She blinked, wondering where he'd gotten his eyes. Were they his mother's? Father's? Maybe he'd gotten them from one of his grandparents? They really were an unusual shade of hazel. Or, were they simply just green? "Hmm?"

A line formed between his brows. "Maybe you should come sit down. Perhaps have a cup of tea?"

"I don't need any of that. I'm fine." When Junior continued to study her like she was about to fall down, she laughed softly. "I'm sorry if I look as off-balance as I feel. But it has nothing to do with my health."

"Are you sure? I mean, I don't know much about being pregnant, but I'm pretty sure you'd rather be off your feet."

"It's good for me to walk around, and I don't feel bad at all. If you're worried about why I look so confused, it has mostly to do with the fact that I've been foolish."

"About what?"

It would be so easy to make up something innocuous, but she didn't want to lie to him. "About my first impression of you. Junior, I'm sorry. I shouldn't have formed so many split-second assumptions about you."

He blinked. Then stuffed his hands in his pockets, like he was trying to pull himself together. "I see."

She shook her head. "No, you don't. I don't mean any disrespect. The problem lies with me, not you."

"Sorry, but I'm not following."

Of course he wasn't! She'd interrupted his day, taken over the reception area, and was now staring at him like a besotted fool.

Swallowing hard, Beth forced herself to utter more truths. "You see, when I look at you and this business and . . . and other things, I realize that I've been fighting with myself for all the wrong reasons. And that it's time I faced some hard truths."

He sat down. "Fighting with oneself ain't good."

"I know it." She chuckled again, because if she didn't do that, she was probably going to cry. "And here I am, once again, only thinking about myself when I barged into your offices and ruined your day."

As if he could sense those tears, he said, "Please sit down."

"Fine. I'm sitting."

"Now, let's talk about what you just said. I don't think you ruined anything. That's putting things a bit much, *jah*?"

"Maybe so," she murmured. She had been exaggerating, which was something she usually tried hard not to do. She liked to tell everyone that exaggerating needs didn't help get anything done or make things easier to accept.

But here she'd been . . . doing the same thing.

"What's going on, Beth Schrock? Why did you come to Walden Wax Works?"

"Well, I could give you a lot of reasons, but I basically stopped by because I was bored."

"You were bored."

He looked taken aback and yes, a bit offended. "Oh, I didn't come over here for you to entertain me," she said quickly. "I came over to see if you could put me to work."

"You need a job?"

"Kind of." His expression turned even more confused—and who could blame him? She added, "You see, I . . . I had a really good job in Cleveland. I worked for a realty company."

"You sold houses?"

"Not really. I mean, yes, I do have my real-estate license, but I did more of the office managerial work. I paid bills, scheduled meetings, helped with insurance, called Realtors in other cities, and developed marketing plans." Thinking of the hundred details she juggled a day, she waved a hand. "And because everything revolved around either land or property that needed to be bought or sold, it was all very much time sensitive."

"You had a lot of responsibilities." Junior leaned back in his chair.

"I did. I had a *lot* of responsibilities. And, not to sound too full of myself . . . I was good at my job. I am used to being busy. And now . . ." Her voice drifted off as she tried to find the right way to describe the way she'd been feeling.

"Now?" he prodded.

"Now, I feel like I'm at a loss. I came to Walden because I needed to reassess my life and my choices. I needed to find peace. Unfortunately, I'm not finding much peace at all."

"How come?"

Figuring she had nothing to lose by being completely honest, she said, "I think Martin, Kelsey, and Jonny are upset with me for being pregnant." And then, of course, she found herself half-holding her breath. Was Junior about to disparage her, too?

After a few seconds, he said, "Last I heard, a woman couldn't get pregnant on her own."

"You would be right," she said as she exhaled. "But, as hard as it's been to face their disapproval, I can't say that I blame them."

"No?"

"I think I've kind of brought it on myself. I mean, I've always been the member of the family who tried to be perfect and pushed and nagged. And now I'm looking forward to being a single mother. An Amish single mother." Realizing what she'd just blurted, she groaned. "And now yet again, I've told you way more information than you wanted to know."

He stared at her intently. "How do you know?"

"How do I know . . . what?"

"How do you know what I want, Beth?"

"I . . . I don't." Turning more embarrassed, she said, "Junior, I came here to see if maybe you could use another hand. I'd love to do something useful. You don't have to pay me. But I could help make candles or pay bills or answer phones . . . that is, if you need help. Which you might not. Or, um, if Cherry doesn't mind."

"Are you concerned about Cherry now, too?" His gaze warmed.

Making her feel even more confused and flustered.

"Well, yes." Deciding to be honest, she added, "I mean, a little bit. How could I not?" Although Beth did think that Cherry should've been just a little bit more understanding. She'd only been trying to help.

"She was acting rather territorial."

"I don't know why. I mean, everything really had been happening so fast." She stopped talking. Suddenly it all made sense. Not only that that cute receptionist thought that Beth was invading her work, but she was trying to snag her boyfriend, too. "Are the two of you a couple?"

It took a second for her question to register. "Elizabeth, are you asking if I am courting Cherry?"

She nodded. "Well, yes. Are you?"

"No!" Realizing he sounded a bit too forceful, he tried to tone things down. "I mean no, I am not."

"Oh. Okay."

"I promise. Cherry is, well, Cherry." Looking like he was trying not to laugh, he continued. "She has one way of doing things and she works at one speed. Deviation is not an option."

"I see."

He stared at her. Glanced at his messy desk and beeping computer. "You were able to pull up information on the computer up front without a problem."

"Jimmy helped."

"But I have a feeling you could've done it by yourself. Could you?"

"Well, yes. I mean, it's a pretty common program."

"You didn't get bothered none when multiple people needed multiple things."

"Like I said, I'm used to that. I thrive on that."

"And you really don't want to be paid?"

"Really. I need something to occupy myself, not fill my bank account."

"Still, that doesn't seem fair."

"It's fair enough. To be honest, I don't need the money. I had a really good salary at my other job and saved a lot. Plus, I'm basically living for free at my grandparents'."

He gazed at her for a long minute. "Actually, I could use some help. Some office help," he clarified. "I'm drowning in emails, phone calls, and production schedules. What Jimmy said in the lobby was exactly right. In some ways I am still trying to run this place like a small business out of my garage."

"It's way past that."

"It sure is. I've been feeling overwhelmed."

She'd never been so glad to hear that someone was in over his head. "I can help with that. I promise, I really am good at being efficient. I'd be happy to help you. That is, if you'd be willing to give me a try."

"We could do that. Maybe we could give it a test run for a few hours a day? How does that sound?"

It sounded good. Very good.

He was going to hire her. She wasn't going to have to sit at her grandparents' house and worry. "A few hours a day is good with me."

"Are you sure you're feeling well enough to work?"

"I'm in the middle of my second trimester, which is supposed to be the easy part. As long as we don't talk about poultry, I should be all right."

"Poultry? You mean chickens?"

Even thinking about them made her feel queasy. "Like I said, please don't mention them."

"I'll be sure to never bring up ch—I mean *them* in conversation again."

"Thank you."

"I'm assuming that includes eggs as well?" His lips twitched, as if he was trying really hard not to dissolve into laughter. She got it, but she was beyond joking about it.

It was all she could do not to make a face. "Junior, I'm not kidding. Do not mention anything that has to do with you know who. *Please.*"

"I understand now. They will not be mentioned again."

"Thank you."

Holding out his hand, he said, "Beth Schrock, as of right now, you are hired."

Shaking his hand, she said, "Thank you, Junior. You won't regret it."

"I never regret hiring workers for free. So, when can you start?"

"Now?"

"You have time?"

"I have nothing but time." Before he could protest, she

pointed to the pile of papers and invoices on his desk. "What are you doing there?"

"Well, I'm answering emails. But I also need to double-check the orders with the inventory and the schedule. If we're short, then I need to go speak to the people on the line and see when they can fulfill the order."

"And if things are good?"

He walked to his computer and wiggled the mouse until his screen turned on. "Then I return their email and make a note in this chart, which goes to Dwight. He's inventory control."

"I could probably handle that. How about I start going through things, and if they are good, fill out the form for Dwight and then email the customer. If it looks like there might be a problem at all, I'll leave the order for you to look at."

"You think you can do that so easily?"

He sounded so doubtful it was almost embarrassing. Did he really think she was so incapable?

But then she remembered two things. One was that they didn't know each other all that well. All he knew about her work ethic and ability was what she'd told him. Secondly, this was his business. Of course, he was going to be wary about having someone else do anything that might jeopardize an order or make one of his customers unhappy.

So she took a deep breath and said, "I think I can. I'd like to try."

His gaze softened. "You . . ."

"Me?"

"You are something else, Elizabeth."

"Elizabeth?"

"I like it." Looking a bit awkward, he stuffed his hands in his pockets. "There's a lot to you, Beth. You're a complicated woman. Elizabeth suits you."

"No one calls me that."

"If you don't mind, I'd like to."

Every time he said her full name instead of her nickname she felt a little buzz. "Only if you think my complications are a good thing."

"They absolutely are. First, you bring in a big sale, which I still haven't thanked you for. Thank you."

"You are welcome."

"Now, you showed up like an answer to a prayer. No matter what happens here at the factory, I'm grateful for you stopping by and offering your assistance. Especially without asking for anything in return."

"I've told you that being here will help me, too."

"Still, working for free is unexpected. No, it's more than that. It's kind of you."

"It's nothing." She blinked back a sudden onslaught of tears. Oh, those pregnancy hormones were no joke.

"It's everything. I've been praying and asking the Lord for guidance and here you are."

"Let's just hope you still feel glad I'm here in four hours," she joked. "I could very well ruin your spreadsheets."

"I hope you don't. But if you do, I'm not going to get upset with you for trying to help."

"We'll see."

"And by the way, you're not going to be here for four hours. After two, I'll take you home."

"There's no need for that. I can get home by myself."

Junior shook his head. "If you are going to work here, then I am going to make sure you get home safe."

"But—"

He cut her off. "That's the deal. You are taking care of the babe, yes?"

"Yes."

"Then there is nothing wrong with taking things easy the first day, right?"

Put that way, Beth knew it would be petty to argue. Especially since he was doing her a favor. "You're right." Smiling at him, she said, "It's a deal."

Junior's expression warmed. "Come sit down and I'll show you what to do."

Beth sat, listened intently, asked questions, and then got to work.

At first, Junior worked on the couch nearby. When his cell phone rang, he held it to his ear and walked out the door.

After an hour sped by, Beth realized that she was happier than she'd been in weeks. She told herself it was because she was finally feeling useful again.

But the way she felt butterflies whenever Junior walked into the room told her a very different story.

She had no idea how she was going to ignore that, but she hoped she figured it out sooner than later.

It would do them both a lot of good.

CHAPTER 9

Now that Kelsey and Jonny were happily married and busy with their new lives in Walden, the four of them didn't get together all that often anymore. As the months passed, Martin began to feel more and more like the odd one out. Unlike the others, his life was still in Cleveland.

And, since he'd come to the conclusion that he wouldn't be able to give it up, he sometimes felt like he was an unwelcome reminder to the way things used to be.

How could it not? His days were filled with things they'd all given up. Even Beth, who was struggling with her pregnancy and her future, didn't always act all that interested in hearing about his work, the Browns, or some of the new restaurants in town.

He understood that they had adopted a different life and were happy, but a part of him wished that at least one of them had made the same choice that he had.

He missed them.

He'd missed them so much, he'd reached out to each of them individually and asked if they could get together the next time he came into town. To his relief, they'd all seemed eager to spend some time together—just the four of them.

Even better, Kelsey had suggested that they meet at Green's Farm Kitchen instead of at their grandparents' house. Martin loved Mommi and Dawdi, but no one felt like they could be completely honest when they joined them. No one wanted to hurt their feelings by admitting that they missed Chinese takeout, watching hours of mindless TV, or listening to music.

Plus, when it was just the four of them having supper, it brought back a lot of good memories. The four of them had supper on their own more times than he could count when they were in their teens. Whichever parent they were staying with would have plans that "couldn't be broken." Next thing they knew, they'd be making their own supper and eating together.

Sure, that dinner alone hadn't always been a happy occasion. But, more often than not, one of them would make a point to make the others laugh.

Because he was the only one still driving a vehicle, Martin had picked everyone up. He was glad he had, too. He'd been able to spend a few precious minutes with Kelsey before they picked up Jonny and Beth. She might be married and an adult, but old habits died hard.

With her sitting next to him, he had to admit that both Amish life and marriage seemed to suit her well.

"You keep looking at me and smiling, *bruder*," she teased. "What's wrong? Do I have something on my cheek?"

"Of course not."

"Hmm."

Not wanting to voice his thoughts, Martin pretended to concentrate on the road. The truth was, she actually had nothing on her cheek. Not a bit of makeup. Not that she'd ever worn much makeup—not that he was aware of, anyway, but sometimes, seeing the way her bare skin glowed caught him off guard. That, and the fact that she was wearing a *kapp* and was so much more contained than she'd ever been as a teenager. She looked adorable.

"Martin, talk to me," she said after he'd studied her a moment too long at a stoplight. "Why do you keep staring at me?" Looking more worried, she fussed with the pins on her dress. "Do I look silly?"

"Of course not. You look perfect. It's just . . . well, I was just thinking about how happy you look."

"Oh. Well, I am happy."

"I'm glad."

She didn't return his smile. "Are you happy, Martin?"

"Yes." He was happy enough. Sometimes.

She frowned. "You don't sound so positive about that."

"Well, I am. And look. We're at Jonny's place."

He and Treva had gotten married right away but had elected to stay on her family's farm. Treva's coffee shop was on the property, so she needed to live nearby. Jonny had seemed happy to be there as well.

Though Martin had asked his younger brother if he felt it was wise to start out a marriage while being surrounded by Treva's family, Jonny had said he was good with it. To everyone's surprise, their father had pushed for that option, too. He'd pointed out that while Jonny might be managing a business and happily married, he was also very young.

With that in mind, Treva's father had cleaned out the back of the barn and accepted everyone's help to make it a comfortable and private first home for Treva and Jonny.

They seemed happy there.

Parking the car out front, he turned to Kelsey. "I'll be right back."

"I can go get him, Martin."

"You stay here where it's warm. I'll be right back."

"Martin, don't be so stubborn."

Ignoring her, because they might be adults but he was still her big brother, he repeated, "I'll be right back."

Just as he started to go around to the side, where they'd installed a door so the newlyweds wouldn't have to go through the barn first, Jonny stepped outside.

"Hey, Martin," he called out as he strode forward. "It's been too long."

"It sure has." Martin hugged him. "It's good to see you." Jonny looked great, too. Ever since he'd started eating differently and taking better care of himself, he seemed to ooze vitality. Of course, it could just be that he was so happy with Treva.

"It's good to see you, too. Thanks for the lift."

"You know you don't have to thank me for that."

Jonny shrugged. "Still, I'm grateful. I'm also happy that you reached out to all of us about getting together."

"I'm glad everyone could make it. It's hard to find a time when everyone is free. Especially when I don't stay in Walden very long."

"I hear you. But maybe there's hope that you'll be driving down more often. After all, I heard that you've made time to see Patti."

"Not as much as I'd like."

"You've been busy."

"Yeah, work's been crazy." That was his excuse, but it was also the fact that he couldn't seem to know what to do with the rest of his life.

Jonny gave him a long look but only opened the door to the back seat and got in.

They didn't speak about anything much until they got Beth in the car. Of course, picking her up meant that all four of them had needed to go inside the farmhouse and visit with their grandparents for a few minutes.

To his amusement, when all four of them returned to his vehicle, they rearranged themselves. Once again Beth was riding sidekick, and Jonny and Kelsey were in the back seat.

"Look at us, together again," he said.

"I'm not sure what made you press for this dinner date, but I'm glad you did, Martin," Beth said. "I've needed this."

"I didn't want to let another month go by without catching up in person."

"We've all said the same thing," Jonny said.

Martin concentrated on driving as the rest of them talked about their grandparents, Mom and Dad, Richard, and Treva. When they arrived at the Green, it was thankfully uncrowded. "Can we get a table near the back?" he asked the hostess.

"Sure." She walked them over, shared the soup specials, and then left them alone.

Jonny scanned the menu, seemed to make up his mind first, and leaned back in his chair. One by one, his sisters did the same.

Then Martin realized they were all staring at him.

"What?"

"You know what. What is going on with you?" Jonny pressed. "What are you and Patti going to do?"

Martin had really hoped they could focus on Beth, at least at first. "Nothing like diving into the hard stuff."

Beth rolled her eyes. "Oh, please. Of course you knew we were going to ask about your plans with Patti. It's not like we could ask her."

"I know." He sighed. "And to answer your question, I don't know what we're going to do. The two of us have kind of come to a standstill."

"I think you know what you want," Kelsey said softly.

Feeling a bit blindsided, he stared at her. "Why do you say that?"

"Because if you wanted to be Amish, quit your job, and move here and marry Patti, you would've already done so," she said with a satisfied smile. "That would have been the easy choice."

He was annoyed that his little sister was acting as if the problems he was grappling with for the last year could have been avoided. "Nothing about any of that would have been easy for me."

"Sorry for sounding so flippant," Kelsey said. "You're right. Choosing to become Amish for the rest of my life wasn't easy at all. But then again, I didn't have a great job and a full life already. You do."

"It's not just about my job," he countered.

"Of course it isn't," Kelsey agreed. "I'm sure you've got a lot of things to consider. I just think that you and Patti would be so good together."

"Wow, Kels."

Beth groaned. "Kelsey, stop talking like you could run the world."

Kelsey frowned. "I didn't say I did."

"Sorry, but Bethy's right," Jonny said. "You're kind of acting like you have all the answers."

"I am not. And come on, everyone. Stop acting so shocked. I know that everything I just said couldn't have come as a surprise. We've all expressed the same thoughts. Martin doesn't want to become Amish like the rest of us."

"Is this true?" Martin stared at the three of them. "You all feel like I've made up my mind, but I don't want to formally make a decision because then I'll be forced to accept that I'm not going to be like the three of you?"

"We haven't said that in so many words," Beth said.

Stung, he turned to her. "I can't believe that you, of all people, are talking about my choices."

"Me, of all people?" Beth's expression pinched. Lowering her voice, she said, "That's pretty low, Martin."

"Come on. My words might not be pleasant to hear, but they can't come as a surprise."

"You are wrong. They do."

"Beth, pull those rose-colored glasses off your eyes and look at the room. The four of us have been through so much. Did you really think none of us would ever ask you about your baby's father . . . or why you don't want to have any sort of relationship with him?"

Beth turned to their sister and brother. "Do you two really have a dying need to know about my one-night stand?"

"I absolutely never want to hear about it," Jonny said. "Like . . . never ever."

When Kelsey looked away in embarrassment, Beth swallowed. "I see."

"You don't," Kelsey blurted. "Martin shouldn't have said that to you. Your private life is none of our business."

"Kelsey's right, Martin," Jonny chimed in. "You have gone too far."

Martin felt like he'd been punched in the gut. As the other three people at his table remained silent and the uncomfortable feeling grew, he started to get the feeling that he'd been reading everything all wrong. "What am I missing? Have you all been talking about this without me? Am I thinking that this man is Beth's big secret, but it's really not a secret at all?"

"You are being ridiculous. I have not been talking about him with anyone."

"You haven't?"

"Of course not."

Jonny cleared his throat. "Bethy, don't you think it's time you did? I mean, I don't need to hear about any details . . . but shouldn't you at least be able to tell us this guy's name?"

"Why?"

"Because he's your baby's father," Jonny bit out.

"It's none of your business, Jonny. I can't believe you're acting as if you have a right to know."

"You're acting as if no one else is ever going to ask you about him," Jonny said.

"If someone is rude enough to ask, I'll tell them the same thing."

Looking pained, Kelsey said, "I'm sorry, Beth, but I am worried that you think you will never have to talk to this man. Or that it will never come up in conversation with your child."

"This baby is going to be fine."

"I don't doubt it. But every child wants to have both a mother and a father. It's human nature."

And just like that, their sister's bluster vanished and in its place was a vacant stare. "I have told the father about the baby. He doesn't want anything to do with it."

"Did he sign away the rights?" Martin asked. "Did you get a lawyer yet?"

"No."

Jonny frowned. "Beth, that isn't good enough. You need to do that."

"Don't worry about it, Jonny."

"Don't brush me off like I'm just a kid. This is important." He waved a hand. "I mean, what are you going to do when it's born?"

"When my boy or girl is born, you mean?"

"You know what I meant."

"The answer is obvious, don't you think? I'll be a mother."

Martin could practically feel the tension emanating from Beth. He felt terrible that they were making her feel uncomfortable, but he couldn't deny that everything they were discussing was important. "What about the birth certificate?"

"We're speaking in circles. Obviously, the baby's last name will be Schrock."

"The father might want the baby to have his name," Jonny said. "Even if you two aren't married or even have a relationship."

"I know he won't. As hard as it might be for you to get

your head around, I made a big mistake and am paying for it. But I've almost made peace with it. Which is more than I can say about any of you."

Kelsey looked like she was about to burst into tears. "All right, Beth. I'm sorry we pushed."

"I can take it," Beth said. "Look, I know my life is in disarray. I know I have a lot of things to figure out, too. But I'm dealing with them. I think you need to deal with you and Patti, too, Martin."

"Whatever we decide is between Patti and me."

When Kelsey frowned at her clenched hands, Martin felt like leaving. He didn't want to hurt his little sister's feelings, but he needed some privacy, too. "Sorry," he muttered. "I didn't mean to snap."

"All any of us wants to do is help you," Jonny said.

Beth nodded. "At the very least, listen."

"Then I guess you and I are in the same place, Bethy," he said. "Both of us are facing situations that we didn't see coming and are going to have to deal with on our own. It's not easy and it's not fun. But there's also very little else that anyone can do."

The four of them stared at each other in dismay. Each of them looking more devastated than the last.

"Are you ready for me to take your order now?" the server asked.

"Not yet," Kelsey said. "I think we're going to need a little bit more time."

When the server moved away, Jonny started laughing. "You are absolutely right, Kels. If there's anything all of us needs, it's a little bit more time."

Feeling sheepish, Martin completely agreed.

CHAPTER 10

Preacher Richard's sermon and stories about Jonah had been inspiring. The Gingerich's barn was roomy and bright, and they were blessed with a quiet, cool breeze from the open barn doors. Altogether, Patti decided that it had been an exceptionally comfortable three-hour service.

All in all, Patti believed that it had been one of the nicest Sundays she'd experienced in several weeks. Maybe it was because the Gingerich family were such organized and re-laxed hosts. That wasn't always the case.

If Martha Gingerich brought out a couple of jars of her delicious pickles, everything would be perfect. Martha was known for her way with pickling cucumbers. No one knew what she put in her secret recipe, but it was just as well. Putting in so much work for a crunchy spear wouldn't be the same.

So, yes, Patti decided, it had been a lovely morning and was destined to be a lovely afternoon, too. Everything would be rather perfect.

That is, if either Kelsey or Sylvia looked as if they weren't about to dissolve into tears.

After closing their eyes in prayer for the last time, everyone started standing up and chatting with friends and neighbors as they headed toward the tables set in the back of the barn. Everyone except for Sylvia and Kelsey.

As much as Patti didn't want to miss out on one of those pickles, she couldn't ignore the fact that something was very wrong in the Shrock family. Walking to Sylvia's side, she sat down. "It's obvious you are upset," she whispered. "How may I help?"

Sylvia reached for her hand and squeezed it with both of hers. "Oh, Patti, I wish there was a way you could help. Unfortunately, there is not."

Glancing at Kelsey, she said, "Is someone sick? Thinking of the most obvious explanation, she added, "Is it Beth? Is something wrong with her babe?"

"*Nee*. As far as she knows, her pregnancy is going well," Kelsey replied.

If she wasn't so close to Sylvia, Patti would stand up and give them space. But Josiah and Sylvia meant everything to her. Some days, she felt as if she was closer to them than her own parents. That meant she must push a little harder.

"You know how much I care about you and your family, Sylvia. Please talk to me."

"I'm sorry to make you worry." Haltingly, she added, "It's just . . . well, I'm afraid the children got into an argument the other evening. Beth returned in tears, and Martin barely said two words. I don't know how it's going to be resolved."

As Kelsey joined them, Patti said, "I'm sure things will blow over. They always do, ain't so?"

"Not this time, I fear," Kelsey replied. "I'm afraid we were all a bit too frank. We haven't snapped at each other like that in years."

Patti looked at Kelsey. "Was it when you all went out to

supper?" Martin had mentioned that just the four of them were going to spend time together. He'd seemed excited about it. She'd been happy for him, too. Though he tried not to act like it, she knew he felt like the odd man out around his brother and sisters.

Kelsey nodded. "We started talking about choices . . . and each probably shared some opinions a bit too forcefully. By the time we parted, Martin was very upset with everyone."

Her heart clenched. As much as she cared about the entire Schrock family, there was no denying that her heart belonged to Martin. "Oh no."

"*Jah.*" Looking even more despondent, Kelsey released a ragged sigh. "I fear things were said that can't be forgotten."

Patti hoped that wouldn't happen. Martin, Kelsey, Beth, and Jonny needed each other. "They'll be forgiven, though, yes?" she asked gently. "After all, that is one of the foundations of our faith."

"I sure hope so," Kelsey said as she stood up.

Sylvia nodded but didn't say a word about that. Instead, she treated Patti to a half smile before walking toward the barn's open doors.

Patti had seen Josiah sitting across the aisle but wasn't sure if he was still there or was waiting outside for Sylvia. She had to forcefully remind herself that their problems were not her own. Sylvia most definitely had not invited Patti to offer advice. Most likely, she'd already tread where she shouldn't have.

Though she completely understood why she was being kept on the outside, she felt a bit dismayed. Over the years she'd opened up about a lot of things to Sylvia and Josiah. She would've thought they would've felt comfortable about doing the same thing.

As she stood by herself, Patti allowed her mind to drift back to Martin. If he'd gotten in a fight with his siblings, it must have been very bad. She knew that he took his role as the eldest seriously and always looked out for the others. If he had left town without saying goodbye, she was going to have to walk to the phone shanty and call him—and bring up her concerns. That was a big risk, though. He would either appreciate her words or resent her interference.

What to do?

"Hey, everything's going to be all right," Kelsey said as she walked to Patti's side. "My grandmother is mostly upset because there's nothing that she can do to help. She hates that."

"What about you? Are you all right?"

Some of Kelsey's self-assuredness faded. "No. I said some things to Martin that I wish I hadn't. He got upset with me."

"I'm sure he'll get over it."

"I reckon he will in time, but his forgiveness isn't going to completely erase my guilt. I should've been more circumspect and thoughtful." Looking upset with herself, she added, "I was so thoughtless, Patti. Martin has given up so much for me over the years. When he was in high school, if he thought I needed him, he would break his plans and stay home. I can't tell you how many Friday or Saturday nights he spent at home with me watching silly TV shows." She swiped a runaway tear from her cheek. "Why had I forgotten that?"

Patti was starting to feel really alarmed. If Kelsey was feeling this guilt-ridden, she must have really hurt her big brother's feelings. "I'll pray for you."

"*Danke.* Pray for Bethy, too, wouldja?"

"I'd be happy to." Tentatively, she added, "I happened to notice that she isn't here. Did Beth not feel like coming to worship?"

"She's been having trouble sleeping and begged off this morning. Dawdi wasn't real happy but understood." Looking toward the open barn door, she added, "I think that's why Mommi is anxious to leave. Even though Beth is a grown woman and used to living on her own, Mommi worries about her. We all do right now."

"That's understandable." She worried about Beth, too. Her good friend had a lot on her shoulders.

After giving Patti a quick hug, Kelsey walked across the room to stand by her husband's side.

Patti sat down again, overwhelmed by the other women's pain and the new set of concerns. Not only about the fight they had, but the fact that Martin left without telling her goodbye. Even though it wasn't helpful, she found herself wondering if the argument had anything to do with her.

Had she inadvertently done something wrong?

Just as quickly, she pushed those selfish thoughts from her mind. She needed to focus on the Schrock family, not herself.

Figuring that the Lord was just as worried as she was, Patti offered a quick prayer. *Dearest Lord, please help Josiah, Sylvia, Kelsey, Beth, Jonny, and Martin work through their problems and struggles. Please be with them as they come to terms with Your will. Help them discover Your grace and find peace. Please help me be the friend that they need me to be and keep my focus on them and not my own selfish wishes. Amen.*

"Everything all right with you, Patti?" Bishop Hershberger asked.

Looking up into the kind man's eyes, she smiled. "I think so," she murmured as she stood up. "I just felt the need to say some extra prayers."

"That's the beauty of the Lord, don't you think? He's always willing and able to be at our beck and call."

She smiled at the idea of the Lord stopping whatever he was doing to listen to her prayer.

"He does wonderous things, for sure and for certain."

"He does indeed." Gesturing toward the tables, Bishop Hershberger added, "My advice would be for you to go enjoy a bit of lunch. Jenna Lambright made some peanut butter chocolate chip cookies that are wonderful. They might make any worry better." He winked. "Then, of course, there are Martha's pickles."

She chuckled softly. "Are there any left?"

"Not many, but I'll tell you a secret. Martha always keeps some in the icebox under the table."

"Do you think she'll mind if I sneak one out of the container?"

"*Nee.* But if you are worried, just tell her that I told you to get one from there. She'll understand."

"*Danke*, Bishop. I think I'll go do that."

"*Gut.* And, Patti?"

She turned back to face him. "*Jah?*"

"I know you are likely worried about your future with a certain special man, but don't give up. I have a feeling nothing is as hopeless as it seems."

"I'll try to keep that in mind." She smiled. But after he walked away, Patti could admit to herself that she now felt as sad as Sylvia and Kelsey had appeared.

Knowing that there was no way she could sit down with the ladies who were eating and make small talk—let alone eat a sandwich or a cookie—she walked to the ice box, found a paper towel and used it to snag a spear, and then walked toward the field where all the buggies and horses were waiting.

With efficient movements, she greeted Ginger, hitched her up the buggy, and then slowly made her way to the main road.

Only then did Patti realize that tears were in her eyes.

She knew why, too. Yes, she was worried about Kelsey and Sylvia. Yes, she wanted to comfort Martin, too. But Patti knew that she was upset by something else—and that was the idea of never having the relationship with Martin that she desired.

She'd never be his wife. Never get to look at him across

the breakfast table. Never get to instinctively make plans for two people, because she was part of a pair.

Never get to tell the whole world that she loved him.

Clicking the leads, she guided the horse to her house but decided that she was going to stop at the phone shanty on the way home.

She needed to speak with Martin. She needed to make sure he knew that she cared about him and that he wasn't alone.

And she needed to talk to him for her own good, too. No matter what he had to say, it was better than the places her mind was going.

She just hoped he answered the phone.

CHAPTER 11

The cell phone's ringing woke him up. Martin had fallen asleep watching the football game, thanks to a sleepless night the evening before. By the third ring, he clutched the cell in his hand and was debating about whether or not he should answer. The number flashing on his phone could only come from one place—the phone shanty near his grandparents' home.

That meant either Beth, his grandparents, or Patti was calling. He didn't know what to say to any of them. Avoiding them all for a few more hours was so tempting.

When his phone started ringing a fourth time, Martin sighed. Then did what he'd known he was going to do all along. He answered.

"Hello?"

"Ach! Martin, you picked up! I'm so glad," Patti said in a rush. "I'd almost given up hope and hung up."

He rubbed his eyes. "Sorry, I had fallen asleep and it took me a minute to grab the phone."

"Why were you sleeping in the middle of the afternoon?" Concern laced her tone.

"No particular reason."

"Are you sick? If so, you can tell me."

"I'm not sick. I promise. I'm just . . . well, I'm just being lazy. That's all," he added as he walked into the kitchen and grabbed a soda out of the fridge. "So, hi."

She chuckled softly on the other end of the line. "Hiya. I guess I forgot to greet you properly."

"You know that I'm only teasing you." After taking a fortifying sip of the Coke, he continued. "Now, what's going on? You sound upset. Was there no church today?" Usually the service combined with the shared lunch with friends lifted Patti's spirits.

"*Nee*, we had services. The Gingeriches hosted this time." Her voice sounded flat. "How was it?"

She paused. "It was all right, I suppose."

"Just all right? Was my brother-in-law not on his A game?"

As he'd hoped, she chuckled. "Oh, Richard was in fine form. No doubt about that. He spoke about Jonah and gave us all a lot to think about."

"Okay . . ."

She continued. "And there was a nice breeze coming in from the outside. It wasn't stuffy in the barn at all. The time flew by."

"If all that was good, what was the problem?"

"I . . . well, I was more focused on Sylvia and Kelsey, if you want to know the truth."

He pulled out a stool and sat down. "What was wrong with them?"

"They were near tears. Kelsey, especially."

"Why was she crying?"

"She was upset about your family get-together." Sounding apologetic, Patti lowered her voice. "She doesn't like it when everyone argues."

"I see." Even though it wasn't fair, he was annoyed with

his sister. Why couldn't she keep anything to herself? Did she have to make a scene in the middle of church? "I'm sorry to hear that."

"I went to talk to them afterward."

He could feel a muscle twitch in his jaw. Now Patti was involved, too? "And what did they have to say?"

"Well, um . . . they didn't tell me everything. But, the gist of it is that Kelsey was upset you left so suddenly. She said that you all had argued about something fierce, and that everyone said things they shouldn't have."

As her words penetrated, Martin closed his eyes. Tried to get a handle on himself. But there were so many things wrong with Patti's story that it was impossible. But most of all, he resented the fact that he felt obligated to explain himself to her. Sure, Patti's call came from a place of concern, but he still thought it was a little gutsy for her to call him about it. "So, you decided to give me a call right away?"

"Uh, yes."

"Why? To make sure I knew how upset my younger sister was?" No longer attempting to hide the smallest bit of sarcasm in his voice, he continued. "Or, was it to let me know that my grandmother is now involved in the argument as well?"

There was a sharp intake of breath on the line, followed by a clearing of her throat. "*Nee*, that's not why I called."

"Are you sure about that?"

Sounding more and more distressed, Patti started talking in a rush. "I was concerned about you, Martin. I called because I was worried about *you*."

And now he was the biggest jerk in the state of Ohio. "Hush, sweetheart," he murmured. "I'm so sorry for snapping at you." When he heard her hiccup, he felt as if someone had just punched him in the gut. "Please stop crying."

"H-How did you know I was crying?"

"Because I know you." Because he loved her.

"Oh."

Martin frowned. He could practically see tears streaming down her face. It was official. He was the biggest jerk in the world. "I'm sorry for speaking to you like that," he said quickly. "It's no excuse, but that fight that I had with everyone has put me in a bad mood. Sometimes I get frustrated because I can't call them on cell phones or shoot off text messages. But none of that is your fault. I . . . I spoke without thinking."

"If that was how you felt, then there's nothing to apologize for."

Patti sniffed, reminding Martin that she was still crying. Man, he would give anything to be by her side right that minute.

These tears were all his fault. Standing up, he walked to stand in front of his roaring fireplace. He had a chill running through him, and he knew it was because he'd hurt her. "I didn't mean to accuse you of anything."

"It rather sounded like you did, Martin."

"I know. I can only apologize and ask you to try to forgive me."

"Of course I forgive you. But, Martin, what is going on?"

He closed his eyes. He wished things were different. He wasn't sure how he could make things better. No, make things different, but he wished he could. "Listen, that's why I went home. I'm not in a good place."

To his surprise, Patti didn't let him off the hook. "So you just left. Without an explanation."

"I don't have an explanation for you."

"You're gonna have to try harder. The last time I saw you, things were far different. You acted . . ."

Even through the phone line, he could tell she was trying not to cry and it was all his fault. "I acted as if I really cared about you?"

"Yes."

"That's because I do," he said, hating every word coming out of his mouth. Not because he was telling the truth, but because the truth didn't necessarily matter.

"Then why did you leave without telling me goodbye?"

He'd reached a breaking point. Both for himself and for everything that he'd been feeling. And regretting.

And trying to ignore.

"I left because I don't want to be Amish, Patti."

He'd done it. At last, he'd uttered everything he hadn't wanted to admit and everything he hadn't wanted to believe. To his shock, his body subtly relaxed just as her heart felt as if it was breaking.

And, because Patti was silent on the other end of the line, he added, "I'm so sorry, Patti. I really wished I felt otherwise. I tried to explain things to my sisters and Jonny, but they didn't understand."

"Oh."

Oh? What did that mean? "That's why I didn't stop by. It was hard enough to tell my family about my decision. I couldn't bear to tell you." And . . . now he sounded completely selfish and wimpy, too. He started pacing back and forth across the living room.

"Is that all you were going to tell me?"

"Yes. I mean . . . I think so. Why?"

"Well, I'd rather know how you feel about me."

He stopped. "Patti, don't you understand? Since I'm not going to change—"

She interrupted him with a sharp tone. "*Nee*, Martin. Stop."

"Stop?"

"Stop explaining things that I already understand. Forget everything but me. *Patti*. Not Amish Patti. Not your grandmother's neighbor Patti. Not even flawed Patti. What do you think about me?"

"There is nothing wrong with you. Don't ever call your-self flawed again."

"Answer me."

Boy, she sounded annoyed. It was adorable. "Patti, you know that we shouldn't—" Not wanting to make things worse, he stopped. What could he possibly say that wouldn't add more hurt?

"Answer me, Martin!"

"Fine. I love you. That's how I feel. I love you. I love all the Pattis you mentioned. I am falling in love with you, but it's like the worst thing that could happen because no matter how hard I try, I can't change my entire life. I tried. Honest to God, I tried." He gripped his phone so hard that he was surprised the case wasn't cracking.

"You love me?"

"Yes. I'm sorry."

She hiccupped a laugh. "Are you apologizing to me or yourself?"

He wished he could see her. Wished he could look into her pretty brown eyes. Maybe then he would get a better idea about how she was feeling—like, was she just saying the words but holding her thoughts inside for safekeeping?

"I'm apologizing for both of those things, I guess. I don't want to hurt you. I never want to do that. But no matter how much I've tried to find a way to wrap my head around it, I can't change my entire life in order to be with you."

"Why didn't you tell me this in person?"

"Because I didn't know how to tell it to you to your face. I don't want to hurt you."

"You're acting as if I don't have a choice in the matter."

"What is the choice?"

"I don't know, Martin. Maybe you could ask me instead of thinking for the both of us."

Taken aback, he tried to think of an appropriate reply. What was she saying? Was she really insinuating that she would leave her faith for him?

Would she actually abandon her whole way of life? Her house? Everything she knew and was comfortable with just to be with him?

It didn't seem possible.

"You're going to have to tell me what you're thinking, Patti," he whispered after he gained his voice.

"I think you know."

But that was just it. He didn't. "No, I'm not sure that I do." When he didn't hear a reply immediately, he rushed to try to explain himself. "This is too important to me. No, to us," he corrected, "to guess."

"Martin."

"What I'm trying to tell you, Patti, is that I need to hear you say the words."

"Oh."

"Please," he added. He was afraid his pushing was going to alienate her, but he also didn't want to let her off the hook.

"All right, then." She took a breath. "Martin, what I'm trying to say is that I think I'm falling in love with you, too," she whispered.

Tears pricked his eyes. Never. He'd never imagined that she'd ever tell him something like that. Even if she did have feelings for him, he was sure that she would have buried them deep.

Because they had no future.

Or did they?

"Martin, say something," she whispered.

He dug deep, trying to find a way to convey everything he was feeling into the right words. "I'm trying." Hearing his weak effort, he mentally kicked himself. "I wouldn't have thought it possible, but you have taken my breath away," he said at last. "I wish I was there so I could hug you."

"I wish you were, too."

"We're on the same page, Patti." He could hardly believe it. They were in love with each other.

She chuckled, though it sounded more dry and brittle than joyous. "You shouldn't have left without telling me goodbye, Martin."

He ran a hand through his hair. "What do you think happens next? What do you want to happen next?" If she was wanting to be with him, then she was going to have to leave her faith.

"I guess we pray and think and talk some more."

"I'll make plans to come see you, too. I could probably come down Thursday night—"

"*Nee*," she interrupted. "I think you need to wait a bit to come to Walden. I'd like us to think about what this means for a spell."

"Whatever we decide can take place whenever we are ready. There's no timeline on this."

"I reckon that's true. So maybe we need to keep things between us. That is, if you don't mind."

"I don't mind. Even if we weren't fighting, my family is going to have something to say about all of this, and I don't want to think about what they want or hear their opinions. I still want to see you, though."

"I'll be okay. Now that I know how you feel about me, I think I'll be all right."

"If you're okay, then I'll be okay, too. I'm going to pray about this, Patti. I mean, pray some more about it."

"I know what you mean."

"Will you keep praying, too?"

"Of course." Her voice was calm and certain.

Amazingly, that tone in her voice made him ease, too. "I'm glad you called, Patti."

"Me, too. I'm very glad. Goodbye, Martin."

"Goodbye, Patti. And don't forget that I love you."

She chuckled. "I won't ever forget that."

After they hung up, he realized that his entire body felt different. He felt buoyant. Filled with hope.

Sitting back down on the couch, he leaned his head back and stared at the ceiling. Breathed deep.

Patti loved him and he loved her.

They were in love.

No matter what happened in their future, being loved by a woman as special as her felt incredible.

It felt like she was the sweetest gift he could ever receive. "Thank you, God," he whispered.

Sure, he was going to have a lot of obstacles to overcome, but for the first time in over a year he felt as if he wasn't fighting to breathe.

He'd always be thankful for that.

CHAPTER 12

Beth was uncomfortable. After wearing loose dresses and tennis shoes for several weeks, it felt strange to have on her regular clothes. In addition, she'd been amazed at how long it had taken her to get ready that morning. She'd gotten used to simply washing her face, applying moisturizer, and pulling her hair back into a ponytail.

Applying eyeliner, mascara, and styling her hair into loose waves with a battery-operated curling iron had been frustrating. Back in high school and college, she'd taken great care in her looks. Honestly, she'd felt the same way in her real-estate job. She'd taken pride in looking put together and comfortably stylish.

She would've never imagined that her former morning routine would suddenly seem silly and like a waste of time.

But it sure did now.

It also felt a little bit odd to be driving again.

She currently had a death grip on her steering wheel as she drove on the freeway toward Lakewood, a suburb of Cleveland bordering Lake Erie. As a couple of cars zipped by her on the left, Beth told herself not to worry about her speed.

She was fine. And she was. She was maintaining a respectable seventy miles an hour and keeping up with the traffic.

She could return to her old life whenever she needed to. She might be currently living in Walden and helping her grand-mother hang laundry on lines in the basement, but she was still the same Beth Schrock that she'd always been.

Maybe.

It was just the relationship with her longtime friend Kiran that was in shambles. But what could she expect when the two of them had too much to drink one night and decided to take their friendship to the next level? She'd woken up the next day hung over and embarrassed. She'd expected to feel awkward around him for a while. And she had.

She'd never imagined she'd also be pregnant.

As much as she wished she never had to see him again, that wasn't going to be possible. They needed to iron things out for the baby's sake. One day he or she was going to want to know their father, and both she and Kiran agreed to even-tually set up a plan in order for that to happen.

All that was why she'd told Junior that she was going to take a couple of days off work and had gone against Jonny's advice to do everything via email.

So this was the right thing to do. It sure wasn't easy, though.

Kiran had agreed to meet her for lunch at Toast, a trendy spot in Lakewood.

The restaurant was expensive and small. The menu catered to a variety of special diets. If one was following a keto, vegan, or gluten-free diet, they had it covered. Toast also special-ized in organic, farm to table fare.

She'd always enjoyed it.

Now she couldn't help but think that there were three or four quaint restaurants in Walden that served many of the same items with a lot less fuss for a lot less money.

Toast was a good spot for her, though. A successful one.

A lucky one. She'd taken at least a dozen clients there, usually when she was trying to impress someone new.

Over sparkling water and appetizers, she would present herself. No, she'd sell herself, unabashedly sharing her successes and the accolades she'd earned.

It was also where she'd closed deals with one set of people and then celebrated with some of her colleagues.

Beth realized that she'd chosen the restaurant in the hopes that the surroundings would spur a little bit of her fortitude. A little bit of verbal muscle memory, if you will. She needed her brain to be working well. She needed to be able to speak clearly, concisely, and with confidence about her needs.

And, perhaps, effectively close out any questions or comments that Kiran might have.

This place was her armor.

After the server brought her a fresh glass of sparkling pomegranate tea, she glanced down at her watch. And realized that she'd arrived ten minutes early.

Too early to appear completely confident and at ease. That had been a mistake.

But at least Kiran wasn't there yet and would never know.

After reminding her bladder that she did not need to go to the bathroom just yet—even though it was doubtful it would listen—she crossed her legs and did her best to appear relaxed in her rather snug dress and uncomfortable heels.

"Beth Schrock, look at you. You're just as gorgeous as ever," Kiran said as he approached the table. "No, don't get up," he murmured as he ignored the place setting across from her and sat down on her left.

Kiran was a surprise. He was dressed in dress pants, a white finely woven cotton shirt with the top button unbuttoned, and an open navy blazer. His shoes were from a popular men's shoe store and recently polished. His cheeks were freshly shaved, and the faint reminder of his aftershave lingered on his skin.

He was just as handsome as she remembered.

No, that wasn't right. He was actually a bit more than that. He was more than she'd allowed herself to remember. More charismatic. More charming. More confident. Nicer. And yes, even more good looking than she'd wanted to think about.

Though she felt nothing toward him beyond a regret for the change in their relationship, she did acknowledge that there would always be a link between them.

She'd been a bit of a fool to imagine that a favorite restaurant to celebrate work success was going to have any bearing on how she felt.

Her personal life was in shambles.

Clearing her throat, she attempted to adopt an easygoing attitude. "Thank you for meeting me here."

"There's no need to thank me. Of course I was going to meet you."

"Kiran." She couldn't help but shake her head. He spoke so smoothly . . . but she had a feeling that he wasn't fake and slick. At least not right at this moment.

Lines around his eyes deepened as his smile deepened. "Hey, why are you looking so surprised? I picked up as soon as you called and agreed to meet the minute you asked."

He had done all those things. "I . . . I'm not sure why I'm surprised. I guess it's because things are different now."

"I know. But it's still just you and me. Have you forgotten that we've been friends for years?"

"Of course not. I haven't forgotten."

"I figure if we can survive all those crazy real-estate deals we worked on together, we can figure out how to manage our future, too." Some of the amusement in his eyes faded as he studied her.

She could practically feel his eyes examine every inch of her. Taking catalog of the differences. Her muscles tensed. She forced herself to look right back at him. Not look away.

Not be embarrassed that her body had begun to change because she was carrying a baby.

No, not a baby. Kiran's baby.

When the server approached again, she smiled at Kiran. "It's nice to see you again, Mr. Gould. What would you like to drink?"

"I'll have a Perrier, thanks."

"Lemon or lime?"

"Lime. Thanks, Carolina."

"Of course, Mr. Gould." The server turned to Beth. "Would you care for another pomegranate spritzer, miss?"

"No. Thank you. One is probably enough. I'll just drink water from now on." No way did she want the server to be the one to tell Kiran that she'd arrived too early.

When Carolina walked off, Kiran tilted his head to one side. "You've been here for a while?"

"No, I just got here a little early."

"What's going on, Beth? When you told me the news, you were pretty matter of fact. When you told me that you didn't want me to be a part of the baby's life, I agreed. Have you changed your mind?"

"What would you do if I said I did?"

Kiran looked slightly taken aback but recovered quickly. "I'd probably do the same thing I did when you called two days ago. I'd agree to meet with you and talk things through."

She blinked. "You mean that, don't you?"

"Of course, I do." He opened his mouth to continue but refrained when Carolina returned with his drink.

"Would you two care for anything?"

"Yeah. Bring us one of those cheese boards with fruit. Do you want anything else, Beth?"

"No, that sounds good."

"Just that. Thanks," he said, not even looking at Carolina. Some of the spark in the server's eyes faded as she turned around. Beth wondered just how close the two of them had been—then decided it didn't matter. She wasn't jealous and had no real interest in Kiran's personal life.

After taking a sip of water, Kiran spoke. "Beth, I'm going to be honest. From the time we first met, we've clicked. I've always liked working with you. Whenever our paths crossed on a real-estate deal, I would breathe a sigh of relief. You're smart and have an easy way about you. I've always considered us to be friends."

"I felt the same way."

Looking a bit relieved, he smiled at her before continuing. "That said, I'm not going to say that I wish our, um, night hadn't happened. But I do wish we'd made better choices when it did. I'm sorry that something must have been wrong with the protection we used. I'm sorry for that."

"I've never held you responsible. There were two of us that night." She swallowed. "And everything we did was mutual."

"I know you're keeping the baby. You haven't changed your mind about that, have you? You still don't want to think about adoption?"

"No. I want this baby." Curving her hands around her belly, she said, "I'm excited to be a mother."

"All right, then." He cleared his throat. "If you'd like me to help support it and give you money every month, or I don't know, a sum every six months or year, I can contact a lawyer and put that into place. But, when you first called to tell me the news, I didn't lie. I don't particularly want to be a father. If our child wants to know me or if you later decide that you want financial support, then I can get more involved." He looked down at the table, then added, "I also can't read your mind. If you want something more, then I need you to be as honest with me as I'm being with you."

"I understand. You are being very honest." Even though

his words still stung a bit, she appreciated how blunt he was being.

"I think we have to be. It's another life we're talking about."

She mentally breathed a sigh of relief. Kiran thought the same way she did. He hadn't suddenly become a jerk.

Now it was her turn. Beth realized once again that as much as she regretted having a one-night stand, she'd come to terms with the pregnancy and was excited to be a mother.

"Kiran, ever since that first pregnancy test came back positive, I've planned to do this on my own. I agree, we've been friends over the years, but it really has been in a professional capacity. I don't want to trap you into doing something you don't want to do."

Taking a deep breath, she continued. "I realize now that I was naïve to not have thought about what this child might want in the future. I should've done that."

"I never thought you were trying to trap me, Beth. It never crossed my mind."

She made a decision. "How about this? Let's go ahead and get a lawyer involved. I don't want or need any money from you, but perhaps you could put a small amount in an account for him or her? I mean, if you wanted to do that. Also, perhaps you could agree that we'll always give the lawyer and each other our contact information in case something happens. What do you think?"

Kiran nodded slowly. "I think that sounds good. If something happens to you, I'll want to know. Just like if something happens to this baby and you need money for the hospital or something, I don't want you to have to do that on your own."

"But otherwise, you won't be involved."

He visibly winced but didn't look away. "Otherwise, I won't. I'd rather not be. I know I sound harsh. I'm sorry, Beth."

As awkward and painful as the situation had become, Beth appreciated his honesty. "Don't be sorry. I'm fine with that."

"If you change your mind . . ."

"I won't," she said quickly. "But if I do, I'll tell you. I promise."

"Here you are," Carolina said as she placed a generously filled tray in between them. There had to be at least four types of cheese, that many types of fruit, and a variety of crackers and nuts. It looked like it should be on some influencer's media page or in a fancy cookbook.

"This is beautiful. Thank you," Beth said.

"It's our most popular app," she said as she handed them each a plate. "Do you need anything else?"

"Not a thing," Kiran said. When they were alone again, he said, "So, are we good?"

"Yeah."

"You going to be okay sharing this meal with me still?"

In spite of how serious their conversation had been, Beth couldn't help but smile. "You know what? Yeah."

"Good. There's a ton of food here. I probably should've ordered something smaller."

"Are you kidding? I'll make a good dent in it. I am eating for two, you know."

Kiran threw back his head and laughed. "How could I forget?"

Eager to talk about anything else, she said, "I saw you got that listing in Rocky River."

His eyes lit up. "The Jamison property?"

"That's the only one I cared about. How did that come about?"

"You're not still in the business, are you?"

"Nope."

"In that case, get ready, Beth. I can give you the whole ugly story."

Taking a bite of brie, she crossed her legs. She finally felt like herself again. She might be living Amish, but she was still the woman who'd spent hundreds of hours working in real estate.

Smiling at him, she said, "I can't wait, Kiran. Don't spare me a single detail."

CHAPTER 13

The park was empty and Junior gave thanks for that. It was Wednesday afternoon and he'd taken off early from work. Monday and Tuesday had been so hectic, he'd not only gotten home late but had been so tired that he'd barely given his dogs much more than a short walk and a couple of distracted pets.

Deciding that he needed a midweek break, he'd worked through lunch, told Cherry that he'd see her on Thursday, and hurried home to take Clyde and Honor out for a long walk. As he'd expected, the Labradors were pleased to see him, wiggling and wagging like he'd been gone for days instead of hours.

The Labs were a brother and sister from the same litter and now twelve years old. He still was surprised that he'd bought the pair of them together. One Labrador puppy was a destructive handful. Deciding to raise two of them at one time was a mistake.

He'd known that and done it, anyway.

Looking back, Junior figured that his decision had more

to do with the way the puppies had snuggled together when they were sleeping. They truly loved each other. Just like he and his brother, Samuel, had been when they were small. Part of him had hoped that one day he and Sam would be close again.

Now, all these years older, Junior was a little older and wiser. He'd also long since given up the hope that he and his brother would ever be close again. Samuel had not only jumped the fence, he refused to grow up. Whenever he visited, he was always talking about some new scheme to make a gob of money.

Which he never did.

Clyde and Honor, on the other hand, were still best friends. They didn't like to do anything on their own. They had also lost most of their wild ways. It had been a long time since he'd found one of his Red Wings chewed or a library book shredded.

Now the pair were slightly rotund, always ready for a nap, and no longer seemed to care what any of the neighborhood squirrels or neighboring cats did. The only things they seemed to move quickly for anymore were dog treats and tennis balls.

The dogs' current favorite method of getting around was a slow, meandering walk filled with lots of smells, stops, and sniffing for chipmunks. Junior had long since given up trying to encourage the pair to "heel." Neither had any desire to walk politely by his side.

Actually, the dogs' general laziness had become a blessing since he'd been working so much. Though he tried to take them to work one day a week, they were usually home. Every morning, either one of his neighbors or his mother would come over and keep them company for a spell. They would pet the dogs, take them out to do their business, and then spend an hour or two reading, knitting, writing letters, or, on occasion, helping dust his house.

After they left, the dogs ate a bit, took a long nap, and then occupied themselves by staring out the front window waiting for Junior to return home.

It was obvious that the three of them were quite content with their lives. But it was also obvious that a little bit of a change of pace wouldn't be a bad thing.

"I fear we're in a rut, dogs," he said as he sat down on his favorite bench in the park. "You two are getting old, but I'm not. Shouldn't I be doing something besides think about candles and you two?"

Neither of his chocolate Labradors replied. They were too busy inspecting every bush and shrub in the vicinity.

Junior chuckled. "Really? That's all you have to say?" he teased.

But then Clyde barked. Then barked again. Honor chimed in and began wagging her tail.

Curious about what had caught the dogs' attention, Junior turned.

And then did his best to hide his shock. There was Elizabeth Schrock, looking as pretty as ever. And, if he was being honest, looking as lost as he felt.

The aura about her was one of the reasons that he'd agreed to have her help him at work. Sure, he needed help. Everyone knew that. But he'd gotten the feeling that she'd needed the work almost as much.

Had she been in a rut, too?

He got to his feet. "Hiya," he said.

"Hi, Junior. Sorry I didn't call out to you when I got close. These Labs caught my eye."

The pair was wiggling and wagging their tails to beat the band. "They do like to get attention."

"Are they yours?"

"Yep. Please meet Clyde and Honor. They're brother and sister."

"They're also so cute." She chuckled as Clyde meandered

over to say hello. "Hello, you," she said as she tentatively held out her hand for him to sniff.

Before Junior could warn her, Clyde licked her hand.

She laughed. "You're adorable."

"He is. He's a good dog, though not the best sportsman."

Bending down to rub his head, she said, "That's okay, Clyde. I'm not the best sportsman, either." Turning to Honor, she held out her hand to greet. "What about you? Are you the sportsman of the family?"

Honor responded by lying on her back.

Junior walked closer and rubbed the dog's tummy. "They're hopelessly spoiled, I'm afraid."

"Maybe not hopelessly. They look loved," she said as she sat down on the grass by Honor's side.

"Well, they are that."

Watching her, Junior took in her outfit. Today she was wearing loose jeans, a baggy sweatshirt, and canvas tennis shoes that had obviously seen better days. Her hair hung loose down her back, looking gorgeous and shiny. Altogether, she looked comfortable and pretty.

Elizabeth also looked very far from what he'd thought she was, which was a woman seriously considering being baptized in the Amish faith. He wondered if she'd had a change of heart.

"Have you been to this park before?" he asked.

"I have. I think my grandmother's neighbor Patti took me here once. Or maybe my younger brother. Jonny is always up for exploring a new park." She smiled at the dogs. "Usually Jonny's on the back of a bike, though."

"It's *gut* you've got so much of your family here."

She lifted her chin. "Yes, it is."

"That's got to be something, all of you intent on becoming Amish."

"Not *all* of us," she corrected. "So far, only Kelsey and

Jonny have gotten baptized. This quest we've been on hasn't been all that easy. It's actually been something of an odyssey for us."

"Of course not. I didn't mean to insinuate that you were living here as a lark."

"You didn't." Taking a deep breath, Beth pulled her hair away from her face. "I'm sorry if I sounded defensive. It's just that . . . well, all four of us have had to respond to a lot of questions over the last couple of years. Everyone we know—whether they're English or Amish—have felt obligated to share their opinions about our choices."

He drew in a breath. It seemed his first impression hadn't been wrong. She did seem to be a little bit lost. And it didn't matter what she was wearing. The important thing was that she didn't look either relaxed or happy. "Do you not like to talk about your family being here? We don't have to."

"It's not that. It's . . . well, I've had a couple of difficult conversations over the last couple of days. I not only drove up to Cleveland to speak to the, ah . . . baby's father, but I also went out to eat with my brothers and sister and it didn't go well. Now my grandmother is involved, too." Looking down at Honor, a wrinkle formed between Beth's brows. "Sometimes I wish that I could spend twenty-four hours tucked away from the world. I'd give a lot to only worry about staying up too late reading a book."

He nodded. "I'm sorry your week has been so tough. It sounds like you've been through the wringer."

"I guess I have, but I'll be fine. I hate personal conflicts. I used to be able to handle any conflict that came up in a real-estate deal. Sometimes I think I even kind of liked it." She turned to him. "It made me work harder, you know?"

"I do know."

"But I have a much harder time arguing with people I'm close to."

"Does that happen often?"

"Arguing with my family?" When he nodded, she shook her head. "No. Luckily the four of us don't usually argue much at all."

"And with the, um . . . father?"

"We didn't argue once. Surprisingly, that went well. Really well."

Junior wondered what that meant. Was she getting together with the guy? Back together? He knew nothing about her story. Sure, it wasn't any of his business, either.

But that didn't mean he didn't want to know about it. He wanted to know a lot of things about her—and to hear all about it from her, too. Not as relayed information.

Deciding to fill the silence, he said, "If you aren't used to arguing with your family, then you should count yourself lucky. Me and my brother rarely see eye to eye." Actually, it was usually never.

"Family is family, right?" Nodding, she sat down on the grass and kicked out her legs. Clyde, who'd been inspecting a bush and then half-heartedly digging a hole, trotted to Beth's side.

"You are so cute. Both of you are," she cooed as the dogs crept closer and closer.

"They're both real cute, but they don't realize that they're each seventy pounds. Plus, they like to cuddle."

"Cuddle?" She raised an eyebrow.

And now he officially sounded like an awkward teenager. "What I'm trying to say is that one of 'em is going to plop down on your lap if you're not careful. You'll be stuck with a slobbery, furry dog in your business in no time."

"That's not a bad thing. Clyde or Honor, if either of you are in the mood to cuddle, I'm ready."

He laughed at her singsong voice. "Something tells me you've been around dogs before."

"Yep. We always had one at our mother's growing up. They were never big and exuberant, though."

"No?"

"My mother favored poodles and terriers. When they weren't barking at the postal carrier, they were generally quiet, didn't shed too much, and were happy to lounge on the couch for hours at a time."

Junior sat down across from her on the grass. "Are you planning to come to work on Monday?"

"Yep. It's one of the reasons I went ahead and drove up to Cleveland."

"You know I would've given you the day off."

"I know, but I didn't want to be thinking about Kiran when I was looking at invoices or answering the phones. One thing at a time, right?"

He chuckled. "I'm not sure that you're going to be ready for life at Walden Wax Works. I have a feeling that we do things at a little slower pace than you're used to."

"Sorry, but that wasn't the impression I got."

"What does that mean?"

"Only that the phone was ringing off the hook, people were walking in for business and deliveries, and you had more work than any one man—or woman—could do. If that was working slow, then a busy day must go at warp speed."

"I guess you got me there. But, um, things aren't usually like that."

"I didn't think it was bad. Do you not want to have a lot of business?"

"I do." When she raised her eyebrow, he groaned. "Fine. I guess I do like things busy. But I also want to honor every-one else's time commitments. Which means if you told me that you needed to be in the big city for personal reasons, I wouldn't have minded." Tossing her a pointed look, he added the obvious. "Especially since you don't want to be paid for your work."

"I'm the type of person who doesn't like to juggle too many things at once. I needed to wrap up some unfinished business."

"Were you successful?"

"I think so. It went better than I thought it would."

"I'm glad." When both dogs stood up and stared at him, Junior knew it was time to move on. "I need to go," he said as he got to his feet. "They enjoy getting out and about, but they're most comfortable at home."

"Ah. And I've kept them from it for too long." When she moved to get on her feet as well, he reached down to help her. Clasping her hand, he gave a little tug.

Her hand was soft and smooth in his. It was a hand that hadn't washed a lot of dishes or scrubbed a lot of floors, he realized.

"Thanks," she said as she got to her knees, then finally got to both of her feet. She paused, trying to steady herself.

He didn't know much about pregnant women, but the frown she was now wearing didn't look good. "You all right?"

"Yes. It's . . . well, I just realized that today was probably the last time that I am going to sit down on grass without thinking about how I'm going to get back up. I'm getting bigger by the day."

"I reckon that's to be expected, ain't so?"

"Yes." She paused. Tucked in her bottom lip. "Ah, I'm fine now."

"Hmm?"

"My hand?"

He was still holding her hand. "Oh, sorry." Junior dropped his like he was in danger of getting burned. "I didn't realize . . ."

"No worries. I'll see you tomorrow at work, boss. Nine o'clock?"

"It's up to you, remember?"

"I know. But I'd still like to pretend to be a decent employee."

He had a feeling Beth had been far more than just a "decent" real-estate agent. "Nine's good. See you then."

Her smile was bright before she turned and walked away. From the back, she didn't look pregnant at all. Her hips were nicely curved and her walk was graceful.

"*Yip!*"

"Sorry, buddy. You're right, buddy. It's past time we were on our way. Let's go, you two." Turning, he headed toward home.

Honor scampered ahead. As Clyde increased his pace, his tail wagged. The dogs were happy. Happy with the walk, happy to have him all day long. The three of them were a good team—there was no denying that.

But that didn't mean there wasn't a part of him that couldn't help but acknowledge that his dogs' backsides weren't near as fun to watch as Elizabeth Schrock's.

His new almost-employee.

"That is a problem, right there," he murmured. "She's your employee and probably someone else's girl."

"Dogs, it looks like it's just going to be us for a while longer," he said. "What do you think?"

To his surprise, Honor whined.

"*Jah.* I was thinking the same thing, *hund.*" It would be nice to have someone like Elizabeth in his life.

Maybe it was time to think about courting again.

CHAPTER 14

It was Monday morning. After looking at her reflection in the bathroom mirror one last time, Beth turned off the flashlight she kept on the counter and headed into her bedroom. There, she grabbed her sweater, put on her tennis shoes, and picked up her purse. At long last, she was ready. Unfortunately, she felt no sense of accomplishment . . . because she was going to be late for work.

She hated that. She'd been an on-time girl all her life. Heaven knew she'd nagged Jonny to get out of bed and get into the shower almost every single morning in high school.

Running against the clock didn't feel comfortable at all. But . . . maybe if she skipped her morning cup of coffee, grabbed a granola bar from her stash in the back of the pantry, and walked along Main Street instead of meandering through back fields, she wouldn't be too late.

Yep, if she did all of those things—and didn't veer off track for even a minute—there was a good chance she'd probably walk in the front door of Walden Wax Works at six minutes after nine.

And, sure. Any minute after nine o'clock was technically late. It wasn't anything to be proud of, but it wasn't horrible. Plus, if Junior said anything, she had a lot of good excuses in her arsenal. She could blame the traffic on the roads. Her grandmother needing her to do something unexpected. Or her pregnancy. Junior would never fuss if she said that was her reason.

Or, Beth could go the teasing route, and remind Junior that he had said that he ran a relaxed office. Didn't that also mean she had relaxed start and stop times, too?

Feeling better about spending most of the morning battling an unwelcome dose of morning sickness with a side of laziness, Beth entered the kitchen. "*Gut matin*, Mommi."

"Good morning to you, child. Come sit down. I made you a nice bowl of oatmeal."

Brown, soggy, warm oatmeal? She did her best not to grimace. "Well, ah . . . that's so nice of you, but I'm running late."

Her grandmother pulled out a chair and pointed to it. "If you're running late, then you'd best get started on your meal. Ain't so?" Before Beth could reply, she bustled to the kitchen counter. "Sit, sit. I'll pour you a cup of coffee and a glass of juice."

"Thanks, but I'm just going to get a granola bar."

"No, you are not. I heard how upset your stomach was this morning. It's obvious that you need to get something of sustenance inside of you." She tapped a foot. "Sit, child."

"Heard" meant that her grandmother had overheard her losing her stomach contents through the thin walls of the house. Even though she hadn't been able to help it, Beth still felt her cheeks heat with embarrassment. On its heels was the reminder that this way of plain speaking was as part of her grandmother's makeup as getting up with the sun in the morning.

"I'm sorry you heard me, but I really do have to leave."

"If you had sat down when I asked you to, you'd already be halfway done with your meal. Sit down, Elizabeth."

"Elizabeth?"

The barest hint of a smile appeared on her dear grandmother's face. "It suits you, Beth."

There it was again. The reminder that Junior Lambright—who steadfastly seemed to only go by his nickname—preferred her given name.

Even more perplexing was the way she didn't mind him using it, either.

Glancing at the clock on the kitchen wall, she winced. It was already nine. Figuring there was nothing to do about it now, she sat down at last. With a sense of foreboding, she took a tentative sip of the coffee her grandmother had just placed in front of her.

To her surprise, it tasted good.

Mommi stepped closer. "So far so good, dear?"

"*Jah*. I . . . think I'm good now."

"Of course. Now eat up."

She closed her eyes and quietly said a quick prayer of thanks. Then, picking up her spoon, she took an experimental bite of the oatmeal. To her surprise, it hadn't gotten too cold. It also tasted delicious. "Did you mix in cinnamon?"

"To be sure I did. I added brown sugar and cream, too."

"Cream?" Wasn't that, like a thousand calories?"

"It's good for your babe. Stop fussing and eat, child."

Doing what her grandmother wanted at last, Beth pushed all thoughts away about weight gain, time clocks, and upset stomachs and focused on the present—which was that she did have much to be thankful for. "Mommi, if I wasn't living here with you, I would have been in the real-estate office for two hours. And, I probably would have been stressing about work right now with only a granola bar in my stomach."

"Umph. This is better, I think."

She smiled up at her. "I think so, too. I appreciate you, Grandma."

Mommi patted the top of her head before sitting in a chair across from her. "Beth, I have something to share with you."

"Yes?"

"Back when you, Martin, Jonny, and Kelsey drove up to this house and then told Dawdi and I that you four were thinking about becoming Amish, I didn't know whether to laugh or cry."

"I get the laughing part. It did have to sound outlandish. But cry? Were you two that upset with us?"

"Not with you. Your situation."

"I don't understand."

"Bethy, all we could think was that the four of you must have been very unhappy with Matt and Helen. That you all must have been might unhappy with your lives if you were thinking to leave it all behind."

"I never thought about it like that."

"We worried about each of you something awful."

"I'm sorry. I do know that holding our hands through all of this has been challenging."

"It has been challenging, but the Lord sure knew what He was doing, ain't so?" she mused. "Here Kelsey, Jonny, and Martin all found what they were looking for. They were meant to be here. And now I believe He has big plans for you, too."

She didn't know about that. In contrast to her little sister, her life was a scrambled mess.

But she wasn't the only one. "Mamm, I know Jonny and Kelsey are happy, but I don't think Martin is settled yet."

"I believe otherwise."

"But he doesn't want to be Amish."

"I know."

She figured she might as well throw it all out there. "And he doesn't want to admit it, but I'm pretty sure he is in love with Patti."

Her grandmother smiled. "I think the same thing."

Feeling like Mommi still wasn't grasping the complete situation, Beth added, "That means that they aren't going to work out. While me, Kelsey, and Jonny are happy, Martin is going to get his heart broken. Patti, too."

"What I know, Elizabeth, is that Martin isn't the only person in that relationship who needs to make some decisions."

"You're talking about Patti?"

After taking a sip of coffee, Mommi nodded. "I am. She's stronger than Martin believes."

Beth smiled. "You really feel that they have a chance, don't you?"

She shrugged. "It's not up to me, of course, but the Lord did give me a fine set of eyes. I can see what is going on."

"Maybe it's just Martin and Patti who are blind."

"Perhaps." She looked down at Beth's empty bowl. "And it looks like you are now ready for work. Would you like me to hitch up the buggy and take you?"

"Thank you for the offer, but no. It will be faster if I walk, and the exercise will do me good. I just have to hope that Junior doesn't get too upset with me for being late."

"I will hope and pray that he doesn't." Walking to the refrigerator, she pulled out a darling insulated lunch box from the bottom shelf. "Here is your lunch. Don't forget to eat it."

"I won't."

"Off you go, then."

Quickly, Beth donned her coat, grabbed her purse and lunch box, and then kissed her grandmother's cheek. "I love you, Mommi."

"I know." She opened the door. "Walk carefully now."

The moment Beth was outside, her grandmother shut the door. No doubt her mind was already on the dishes, the laundry, and everything else she did to keep her house and yard spotless and well organized.

Beth sighed. She didn't know if she was ever going to be that good at domestic chores, but she figured there was room for improvement. She didn't dislike housework; she'd just never taken the time to focus on it much.

In that way she took after her mother, Beth realized.

As if her mother had read her mind, the phone rang.

"Hey, Mom."

"Beth, I'm so glad that I got hold of you."

"Why? Is something wrong?"

"With me? Of course not. I was thinking of you, sweetheart. How are you feeling?'

"Pretty good."

Worry entered her tone. "Uh oh. What's going on?"

"Nothing too exciting. I, um, just had an upset stomach this morning when I woke up. I had hoped I was done with that."

"Pregnancy is a funny thing, isn't it? It's like your body has a mind of its own."

Her mother's comment took her off guard, which was a mistake, she reckoned. Over the last few years they'd grown apart and while some of her other siblings had spent time with her at least once a month, Beth never had. She'd told everyone it was because she was so busy. She'd worked with clients who were either buying or selling million-dollar homes. The majority of them had been both needy and demanding, and she'd been only too happy to cater to their every whim.

But the other, more personal reason for her distance from her mom was that she was still harboring resentment about how her mom had placed her own needs in front of her kids' needs and wants after the divorce. Because of that, Beth had stepped into the role of mother for Kelsey and Jonny. She'd been the one they went to when something was wrong. Or they had a school project. Or they just wanted someone to hang out with.

She'd loved being needed, but there had also been plenty of times when she'd been forced to give up her plans in order to see to the needs of Jonny or Kels.

Now, though, Beth was wondering if maybe she'd been too hard on her mother all this time. "I guess you would know about all the changes that go on during pregnancy."

"I'm afraid I do. If you are experiencing anything odd, chances are pretty good that I've experienced it, too."

"Even heartburn?"

"Yep."

"Headaches?"

"I'm afraid so, dear. Each pregnancy was unique." She chuckled. "With Martin, all I wanted to eat was baked potatoes, but with Jonny, the only thing that would make me happy was Graeter's ice cream."

"What? The fancy ice cream from Cincinnati?"

"The one and only. Near the end of Jonny's pregnancy, I was miserable. I had three toddlers and your father's career had gone into hyperdrive. The only thing that made me happy was chocolate chocolate chip ice cream from Graeter's. Your father got so tired of hearing me whine about it, he called up the store and had them ship us six pints in dry ice."

"Dad did that?"

"He sure did. Of course, it wasn't like he had much of a choice. It was either take care of my ice-cream addiction or take care of three toddlers while I cried."

She not only couldn't imagine her mother crying over lost ice cream, but even thinking about her father coddling her mother was strange. "Mom, I had no idea."

"Why would you?"

"But still . . ."

"I didn't like talking about all that after Dad and me got divorced. And, well, I never wanted you kids to think that I didn't want you."

"You just wanted to feel better."

"Exactly."

"Mom, I can't believe you went through it four times."

"Those were some crazy years, to be sure. But good ones. I have a feeling you'll look back on these days the same way."

"Do you really think so?" She hated to feel so vulnerable, but she was aching for reassurance.

"Beth, what's wrong?"

"I don't feel like myself."

"Is it because your body is changing? Because that's normal, Bethy."

"No. Because I'm not really working and I'm not in love. I'm not near in love."

"I have a feeling if Kelsey called and said such things, you'd have some good advice for her."

"Maybe. But Kelsey is fine." And happily married to Richard, who adored her.

Her mother didn't say anything for a few seconds. "Beth, honey, I'm going to tell you something, but I feel like I should tell you first that you are welcome to ignore any advice I try to offer."

"What, Mom?"

"If I've learned anything, it's that you can't change the past."

Against her will, Beth felt defensive. And maybe a little scornful? "What do you mean by that?"

"Nothing secretive, dear. Only that it's easy to feel regret about a bad decision, or something you said when you were upset, or even a mistake that you're having to live with the consequences about. And I'm not going to say that isn't hard. Sometimes life really is hard."

She paused, then added softly, "But no matter how hard you pray or wish that you had done or said something differently, you can't go backwards."

"You think I should stop beating myself up about getting pregnant, don't you?"

"I think you are excited about being a mother. And I, for one, believe that you are going to be an exceptional mother. Perhaps it's time you focused on that?"

"That's good advice. Thank you."

"You're welcome."

"Hey, Mom?"

"Hmm?"

"Would you come down here sometime?"

"To see you?"

Admitting that felt a little weak. "Yes. Or to see Jonny and Kelsey and Martin."

"If you'd like to see me in Walden, all you have to do is ask, Beth."

"Would you come down soon?"

"I'd love to. Let me look at the calendar and text some dates."

"Thanks."

"No, thank you, honey." She inhaled a shaky breath. "This phone call meant a lot to me. I appreciate it."

"It meant a lot to me, too. Love you. Bye."

"Love you back, Beth. Bye."

When only silence filled her ear, Beth felt tears in her eyes. Maybe she was crying because she was hormonal. Or maybe it was because she'd just had the conversation with her mother that she'd never known she needed.

Whatever the reason, a ten-minute phone call had put her to rights and made her feel as if she was ready for anything.

Even her new job.

CHAPTER 15

About fifteen minutes ago, Junior had given up attempting to look like he was doing anything else but waiting for Elizabeth Schrock to arrive. At first, he'd tried to tell himself that he was loitering in the reception area because she was his friend.

That excuse didn't last long. Yes, she was his friend. But Elizabeth was also slowly becoming his crush.

Next, he'd decided that he was waiting for her because she'd looked so upset when they'd crossed paths at the park. He wanted her to have a good day. Not make her life harder.

But, as the minutes passed and nine turned into nine fifteen and then nine thirty, Junior decided that he didn't need an excuse, after all. Walden Wax Works was his company, and he could stand or sit wherever he wanted. He could certainly greet anyone who walked in the door without having to explain himself.

Cherry didn't agree.

She was glaring at him after he'd signed for a package that had just been delivered. "That's my job, you know."

"Signing for deliveries?" When she nodded, Junior was tempted to laugh. "Come on, Cherry. We both know you do a lot more around here than that."

Her chin lifted, making the ties on her *kapp* flutter slightly around her neck. "You're right. I'm the office's receptionist. I have a lot of responsibilities, all of which center around the *reception* area."

"I'm not disputing that." He was also doing a good job of not rolling his eyes, which he counted as a win.

"Maybe not, but you're still in the way. You're in my way."

"All I did was sign for a package. You should be thanking me, anyway, because I greeted Chad; you didn't even stand up."

Twin blotches of color appeared on her cheeks. "It doesn't matter if I did or didn't get out of my chair. The point is that I can't concentrate when you're watching me and pacing in front of the door like a caged tiger."

"I'm hardly doing that."

"I disagree." Making a shooing motion with her hands, she added, "Go on back to your office and let me take care of my reception area. I'll escort Beth Schrock to your office as soon as she arrives." She looked pointedly at the clock on the wall. "Since she is late."

Junior was just about to finally tell Cherry to watch her attitude when he spied Elizabeth coming up the walk. Today she was wearing a long-sleeved dark teal dress, tennis shoes, and her regular purse that happened to look a lot like a small backpack.

She also seemed to be looking a bit pale.

Was she sick?

Unable to help himself, Junior strode out to meet her. "*Gut matin.*"

Her blue eyes widened before she regained her composure. "Morning, Junior. Ah, what are you doing out here? Are you about to leave?"

"Not at all. I was, um, talking to Cherry about something when I happened to notice you were on the sidewalk. You looked like you could use a hand, so I came on out." Ashamed at how easily the lies kept coming, he held out a hand. "How about I take that backpack from you?"

"Usually I'd say that I was fine, but I really would love some help. Thanks."

When he pulled the pack off her shoulders, Junior couldn't resist moving her hair out of the way. It was the first time he'd seen her wear it down about her shoulders. Previously, she'd had it either pulled back in a ponytail or secured in a bun at the nape of her neck.

When a strand of hair got caught in a strap, he'd gently freed it. And tried not to think about how the light blond strands felt like silk.

When he felt her shoulders tremble slightly, he paused. "Sorry, but some of your hair was caught. Did I hurt you?"

"Not at all. I was, um . . . just being silly."

He wondered if her "being silly" was her way of describing the same zing of attraction that he did.

Or, maybe he'd just lost his mind.

Embarrassed at his train of thought, he focused on the surprisingly hefty backpack he was now holding. "Elizabeth, this is heavy."

"It's not that heavy." But the way she was rolling her shoulders belied her words.

"It's probably too heavy for a pregnant woman to be lugging around, ain't so?"

"Usually, I'd say that I can carry whatever I want on my back, but today it sure did feel like a lot."

"What do you have in here, anyway?"

"Lunch. Water bottles. A smaller purse. My phone. A book." She chuckled. "Stuff."

"Hmm." He opened the door and shuttled her inside. Worried that she might be chilled, he glanced at the coffeepot in the corner of the space. "Cherry, how fresh is that coffee?"

Turning to peek at the machine, she said, "Not very, since the pot is off." After giving Elizabeth a scathing look, she added, "It's practically lunchtime, you know."

It still wasn't even ten. "Isn't it kind of early to stop making it?"

"Why? Do you want me to get up and make more coffee?" She sounded put-upon.

It was all he could do not to point out that making coffee was part of her receptionist duties. "I want some for Elizabeth."

Cherry turned to Beth. "How much coffee do you want?"

"Just make a fresh pot," Junior said before Beth could say a word.

"If you're going to do that just for me, please don't bother," Elizabeth said. "I've already had my one cup of caffeine. I probably shouldn't have any more."

"Do we have decaf, Cherry?"

"Nope."

"I promise, I'm fine, Junior," Elizabeth said. "Thanks, anyway, Cherry."

"You're welcome." Thawing a little bit, Cherry smiled at Beth. "I hope you have a good day."

"Thank you."

Just as they turned away, Cherry added, "By the way, do you go by Beth or Elizabeth?"

"Beth."

"Hmm." After darting a look in Junor's direction, Cherry added, "I would offer to show you around and tell you where to stash your stuff, but the boss wants to do it."

Some of Elizabeth's smile faded. "Oh. Okay."

"Don't mind her," he said as he opened the glass door that led to the main manufacturing wing. When the door closed behind them, he said, "Cherry's not real pleased with me right now. I'm afraid that she decided to take it out on you. I'll speak to her about that."

"There's no need."

"There's every need."

"What did you do to get on her bad list?"

He chuckled. "I got in her way," he said as they headed toward his office. "It seems she's territorial."

She wrinkled her nose. "I'll make sure to stay out of her way, then."

"You don't have anything to worry about. Cherry usually only gets snippy with me."

"I know I was late. Were you waiting on me? Is that why you were in the reception area?"

"Guilty." Not wanting to dwell on that any longer, he pointed to the work area on the other side of the plexiglass wall. "You might remember that this is where we make the candles."

Stopping to watch the two dozen men and women melting wax, mixing in scents and colors, and placing wicks, Elizabeth smiled for the first time. "I would never forget this area. It's fascinating."

"You know what? I think so, too. It never fails to amaze me that we can take a couple of boxes of wax and change them into something that's pretty and smells good." Seeing that her smile had widened, he blurted, "Sorry. I tend to get a little too syrupy when I talk about the business. I know all we're doing is making candles. Not changing the world."

"I didn't think you sounded syrupy at all. But if you were, that's a good thing. After all, this is your baby."

"This place matters a lot to me, but it's just a business. I think a baby is a little bit more special."

"I have a feeling all the families who receive a paycheck from here might have something to say about that."

"Maybe so." After gazing at the workers, he turned to her again. Noticed how easy it was to get lost in her dark blue eyes.

Then reminded himself that he was her boss. Nothing more, nothing less.

"Let's get you settled. Since you're going to be helping me organize all the paperwork, I thought it would be best if you worked in my office."

"All right." She followed him down another hall and finally into his office. "So, here?" she asked, pointing to the slightly scarred cherry desk that he'd found in a back warehouse.

"Yep. The computer I ordered you came in over the weekend," he added as he placed her backpack on her chair. "I unboxed it yesterday and turned it on, but you're probably going to have to spend some time organizing everything."

"That won't be a problem." Walking to the desk, she ran a hand over the wood before putting her backpack on the floor. "Everything looks great."

"If it doesn't, let me know."

"I will." After a second's pause, she added. "I think I'll get started now."

He felt his cheeks heat. Yep, he'd been staring at her like he was a kid and she was his new puppy. He turned away, already beginning to regret his decision to have her work in his office when he remembered her queasy stomach.

She likely needed to eat often.

"Wait. I, uh, forgot to show you where to put your lunch. I'm assuming there's one in your backpack?"

"There is. But it doesn't need to be refrigerated. Do you mind if I just eat here at my desk?"

"You can eat wherever you want, but are you sure? Everyone gets a thirty-minute lunch."

"I can do that here."

"All right. That's, um, fine."

"Hey, Junior?"

"Yeah?"

"I am sorry that you felt you had to wait for me in the reception area."

How could he explain that he'd wanted to be the one who greeted her without sounding creepy? Realizing that wasn't possible, he shrugged. "We already talked about this. I wasn't waiting. I was in there, anyway. And stop worrying about the clock. I told you that I wouldn't put you on a punch card."

"I know. I just wanted you to know that I didn't mean to come in almost forty-five minutes late. I had to deal with some morning sickness, then my grandmother insisted I eat breakfast, and then my mother called. I hadn't talked to her in a while and didn't feel like I could put her off yet again."

"Are you feeling all right now?"

"Yes, I'm fine now."

"That's all that matters, then. I think it's time you sat down and took a breath."

Looking relieved, Beth nodded as she sat down. "I think so, too. I might have just gotten here, but it's been a long morning."

Junior felt the same way, but not because of anything but his attraction to Elizabeth. He was going to need to find a way to deal with that.

She had enough on her plate without her new boss mooning over her.

He needed to work on that.

CHAPTER 16

Willard Luft was well known for a variety of reasons in Walden. He was a master carpenter, raised champion horses, and took good care of his mother. He was also known to be a confirmed bachelor and a rather persnickety person.

Patti had known Willard for most of her life. Because he was a bit older, they'd never had much of an occasion to converse about anything other than the usual pleasantries whenever they passed each other on the street or spoke in church.

That was why she was mighty surprised when he showed up at her house on Thursday evening. In a clean shirt and freshly shaved face, no less.

"Hiya, Willard," she said when she answered the door. A half-dozen questions hovered on her lips, but how did one go about asking if there was a reason a man stopped by unannounced? Every word on the tip of her tongue sounded rather rude.

That said, she felt flummoxed. No one in need of her bookkeeping services came over in the evening. Then, too, was the way he was studying her. She felt as if he was cataloging her face, hair, teeth, and greeting. It was disconcerting! At least she was wearing a fairly new dress that fit her well. The dove-gray color wasn't her favorite, but she did like that it looked neat and clean.

After a pause, Willard inclined his head. "Good evening, Patti. May I come in? Or, would you like to come out to the front porch?" Before she could answer, he pursed his lips. "Now that I think about it, you'd best come out. It wouldn't be seemly if I went inside."

Seemly? She was tempted to giggle. And, if she was being honest, she was also tempted to close the door in his face. Who was he to say what she should do in her own house?

But, of course, neither option was going to happen, especially since she was starting to get the feeling that he was nervous.

"Willard, I'm afraid you're going to have to backtrack a few steps. Are you in need of a bookkeeper?"

His chest puffed up a bit—as if he needed to emphasize his manliness. "I am not, Patti."

"Then . . . ?" When he simply stared, she decided to be more forthright. "Is there something you need?"

"I realize that you have been off the shelf for quite some time, but surely you can remember what a caller looks like?"

He'd come calling. He'd come courting. *Willard!* Where was Kelsey or Beth when she needed them? Or even better, Sylvia! She and Sylvia had exchanged amused looks more than once when he acted full of himself.

Yes, she absolutely needed someone to exchange an incredulous look with while she did her best not to giggle. "Oh. I see."

He exhaled as he folded his hands behind his back. "If you do, then you also must understand why we shouldn't be alone in your house. People will talk."

About what? she wondered. Oh, she wanted to be a good

and proper woman! The type to graciously nod and invite him to take a seat on the porch while she prepared coffee or hot chocolate for them to sip on a chilly autumn evening.

Unfortunately, she just wasn't quite that good or proper. "Willard, I run my own business. I have clients come over all the time to discuss their companies or their ledgers. Some of those clients are single men."

"I am not like that. Please, get a shawl and join me on your porch. The chairs look somewhat clean. I'll sit down and wait."

He was ordering her about. "Yes. Please sit. I'll be right there," she said in a sweet tone. Right before she closed the door.

Leaning against the frame, she gazed up at the ceiling. "What in the world am I supposed to do with him, Gott?" she asked. "Willard is being insufferable and he's only been here a couple of minutes."

The Lord didn't answer, but it didn't matter, because it felt as if her mother was chiming in her two cents from up above. Her directions were simple and direct, too. Patti needed to put on a shawl, go sit outside on one of her somewhat-clean chairs, and entertain Willard. She needed to be polite, too. After all, he'd come all this way. She couldn't send him home without sitting with him for thirty minutes.

Hurrying to the kitchen, she grabbed her shawl off a peg near the back door and then strode to the front of the house. While she did, Patti purposely did not look at her kettle on the stove. She might owe Willard her time, but she was not going to make him hot chocolate or fresh coffee.

"Sorry it took me a moment," she said in her best breezy tone as she joined him on the porch. "I couldn't remember where I left my shawl."

He did not stand up when she moved to the chair next to him. Instead, he crossed his ankles in front of him. "Do you normally misplace important items?"

"*Nee*, I do not."

"Do you not consider your shawl to be important?"

"Willard, do you really want to talk about my shawl right now?" She smiled brightly. Just to take the sting out of her question.

"I suppose not." His lips pinched before he chuckled. "I guess it's obvious that you ain't the only one who is out of practice."

She kind of wasn't, though. Martin had come calling quite a bit. And he had made no mistake about his appreciation for her. Especially when he kissed her. But how could she admit that without sounding like a hussy? "Hmm."

"Hmm?"

"Willard, please forgive me. Even though we've known each other for years, I was surprised to see you on my doorstep. I never imagined you might be interested in me." There. She sounded modest yet in need of an explanation. Her mother would be pleased.

After crossing his legs, he said, "When I reached my fortieth birthday, I realized that if I didn't do something soon, I would grow old alone."

"So, you decided to start calling on different women?" It might be a little odd, but she supposed it did make sense. Desperation did make a person do things that were out of the ordinary.

"*Nee*, Patti. I made a list, thought about who might best suit my needs, and decided that you would be the best choice." He bared his teeth then, which she slowly realized was his attempt to smile.

And then he stared at her intently.

Just like he'd declared Patti the winner in a Publishers Clearing House giveaway!

She was becoming a little bit uncomfortable. "Wow, Willard. That is flattering, for sure. But, um, I don't believe we would suit."

"Why not? I am single and have a good job. I also want children. If the Lord decides that we could be fruitful, then you could be a mother."

She did not want to ever think about having children with Willard. She also didn't like him bringing up the possibility of her not being able to give a man a babe. "I do hope to be a mother one day. And, God willing, you will also be blessed to be a father."

"Well, of course." Up went an eyebrow. "What do you think?"

"About the two of us being together?"

"About us getting married."

"I'm sorry, but your employment and single status isn't a good enough reason to marry." Not wanting to beat around the bush—or converse with him on her front porch any longer—she added, "Besides, I'm already seeing someone. I'm not actually available. I'm sorry you didn't realize that."

"Who are you seeing?"

"I fail to see how that is any of your business."

"I think differently. I had plans for us."

When he folded his arms across his chest and stared hard at her, Patti realized it was silly to keep Martin's identity a secret. Taking a deep breath, she said, "It's Martin Schrock."

Willard's eyes narrowed. "The *Englisher*?"

"*Jah.*"

"That's impossible."

"No, it's not."

"Patti Coblentz, I thought you were baptized."

"I am."

"When is he joining our faith?"

"I don't know."

"What if he doesn't? Have you thought about that? Or, are you so smitten with his muscles and good looks that you've forgotten your vow to the Lord?"

"I have not forgotten anything." Not her vow to the Lord . . . or Martin's fine physique. Standing up, she said, "I will also not forget the way you came over unannounced and then very rudely informed me about your plans."

"I haven't been rude, Patti. Only direct."

"I beg to disagree."

"I am shocked by your news, though. I think most everyone we know would be."

And . . . now she had no choice but to throw all of her mother's good manners out the window. Folding her arms over her chest, she glared. "What does that mean? Are you going to gossip about me?"

Just as he was about to say something else, the now unmistakable form of Martin appeared.

"Patti?" he called out. "Are you all right?"

She walked down the steps eager to greet him. "I am now."

He reached out for her hands. "What happened?"

"It's a long story." After taking comfort in his touch for a few seconds, she pulled her hands from his. "I promise, I'm fine."

"I hope so." After scanning her face again, he turned to Willard. "Hi. I'm Martin Schrock."

"I know who you are." At last, Willard stood up. "Willard Luft."

Martin glanced her way. When he faced Willard again, he looked far less friendly and a good deal more irritated. "What brings you to Patti's house at this time of the evening?"

"That is no concern of yours," Willard said in a low voice.

Martin continued to stare at him. "I think differently."

Patti supposed it was time to intervene. "Willard came courting, Martin."

"Oh?" Turning to her, Martin scanned her face. "Did you invite him here?"

"I did not. I was just telling Willard that you and I were seeing each other when you walked up."

"Good." His blue eyes warmed.

"*Nee*, it isn't good," Willard said as he tromped down the front steps. "You are leading Patti on and encouraging her to break sacred vows. You are leading her down a very dark and terrible path."

Some of the confidence in Martin's expression faded. "Do you feel that way, Patti?" he asked her in a low tone.

"*Nee*. He dreamed that up."

"I did not dream up the consequences you will face when you disappoint your entire family."

Martin flinched as if he'd been struck.

"It's past time you left," she said.

"I'm going. I'm going. But listen to me, Patti Coblentz. You might choose to ignore my interest and disregard everyone else's opinions, too. But it is wrong to pretend that these vows you made when you were baptized didn't mean anything. It wasn't just a promise, Patti. It was a solemn vow. And if you can't keep that vow, how are you going to keep anything else?"

Her mouth had gone dry.

Both she and Martin remained silent as Willard reached for his bicycle and pedaled off.

The scariest part was that she had no idea what she was going to say to Martin.

Because a part of her knew that Willard was right. She knew she was falling in love with Martin. She might be already there. But if she acted on those feelings and left her faith, it would be very hard.

No, almost insurmountable.

But if she broke things off with Martin, she had a feeling she would be spending the rest of her life alone. Substituting Martin for someone different wasn't a possibility.

She'd be an old maid.

Staring into Martin's eyes, she ached to step into his arms and relax against him. Admit her feelings. But if she did that, trouble would follow.

Her heart felt like it was breaking. How could something that was so right feel so wrong?

CHAPTER 17

Martin figured there were only a few moments in one's life when every word uttered determined the future. The first time his father had asked him to tell the truth about a broken vase. The first time Kelsey had been crying in the middle of the night and he'd been the only one to sit with her.

The moment when Angie, his first girlfriend, had asked if he loved her.

This was one of those times.

He'd felt the same sense of importance when he'd interviewed for his first "real" job out of college. He'd felt it again when he'd confessed to Beth, Jonny, and Kelsey that he was thinking about being Amish. Also when the four of them had faced their shocked grandparents and tried to convey their feelings in true and concise ways.

All of those conversations had mattered a lot.

Now, as he stared at the woman sitting across from him, Martin knew, down to his core, that this was another one of those times. Maybe it even mattered more than the others—because his heart was involved. He loved Patti Coblentz and he wanted to spend the rest of his life with her. No, he wanted to marry her.

But he couldn't press her to live the rest of her life in the English world if she was going to regret it for the rest of her days. Those regrets would fester and taint their relationship. She'd grow to resent him.

And he, in turn, would feel so helpless and guilty that he'd grow bitter.

As each minute passed, the tension between them grew, reminding him of a wire on a musical instrument that was strung too tight.

"I had thought you'd have a lot to say right now," Patti murmured.

Patti's eyes held a splash of humor. She wasn't mad at him. That relief allowed him to be frank. "Why? Because I'd felt like knocking that smug expression off of Willard's face when he declared that he would be a better choice for you than me?"

Patti's lips twitched. "Maybe. Or . . . maybe because you seem as if you have some thoughts about what he said."

There it was. In true Patti form, she had taken the subject at hand, weighed the challenges about broaching it, and then forged ahead.

He swallowed, wishing for a little bit more time. "You are pretty brave to bring that up."

She looked down at her feet. "Hardly that."

Unable to resist, he carefully lifted her chin. "I happen to think differently. I like how you aren't afraid to bring up hard subjects."

"Some might describe that as being foolish, not brave." Before he could comment on that, she stood up. "Would you like to come inside? I could make us some hot chocolate. Since you walked here, you're likely feeling a bit chilled."

"I was. Hot chocolate sounds perfect." Following her inside, Martin realized that Patti had likely been feeling chilled, too. "Speaking of being cold, why were you two sitting out here in the first place? It's not that warm out."

Looking back at him over her shoulder, she smirked. "Willard didn't want to be improper."

"It was more proper to have you sit in the cold?"

"He's a stickler for rules of all kinds. And, even though he's forty, it appears he believes in chaperones."

Martin felt like rolling his eyes. First of all, if a forty-year-old man couldn't trust himself to respect the woman he was with, then he needed something more than a chaperone. Secondly, Willard's reasoning felt contrived. Patti didn't live in a row house in the middle of town. Her farmhouse was surrounded by acreage. "If he wanted to steal a kiss, I think he could've done it on the front porch."

"I suppose." Mirth lit her eyes as they walked inside. "Willard is so very determined to be an upstanding man that he often neglects common sense. With the wind picking up, it was rather uncomfortable outside. It was obvious that no one would be here to notice where we were sitting."

"I still don't understand why he was here. Did he come over unannounced?"

"He came courting. And, before you ask, it was a complete surprise to me."

"That was gutsy." Looking off into the distance, he scowled.

"I agree." She gestured toward the living room. "Please have a seat. I'll be right back with our drinks."

"I think I'll help you instead." Her expression was too grim. He didn't want her to have even a minute to decide to push him away.

Or break up with him.

He followed her into the kitchen, which was as neat and clean as ever. "What do you do first for hot chocolate?"

"Get out a pan," she said as she did just that. "Isn't that obvious?"

"Not to someone who's only made it with microwaved hot water and a packet from a box."

She pressed a hand to her chest. "You are shocking me!" she exclaimed as she poured a generous amount of milk into the saucepan. "That is not making real hot chocolate. You'll be making hot powder."

Martin watched as she opened a cupboard and pulled out a combination of chocolate bars. "It's still pretty good." To be honest, he couldn't remember the last time he'd had hot chocolate. Maybe in high school at a bonfire before a game or something?

After chopping the chocolate on a cutting board, she poured it into the pan. "I promise, my hot chocolate will make you wonder why you've been missing out on it for most of your life."

If he thought that, it was because he'd been missing out on Patti. "I guess I'll have to take your word for it."

She handed him a plastic spoon. "Stir."

Doing as she asked, he watched Patti open up a container filled with neatly cut marshmallows. "Did you make those?"

"Of course."

"Of course," he murmured. Right then and there he made a vow to himself to act as if he loved her hot chocolate, when the truth was that the drink was nothing that he would have ever craved.

"I think it's done now, Martin. See how the chocolate has melted and the milk is steaming?"

"I do." He turned off the gas burner and turned to her. She was standing close. Close enough to smell a hint of lavender and vanilla on her skin. Close enough to notice that the port-wine stain on her neck was more than one shade—and he thought it was sexy. It reminded him of a couple of his buddies whose girlfriends had a tattoo on their shoulder. They thought the marking made their women even more unique.

Patti didn't need anything artificial. No, her birthmark was original and attractive. She wouldn't be the same without it.

Tearing his gaze away from her neck, he lifted his head.

And saw tears in her eyes.

"Patti, what's wrong?"

"You were staring at my neck."

"I know." He smiled at her. "I couldn't help it."

But instead of making her feel better, he'd done the opposite. One of the tears fell. Slid down her cheek. He reached out to brush it away. "What did I do that upset you?"

"You know."

"Mmm, I don't."

"Martin. You know I can't help my birthmark."

"I don't want you to help it. I love it."

Two more tears escaped. "Don't tease."

He swallowed. It looked like it was time for some honest words—even if they were inappropriate and probably shocking. "I'm not teasing." Lowering his voice, he continued. "Do you really want to know what I was thinking about just now?"

When she nodded, he ran a finger along the line of her neck. "I was thinking how much I would like to one day kiss every inch of that mark." He lowered his voice. "I want to taste your skin. I want to discover if the nape of your neck tastes as sweet as your lips. I want to hold you close and run my hand along your body. I want to find out if you can get chill bumps in other places besides your arms. If the scent of lavender and vanilla smells just as strong at your neck as it does on other parts of you."

Her mouth opened. Shut.

He knew he should feel regret. No, he knew he should apologize and take a step backward. But he wasn't a kid and he wasn't going to pretend his feelings for her weren't real. "Patti, that is how I was feeling. That is what I was thinking."

"Oh."

"'Oh' is right. I think you're sweet and pretty. I think you're smart. I think you're a hard worker, too." He paused, then added, "I also happen to think that you're attractive and sexy as all get out."

"You mean it, don't you?"

Her words were soft spoken. Filled with wonder, making his heart soften. "I mean every word. Please, don't ever hide from me. I . . . I love every bit of you."

"You love me."

He leaned over and kissed her forehead. A spot right under where her hairline ended. Then, because the spark of interest that he'd been waiting for flared in her eyes, he wrapped his hands around her middle, pulled her in close, and kissed her.

It wasn't their first kiss. The first one had happened over a year ago.

But as sweet as it had been, it wasn't like this. Now, there was a new sense of awareness for each other. A new aware-ness of how meaningful their relationship was—and how precarious it was. It would crush him if he had to break things off with her.

No, it would come very close to killing him. Patti Cob-lentz was *it* for him. He knew it. He knew it down deep in-side of him and with the certainty that had come with his need to take his driver's license test, to take care of his sib-lings whenever they needed him.

When he used to pull an all-nighter in college in order to get an A on the exam instead of just a B.

When she pulled away, he released her instantly. She was panting, like he'd taken her breath away.

Martin had to force himself not to apologize for the kiss. Because he couldn't do it. He wasn't sorry.

When seconds passed and she didn't say a word, only stared at him, he broke the silence. "Patti, I've been coaching myself for the last minute about what to do next. About what to say."

"And?"

"I don't think there's anything more that I can tell you or do. You know how I feel about you. And, I think it's also obvious about how much I desire you, too."

"You . . . you come here at night and say all this. On the heels of Willard's visit." Her cheeks pinkened as she continued. "It's hard to believe."

"What do you want to believe? What do you want to happen between us?"

She blinked. Seemed to wage war with herself about what to say. "What I want isn't the same thing as what is possible," she said at last.

"Are you sure about that?"

"Martin, I . . . I would love nothing more than to be your girlfriend. To share more kisses like the ones we just shared. To stay by your side and plan a future together."

"But . . ."

"But I can't promise you a life together."

"Because you got baptized."

"*Jah.*"

Had he ever felt so torn? He doubted it. "Patti, God knows how much I wanted to be able to change my life and become Amish. I wanted to honor my grandparents. I want to feel close to the Lord and live simply. Now that Kelsey and Jonny have been baptized, I feel as if there's an invisible wedge between us. I'd love to remove it. But I can't."

"I know."

"I'm . . . It turns out that I can love my family very much but still need to be myself. I belong in my regular world. I'm good at it. I'm successful at it."

"It makes you happy."

"Yes, but a better way to describe it is that it fits me. Trying to fit in here felt like I was walking around in shoes on the wrong feet. I could do it, but it wasn't comfortable, I could never go very far, and it hurt."

"Your parents jumped the fence."

"I know."

"And you are expecting me to leave."

He shook his head. "No. I'm not expecting you to do anything." Taking a fortifying breath, he added, "But what I am saying is that I want to mean so much to you that you'd be willing to break an earlier vow in order to be happy."

"You mean an awful lot to me, Martin."

"Do you love me?"

She inhaled. Averted her eyes. And didn't say what he'd hoped she would.

And it hit him hard. Smack in the middle of his body. For a moment, he was afraid he wasn't going to be able to breathe.

But then he could.

It enabled him to stand up. To take the drink she'd so carefully made him and put it on the counter. Most of it was left.

"I think it's time I left, don't you?"

Tears were back in her eyes. "*Jah.*"

It hurt to look at her. He couldn't do it. So, he turned away and walked to the door. Grabbed his coat with one hand and the door handle with the other.

And then two minutes later, he was walking back down Patti's driveway. Clouds had come in, covering up a lot of the stars in the sky. It was hard to see anything beyond a few feet in front of him.

But that was okay. After all, he was alone.

CHAPTER 18

Not only would Beth have never imagined that her mother would visit her in Walden, she *really* never would have imagined that her mother would be staying at Mommi and Dawdi's *haus*. Sylvia and Josiah Schrock were not Helen Schrock's parents. They were her in-laws. Technically, they were her former in-laws, and as far as any of the kids knew, Mom hadn't seen them in years.

Then there was the fact that her mother had never spoken the least bit fondly about the homestead. Though Beth did remember the six of them visiting her grandparents, it didn't happen often. She didn't remember her mother being all that comfortable, though.

But maybe she had been? After all, her mom had been raised Amish, too.

Not for the first time, Beth wondered if her childish perception had been skewed. Maybe her mother had been happy there. Had other things been going on in her parents' lives that she hadn't been aware of? It stood to reason, but for some reason it made her feel a little guilty. Like maybe she'd held on to so many slights and hurt feelings when she'd actually been the one who had been in the wrong.

But none of that mattered now.

Not when Beth was standing on the front porch next to her grandparents as her mother easily pulled her Cadillac into the driveway near the barn. After she parked, she tapped something on her phone.

Glad for the few seconds reprieve, Beth glanced at Mommi and Dawdi. They were smiling. "I still can't get over the fact that you two knew Mom was coming here before I did."

"Now, I don't think that's completely true," Dawdi said. "Helen told us that she'd already discussed this visit with ya."

"She asked if I minded if she came," Beth corrected.

"And?"

"And . . . I told her I'd be glad to see her." When Mommi raised her eyebrows, Beth snorted under her breath. "All I'm saying is that it would have been nice to have been included in the final details."

"Not sure why," Mommi murmured.

"Ah. She's getting out now. Go on down and help your mother, Bethy," Dawdi said.

She started forward, but almost gasped when she saw the trunk pop open and her mother pull out a suitcase. Turning back to her grandparents, she whispered, "Did you know she was staying here?"

"Of course, child," Mommi replied. "I invited Helen to stay a spell."

"You just called her out of the blue?"

"*Nee*, dear. She called us." She lowered her voice. "Now, stop stalling and go."

Beth hurried toward her mom, who was putting away her cell phone in her purse. "Hi, Mom!"

Her mother's smile seemed frozen for a brief moment.

But then her entire body seemed to relax. "Beth, look at you. You look so . . ."

"Pregnant?"

She chuckled. "Yes, but it's more than that. You look at peace," she said as she pulled Beth into a hug. "Boy, I've missed you."

Her mother's slim body and signature perfume felt familiar. Not homey, but good. So did her pleased expression. "I'll take looking like I'm at peace."

"You should. It's a good thing. You look beautiful, too."

She chuckled. "You always say that."

"That's because it's always true." Still gazing at her from head to toe, her mother said, "When I first saw you, I felt like I was going back in time. You look so much like a teacher I used to have at the Amish school."

"I'll take that as a compliment?"

"Of course. Miss Janie was a super teacher. One of the prettiest women in the community, too. Just like you."

"Thank you, Mom."

"Wait here. I have some things for you. For all the kids, actually."

"Want some help?"

"Not yet."

Her mother had been adopted as a baby by an older couple. They'd long since passed. Though her mother never had gone so far as to say that she hadn't been close to her adoptive parents, she rarely mentioned them. Well, not beyond her saying that her parents had been taskmasters and not very affectionate.

Beth had always been sad about that, though her mother had shrugged it off. She'd found a lot of love in her neighbors, friends, and Dad, of course.

Once her mother had all of her gifts organized in two large canvas tote bags, she walked to Beth's side. "Could you take in my suitcase?"

"Of course." Pulling on the handle, she started walking to the house. "So you really are staying here?" She probably sounded as skeptical as she felt, but what could she do? She'd never imagined that her mother would be visiting Walden for more than a few hours.

"I really am, Bethy," she teased. "And stop worrying."

"I'm not worried." Much.

"Everything will be fine. I promise. When I called Sylvia to ask if she'd mind if I visited you here, she invited me to stay for a few days. It sounded so perfect, I couldn't say no."

"I'm kind of surprised you were good with that. They don't have electricity, you know."

"Oh, honey. Of course they don't. I haven't forgotten that."

"You'll be okay without the internet and plugs? Dad had to move to a hotel so he could get some work done."

"Well, I didn't come here to work. I came here to see my kids. Plus, I brought some books. I'll be fine."

"Well, I'm glad you're staying. We'll get to see a lot more of each other."

Looking pleased, her mother said, "I was thinking the same thing."

"Helen, *wilcom!*" Mommi said. "It's been far too long."

"*Danke.* And *jah.* Too many years have passed indeed." When Dawdi reached out to take one of the bags, he grinned at her. "It's nice to know some things never change, Helen. You never could travel lightly."

"Obviously I still can't," she said with a chuckle. "But don't be too hard on me. In my defense, everything in these bags are gifts."

"We have plenty of room, Helen," Mommi said. "Our *haus* is your *haus.*"

In short order, the four of them got the three suitcases into the house.

Looking around at the entryway, with the smell of lemon

oil and vanilla candles surrounding them, her mother breathed deep. "I've always loved this smell. I think I feel more relaxed already. Sylvia, Josiah, thanks again for letting me stay."

"It ain't a problem. Plus, you need to be close to Bethy," Dawdi said.

Reaching out, Mom ran a hand down her back. "This is true."

"Beth and I prepared some snacks," Mommi said. "We can sit at the kitchen table."

"That sounds wonderful. I came hungry. Let me run upstairs and freshen up."

"I'll carry your bag upstairs, Helen," Dawdi said.

"Thanks. I'll be down soon."

Mommi shrugged. "Take your time. Would you like water or coffee or both?"

"Both?"

"I'll have it ready. Come along, Beth."

After watching her mother follow Dawdi up the stairs, Beth hurried after Mommi to put out everything that her grandmother had arranged on plates early that morning.

"Do you feel better now?" her grandmother asked.

"Yes. She seems to be okay, doesn't she?"

"Your visit is going to be fine. Just because you and your mother haven't always been best friends, there's still love there. Focus on that, *jah*?"

Beth exhaled. "Yes."

True to her word, the conversation around the table after her mother returned was easy and relaxed. Her mom caught up with Josiah and Sylvia, and ate a heaping plate of the cheese, crackers, chicken salad, and fruit that Mommi and Beth had set out.

After about an hour, her grandparents left. They'd claimed that they needed to check on something in the barn, but Beth knew it was a flimsy excuse.

"I guess Mommi and Dawdi decided that we needed some time alone," Beth said.

"I agree. They weren't very subtle, were they?"

"I don't think they know how to be."

"I dare say you're right." After walking to the percolator on the stove and filling her cup, her mother's stance seemed to ease. "How are you doing, really?"

Thinking about Junior and her new not-job, Beth said, "Good."

"You're feeling all right?"

"I am. With the exception of a few lightheaded moments and a couple of bouts of nausea, I really only just feel big."

"That's to be expected."

"I know I've told you this many times, but I can't believe you went through four pregnancies."

"It was fun. I wanted a big family. Plus, your father helped a lot. It was only when we got older that things changed."

That was putting it mildly. But she didn't want to go there. Not during the first hour of her visit. "Do the others know that you're here?"

"They do. I called and left messages with everyone last night. All three of them called me while I was driving here."

"They didn't tell me."

"I asked them not to."

"Why?"

"I feel like I have a little bit more work to do with you than with the others. I guess I'm treading lightly."

"What do you mean?"

"I mean that I know you looked out for Kelsey and Jonny a lot when you were growing up. I should've done better after the divorce."

"I don't want to talk about that."

"Why not?"

"Because it's not going to change the past and it probably doesn't even matter."

"It does matter. I should have tried to do more motherly things with you all instead of dating so much."

"You were still around, Mom."

"I could have been more present."

Remembering those days, Beth realized that while their mother might have been hurting from the divorce and wanted to go out with her friends a lot, she'd also done a lot for her kids. She'd still cooked and cleaned and done their laundry and helped them get what they needed for school. Did she hang out in the evenings with them and watch shows? No. But the four of them had. And because the four of them had each other, they'd been okay.

"Mom, we're all fine now."

Her mother studied her face for a long moment. "You're right. All of you are fine now. Better than fine." She stood up. "What do you think about us working on these dishes?"

"That sounds good."

Walking to the sink with a handful of plates, her mother said, "I'm glad I came to stay for a few days."

"Me, too." She meant it, too.

"If your grandmother doesn't make liver, everything is going to be just fine."

"I think she knows better than to feed that to me," Beth joked.

When her mother started giggling, she felt the last of her worries float away. A lot of things might be at loose ends with her mother, but they still loved each other.

That was a good place to start.

CHAPTER 19

Martin was pretty sure the brunch was going to be a disaster. How could it not be with so many people in attendance? He couldn't believe it when he'd heard that not only were he, Kelsey, Beth, and Jonny going to be eating with their mother, but Richard and Treva, too. And Patti. And their grandparents. And Treva's parents! That was twelve people, thirteen, if he counted baby Belle, which he supposed he should.

When he and Kelsey had talked about seeing their mom, he'd suggested they do something simple and easy. Kelsey had said not to worry.

Obviously, he should've checked in with her two days ago and told her to cut back the numbers.

Or, at the very least, he should have told Kelsey that he couldn't make it when she'd called last night to tell him the details.

But, of course, he hadn't. Even though she was married and had a baby girl of her own, old habits died hard, and he liked taking care of her. Or at least, doing his best to make her happy.

All that meant he was now stuck trying to make the best of things. The problem was that he couldn't decide who to look out for the most. Mom? Kelsey? Beth? Mommi and Dawdi? He didn't want anyone he loved to get their feelings hurt, but chances were very good that was going to happen, anyway.

Then, to make matters worse, his grandmother had shared that she'd invited Patti to join them as well. And . . . she was going to need a ride.

As much as he'd wanted to tell his grandmother that picking up Patti wasn't possible, he hadn't. No way could he deny his grandparents anything, not when they'd completely upended their lives for him, Beth, and the others.

After worrying about what to say to Patti all morning, he'd attempted to shake off his trepidation when he headed to Patti's house to pick her up.

It turned out that Patti was obviously feeling the same way that he did. After a rather stilted greeting, she cleared her throat. "Thank you for picking me up."

"It was no problem."

"Still . . ." Her voice trailed off, reminding him that he wasn't the only one who was feeling awkward and disappointed.

"Patti, if you'd like to change your mind, I can tell everyone that you had a change of plans. I could say that you needed to work."

"It's too late to do that," she stated as she picked up an insulated carrier from the countertop. "I already made my casserole."

"I could bring it for you."

"Nope. I'm coming. I'm looking forward to it, Martin."

Maybe there was hope for them, after all. "You are?"

"To be sure. I mean, I like everyone in your family . . . and I heard Treva was making pumpkin scones."

He supposed Patti had a point. She was as close to his grandmother as he was. And she'd become good friends with Kelsey and Beth, too. Plus, anything Treva baked was pretty amazing. "Fine."

She frowned at his curt response. In typical Patti-style, though, she'd held her tongue until they'd left her house and he'd stowed her hashbrown potato casserole in the back seat.

"Martin, you need to take a deep breath and relax," Patti chided as he started the car. "Just because you and I are having some trouble, we are still friends, right?"

"Yes."

"Then everything is going to be just fine."

"You can say that because it isn't your family that is getting together." Or because she wasn't the one who was hoping to hear a profession of love.

"*Nee*, I can say that because I know in my heart that this brunch your sister is hosting is going to be enjoyable. Both the food and the company."

"What about us?"

Patti's expression clouded before she replied. "Martin, as much as I wish things between us were settled, perhaps we could continue on the way we've been?"

"Do you think it's possible?"

"I think that no matter what the Lord has planned for our future, we can agree that we can still be friends."

She was right. They'd waited this long to figure things out, they could wait a little longer. "I agree."

"So, friends?"

"Yeah." Amazed that some of the tension that had been between them had dissipated, he chuckled. "Patti, you always know what to say to me. It's amazing."

"I don't always know anything. All I know is that I don't want to lose you."

"You won't."

Curving one slim hand around his forearm, she smiled softly. "Then everything will be okay. Between us, and with your family. Stop worrying so much."

He loved Patti's smile, and he loved the way one touch from her could improve his mood. But in this case, he was pretty sure that even her sweet help wasn't going to make much of a difference. "Okay, but if things at Kelsey's go south in a hurry, don't blame me."

"Nothing is going to go south."

"Just warning you, there's a weird dynamic with my mom and my grandparents."

"I don't think so. I've seen them together. They don't fight."

"Of course they don't. Everyone is too well mannered for that. But there's an underlying tension there."

"Perhaps, but what does it matter?"

Glad that they were still parked in Patti's drive, Martin caught Patti's small shrug. He was taken aback. "It matters because it's going to be me who has to diffuse things."

"Why is that?"

"Because Kelsey has gone to a lot of trouble. If things go badly, she'll be upset." And he'd feel guilty.

"If she's upset, I reckon Richard will make things right," Patti said in a light tone. "He is her husband, after all."

"Yeah, maybe." When he realized that Patti was actively trying not to laugh, he blurted, "Do you think I'm over-thinking everything?"

"Maybe. But what I'm trying to get you to see is that even if your mother and grandparents don't become best friends, that's not the point. What matters is that your mother gets to see her *kinner* here in Walden. I think that's why she came, Martin. Helen has seen each one of you a time or two over the last year, but the only time she's seen you all together was at Jonny's and Kelsey's weddings."

"Maybe so."

"I like that Kelsey is hosting, too."

"I couldn't believe that she wanted to host."

"Why? She and Richard are very happy and have their cute baby. She's the most settled of the four of you." Lowering her voice, Patti added, "Maybe Kelsey wants to show you and Beth that she isn't just your little sister anymore."

He rubbed a palm over his face. He did go into big brother protective mode a little too often. She'd called him out for doing that, too.

"I hadn't thought of it like that, but you might be right."

"I know I am. Now stop stalling and start driving, Martin Schrock."

Backing down her drive, he said, "You aren't near as biddable as I thought you were, Patti Coblentz."

She smiled. "I get that a lot."

Two hours later, Martin was very glad that Patti hadn't backed out like he'd suggested. Maybe it was because she knew everyone except for his mother well, but she'd been chatty and relaxed the entire time. And because of that, everyone else seemed to take a collective sigh and become more at ease, too.

Sitting in Kelsey and Richard's living room, Martin had to admit that things weren't going all that badly, after all. His mom was currently holding a sleeping Belle while chatting with Treva about her coffee shop. Jonny was sitting on the other side of Treva, but his attention was on a crossword their grandfather was trying to solve.

Beth had disappeared with Kelsey into Belle's nursery, and Patti and Richard were joking around with his grandmother in the kitchen.

Everything was fine.

So, why could he not relax?

"Martin, you've been watching the going-ons more closely than a hawk circling a nest of field mice."

Hating the scene that had just appeared in his head, he grimaced. "Dawdi, way to paint a picture of death and destruction."

"I did not. And I wouldn't exactly say a hawk looking for his supper was that. It's more like he's going to snap up a mouse and deliver it to his family."

"Still."

Dawdi shrugged. "It was apt."

"It is not. I'm not eyeing my family like one of them is my next meal."

"I reckon that's true." Looking back down at his crossword, he added, "Ah. Here you go. Caregiver."

"What?"

"I've been wracking my brain, trying to think of a nine-letter word for 'guardian.'" He frowned. "Sometimes I get stuck on the long words, you know?"

"No, I didn't know." Noticing that the crossword was already half-filled in, he added, "Dawdi, I didn't know you liked to do crossword puzzles."

"That's because I don't like them. Not especially. They're good for my brain, though. Gotta keep sharp."

"Hmm."

"Sometimes doing something uncomfortable is good for you."

"Like getting all together?"

"*Jah.*" His grandfather darted a look his way, then added, "And letting go of control."

"Dawdi, is that what this conversation has been about? That I need to stop trying to take care of my siblings?"

"Of course not, son. You're a grown man. I wouldn't think of telling you what to do with your life." He stood up. "I think I'd best go see what kind of trouble your grandmother is getting into in Kelsey's kitchen."

Feeling flummoxed, Martin watched his grandfather wander off. He picked up the crossword, looked for "caregiver" and then at the clue. He wouldn't have put it past him to have made the whole thing up, just to have the opportunity to give him advice. But sure enough, there was the clue—a guardian for a loved one.

Amazing.

When he heard his mother chuckling, he glanced her way. "Did you overhear our conversation, Mom?"

"Only a bit of it. Treva here heard most of it."

Treva was grinning. "Sorry, but I couldn't help but eavesdrop. Your *dawdi* had me from the moment he compared you to a circling hawk."

"What's this about a hawk?" Beth asked.

"You don't want to know," Martin said.

"Your grandfather was doling out a bit of Amish wisdom," Mom said.

"To Martin?"

"Of course."

"I'm sorry I missed that," Jonny said.

"What is that supposed to mean?"

"It means that you, big brother, are a chip off our grandfather's shoulder. It would be a treat to listen to you get your just desserts."

"Thanks, Kelsey." And here he'd thought she'd always appreciated his help.

"Don't get your feelings hurt," she said as she gave him a hug. "You've done more for me than I can ever repay. But I'm a grown woman now, right? I'm a wife and a mother."

He swallowed. "I haven't forgotten." Sharing a glance with their mother, she gave him a sympathetic look.

"Don't worry, Martin," she said. "They leave the nest, but they're still yours."

"I was so worried about everyone getting along, I didn't stop to think that maybe the person that would be having the most difficult time would be me."

"I wouldn't worry too much about everyone else, Martin. No matter what happens, our family always seems to muddle through." Looking over his shoulder, she added, "Plus, I think you've got someone pretty special on your side. If you have her, you're going to be able to get through just about anything."

Martin didn't have to turn around to know that his mother was referring to Patti. She was right. Patti was pretty special.

It was just too bad that he had no idea how long he'd get to keep her by his side.

CHAPTER 20

Junior was proud of his company. Walden Wax Works produced quality candles and had developed a dedicated, vocal following. His customers' praises on various sorts of social media had gained their entry into a number of well-known high-end retail chains. In addition, their direct sales were increasing every year. The company that he'd started in his garage had surpassed his greatest dreams, which was saying a lot, since he'd had awfully big dreams when he'd started.

He couldn't take much pride in the accomplishment, though. All of the company's success was due to his employees. From the designers, to the workers on the line, to the sales staff, everyone played a part in the company's reputation and success. He was grateful for every person's hard work and skills.

Just as he was grateful for their customers who continued to support the business.

Unfortunately, at that very moment, all he wanted was for every single person to leave him alone. Better yet, he'd love it if they just went on home. They were driving him crazy, which was kind of a shame, seeing as it wasn't even noon yet.

Looking down at Honor and Clyde, he was fairly sure his old chocolate Labs felt exactly the same way.

Shifting on the dog bed, Clyde looked up and groaned.

"I hear ya, *hund*," he murmured. "What could be going on with everyone? Was there a full moon out last night or something?" He'd never thought such a thing would turn his employees and customers off-kilter, but he had heard of such things affecting patients in an emergency room. "What do you think the chances are for that?"

Clyde stared up at him a moment longer before shifting and closing his eyes again.

Junior wished he could do the same thing.

He was just about to close his office door when Raymond, one of the company's designers, waylaid him. "Oh good. You're not on the phone," he said. "We've got to talk."

"I'm kind of busy right now, Raymond. Can we talk later?"

Raymond put his hand on the doorframe, effectively stopping Junior from going anywhere. "Sorry, boss, but this is important."

Becoming concerned, he gave Raymond his complete attention. "All right. I'm all ears."

"It has to do with the summer catalog."

They weren't supposed to finalize the summer catalog for another week. "What about it?"

He scratched his head. "See, I was thinking that maybe we should rethink the layout of page fifteen."

"Page fifteen?" Yes, he'd lifted his eyebrows, and yes, his voice had turned snippy.

"Oh, for sure. You see, I started thinking that maybe we should do less primary colors and concentrate more on greens and maybe geranium." Raymond droned on, carefully describing a dozen details about a display. Junior reckoned it was important, but the guy had lost him at "geranium." He turned to look at his dogs.

Honor's eyes were halfway closed.

They seemed to be feeling the same way as him.

"Junior. Junior!?"

"No need to yell, man. What?"

Raymond's eyes narrowed. "Are you even listening to me?"

"Sure. Of course." He crossed his fingers, felt bad for lying, and attempted to give the man the attention he deserved. "Listen, why don't you do mockups of the two choices and we'll choose the best layout at the team meeting." He smiled, pleased that he'd solved Raymond's dilemma fairly easily.

Unfortunately, Raymond only looked irritated.

"Ray, what's the problem?"

"The problem is that I don't understand why you're acting so put out about me asking you a few simple questions."

"You know catalog design ain't my forte."

"Junior, I know. That's why I asked you where Beth was."

"She isn't here."

"I know that."

Something in his tone was starting to send off warning signals. "Correct me if I'm wrong, but I'm starting to get the feeling that you're not as worried about the catalog as you are about something else."

Looking sheepish, Raymond shrugged. "Perhaps. See, it's Beth."

"Beth?"

"*Jah.* You see, I don't—"

"Let me be real clear. Elizabeth is none of your business."

"That isn't fair. We're friends, not just employer and employee."

"We are friends, but that doesn't mean we need to talk about her."

"All I said was that we never know when she's going to be here." He lowered his voice. "And that there's a chance that she's taking advantage of your good nature, Junior."

What good nature? "Don't worry about me, Ray."

"Junior, I think you should listen to what he says," Cherry announced as she approached down the hall. "After all, Raymond didn't do anything but voice what most everyone in the company is wondering."

"There are almost a hundred people here. All hundred of them shouldn't be thinking about the comings and goings of Beth Schrock."

"All I'm saying is that her absence is a concern," Cherry said as she walked to Raymond's side. "After all, she talked her way into here and now can't seem to show up."

"She shows up, Cherry."

"Late," Raymond said. "I've noticed her come in late more than once."

Raising her chin a bit, Cherry continued. "But I've never heard you chastise her for being so disrespectful."

He would give anything to shut his office door. "She hasn't been disrespectful, Cherry." He also couldn't imagine "chastising" Elizabeth for anything.

After exchanging glances with Cherry, Raymond cleared his throat. "All I'm saying is that I think you've been blindsided by her beauty. She might be pretty, but she comes in late and sometimes leaves early, too. I don't think that says much about her work ethic."

He'd had enough. More than enough. "Don't talk about Elizabeth." When Honor flinched at his caustic tone, he took a breath. "It's all right, Honor. No worries," he soothed.

"I'm not talking about *her*."

"Sounds like it."

Raymond harumphed. "All I'm saying is that we were all expecting Beth to do some work and she hasn't shown up yet." He pointed to the clock on the wall. "An hour ago."

Cherry popped a hand on her hip. "You know, it could be

she changed her mind. A fancy woman like that? She's likely used to something different than our little place."

He wasn't all that happy to hear Walden Wax Works being described as a little place. Junior counted to five. Reminded himself that he liked Raymond and Cherry and that they were good employees, too. It would be a really bad idea to yell at them. "She'll come. I think she had some personal business to attend to first." She was pregnant, after all. Didn't expectant mothers get morning sick or something?

"So that's it?" Cherry asked.

"It is. Now lower your voice. You're scaring my dogs."

"Must be nice to be most worried about two old Labs instead of things that matter," she said under her breath as she walked away.

"Cherry has gotten awfully opinionated," he muttered. "And my dogs do matter."

"That's true, but she also ain't wrong," Raymond pointed out. "All of us have things to do, but we still come to work on time."

"Did you need anything from me, or did you come in just to point out that Beth is late?"

"Ah, well . . ."

"Just for the record, I'm well aware that she is late. I can read the clock as well as anyone around here."

Raymond's eyes widened. "Junior."

"Why? You're the one who came in here, all flutter and griping about schedules."

"*Nee.* Junior. Stop."

"Why?" Only then did he notice that Raymond was tilting his head to one side. When he turned, he found Beth standing in the doorway with a confused—and yes, angry— look on her face.

"Hey. I didn't know you were here."

Honor and Clyde lumbered to their feet and approached her.

He held his breath. She'd been just fine around them when they were at the park, but some people got a little worried when they were in an enclosed space with them.

But instead of flinching, her expression eased. "Hello again, you two."

Honor and Clyde nudged her hand. Leaning closer, Elizabeth gifted both with lots of pets and attention. "They're so sweet."

"I'm happy you don't mind them being in my office."

"Not at all. You two are good company," she cooed as she rubbed their ears again.

Beside him, Raymond looked a little shamefaced.

Deciding to address it openly, Junior said, "Hey, I'm sorry you heard that conversation when you walked in. I didn't realize you were here."

Looking up at him, she shrugged. Like it didn't matter what anyone said about her.

"Seeing you took us all by surprise," Raymond muttered.

"I noticed." One dark blond eyebrow rose. "It seems that Cherry must have forgotten to buzz to let you know that I was on my way," she said as she straightened.

"It would seem so." Junior felt his cheeks heat with embarrassment.

The dogs, after staring up at him with twin disappointed expressions, walked back to their bed, circled each other, and then curled back down onto the plush spot.

Raymond edged to the door. "Well, now. I, ah, think I'll be heading on my way. I've got a lot that needs to be seen to. I'll work on those sample layouts, boss."

Junior nodded but didn't take his eyes off Beth. She looked as pretty as ever in her pale-green dress, dark stockings, and black boots. He also couldn't deny that her spark of temper had added a spot of color to her cheeks.

When they were alone, she folded her arms across her

chest. "So, when you said that it didn't really matter when I was coming in, it must have not been the truth."

"*Nee.* It was the truth. I, um, I neglected to tell that to anyone else."

Hurt flashed in her eyes. "Why did you keep it a secret? Did you need me to look lazy or something?"

"Of course not."

"Then why was everyone acting like I committed a cardinal sin?"

"Hardly that."

"Cherry would barely let me in the door."

"I'll speak to her. She shouldn't have been so rude to ya."

"I agree. So, why didn't you share our agreement about my hours with Cherry?"

"I don't know. I didn't want to start telling everyone in the plant your private business. It weren't anyone else's business."

"I'd believe that if I hadn't walked in on your conversation with Raymond."

There was nothing he could do to erase what he said—or to have her forget it. "Would you like to get started now, or would you like to talk some more about how I should've handled your first day better?"

"I'd like to get started. Please."

"*Gut.*" Standing up, he pointed to the small pile of papers he'd set on her desk two hours ago. "Here you go."

She'd stepped closer. Close enough for him to realize she had perfume on. Or scented lotion. Something that clung to her skin and filled the air around him. Made him think of all sorts of things that had nothing to do with work, duty, or friendship.

"Junior?"

He cleared his throat. "*Jah?*" he said.

"Are we good?"

"Of course. Don't worry about what you heard. My employees are hardworking and professional. But they're also as human as any other office staff. Sometimes they like to gossip or stir up trouble when things get slow."

"You know, maybe it would be best if I worked someplace else besides in here with you. Like, I could be off to the side in either the reception area or in the production area."

He couldn't think of two worse places for her to be. Cherry would eat her for lunch, and the men in the back wouldn't appreciate having a young woman in their midst. Not all day long, anyway. "It's best for you to be here in case you have questions."

"That makes sense."

"In addition to those papers, I put out a good calculator."

"Thanks. I kept meaning to buy one."

He scratched his head. "Well, there's a story there. You see, when I first started this company, I made a vow that I'd be modern when it came to dealing with the outside world. But for my finances and such, I'd try to work with a minimum of technology."

"All right, then."

He could practically feel her dismay, but it couldn't be helped. It was what it was. "It ain't too late to change your mind." He'd feel regret, but he wouldn't blame her.

"Looks like I better get busy, then."

"Let me know if you have any questions."

"I will. Thanks." Her smile was tight and didn't reach her eyes.

He'd likely messed everything up between them. Not that they had anything between them. Not really. They were practically strangers.

Taking a deep breath, he turned to the work piled on his desk and forced himself to ignore everything else around him. Raymond's knowing glances. Cherry's confusing jealousy. Instead, he focused on the orders on his computer and the phone calls he needed to return.

There was only one thing to do, and that was to tackle one item at a time.

Tackle work and not the temptation that was Elizabeth Schrock.

CHAPTER 21

Junior liked to call her "Elizabeth." No one had called Beth that in years. Well, no one did without her correcting them. So, she should've already reminded him that she went by Beth.

She hadn't. For some strange reason, she kind of liked how her full name sounded out of his lips. It made her feel special. Or, maybe as if Junior thought she was?

Though she would never admit it, Beth really liked that idea. Ever since she'd gotten pregnant, rearranged her life, and then still felt unsettled and unhappy, she'd been struggling.

Struggling hard.

For as long as she could remember, she was the person who always did everything right. She made good grades. She didn't cause trouble. She looked after Kelsey and Jonny. She'd gotten an academic scholarship, gotten her degree, and was successful in her chosen field.

But she didn't feel like that girl anymore.

While everyone in her former life seemed intent on questioning her about everything, Junior simply accepted her as she was.

He had low expectations of her. Junior didn't seem to mind that she came in late. It was as if she was his charity case. His effort to help someone in need and because of that, he didn't act all that worried about how good of a job she could do. He wasn't impressed with how successful she'd been in her former life.

Or maybe he had no idea.

Which would be something else that was new for her. Before this pregnancy, she'd begun to view her identity only by her success in real estate. Her reputation had gained her clients, and the money she'd made had won her awards in the company.

The fact that it didn't matter now was difficult to get used to. Almost as much as the person she seemed to be becoming—whether she wanted it to happen or not.

All her life, Beth had been the steady one. The dependable one. No, that was her version. Her brothers and sister would say that she'd always been a stickler for rules and unafraid to point it out when she got caught doing something good and one of them had messed up.

She'd actually been kind of insufferable.

Was she just noticing that—which was why she kept fumbling around in her current state? Running late. Doing jobs that she could have handled ten years ago.

Mooning over her new almost-boss?

"Elizabeth, is something wrong?"

Junior had caught her staring at him. "No."

"Are you sure? You were frowning."

"I sure didn't mean to be." Thinking quickly, she said, "Oh, I think you caught me staring off into space. Sorry. I'll get back to work."

He chuckled. "If I caught you doing nothing, I guess it

means that you caught me doing the same thing." His hazel eyes warmed. "Don't rush back to work on my account."

"For what it's worth, I do have a good reason. I'm pregnant and was nauseous all morning and it's seemed to have made me off-kilter. What's your excuse?"

"Umm . . . maybe that I almost hired a woman to clean up my backlog of paperwork."

"Almost hired, hmm?"

"I'm not sure what to call you. Saying you're working for free don't sound quite right."

"I don't mind the phrase. I've been thinking of you as my almost-boss," she admitted with a smile.

"I reckon our new titles fit."

Clyde, who was now stretched out in the middle of the room, thumped his tail in agreement.

"I like that you take your dogs to work."

"I like when they're here, too. I don't take them all the time, but on some days, I just can't refuse when they walk to the door with me and wag their tails."

"I couldn't do that, either."

Standing up, he crouched next to Honor and ran his hand along her spine. "When I started this company, I was kind of at loose ends. Clyde and Honor were still rambunctious—just a couple of years old. They'd get in terrible trouble if left to their own devices."

Her eyes lit up. "Uh oh. What did they do? Get into the trash?"

He waved a hand. "The trash, the closet. Any food that was on the counter." Remembering a certain pair of Red Wings, he added, "My shoes."

"Uh oh. They were handfuls."

"They sure were. My Aunt Rhoda said it was because they were bored. They were like little kids, needing constant companionship."

"I could be wrong, but I'm guessing that you weren't too keen about leaving them home alone all day, either."

"You caught me. I reckon I was just as needy as they were. They needed me and I needed them."

Studying his face, Beth wondered what had made him want to get two dogs. Then, practically on the heels of that, start a new company. She had no idea what it could have been, but she was pretty sure that the story wasn't a short one.

"I guess I better get back to work."

"Is it going all right?"

"Matching invoices to the ledger and making file folders?"

"*Jah.*"

"Yes, it's going fine." Her former self would have told him that she could do something so easy in her sleep.

"Sometimes my handwriting could be improved. If you canna read something, let me know."

"I can read the numbers very well. And your handwriting is fine." She felt like rolling her eyes. Could she not think of anything more interesting to say?

The phone's ringing came as a welcome relief.

Getting to his feet, he strode to his desk. "Walden Wax Works."

Half listening to him talk about sizes and prices, Beth drifted back to the job at hand.

Over the next hour, Junior received two more calls about orders. He answered each person's questions easily and somehow made it sound as if their questions made his day.

She wondered if he did that on purpose or if he treated everyone around him like they mattered.

When the phone rang yet again, he groaned. "Walden Wax Works, how may I—Oh." His voice turned pensive. "Hiya, Sam. How are you? . . . Today?" He paused, glanced in her direction. "Well, now . . . I wouldn't say I'm too busy but—" He stopped in midsentence. "Yes, I understand. Well, come

on over, then. *Jah.* Yes. I will see you then. Uh huh. Bye."
He set the earpiece down with a *thunk*.

It was obvious that he was upset. Beth looked his way, but
he didn't meet her eyes. Instead, Junior stood up again and
ran a hand through his hair. Then he sighed.

"Is everything all right?" she finally asked. She hadn't
seen him act that flustered the entire time she'd been there.

"Yes. It's just . . . well, that was my brother. Sam. He's
coming over."

"Soon?"

"*Jah.* Now."

She was surprised. She'd been sure he was an only child,
though she wondered why. It wasn't like he'd spent much
time telling her about his family. "I didn't know you had a
brother."

"I do. He's younger." Still looking agitated, he rearranged
some papers on his desk. "He's also not very reliable. We're
not close."

"I'm sorry."

Junior shrugged. "Me, too. But he hasn't wanted to change."
Lowering his voice, he added, "Or maybe it's me that is always hoping he will."

Since she had two brothers and a sister, she could relate.
Well, she could to an extent. But even when they argued she
still loved them fiercely. It was rare that she didn't call each
of them once a week. "Where does Sam live?"

"Currently in Millersburg with a couple of other guys
who are former Amish."

"That's close."

"*Jah.* Sam shares an apartment with them."

Junior was frowning. Beth wondered what the reason was.
"Are you upset that he didn't want to be baptized?"

"Not particularly. He was never one to follow rules. Even
the simplest ones seemed to disagree with him."

"Then what's wrong with him?" Realizing how nosey she was sounding, she added quickly, "Sorry, it's none of my business."

"No, it's fine. And Sam is fine, too. I mean, there's nothing wrong," he added. "I mean, nothing beyond what he is."

"Which is?"

"Confused."

"I see."

"No, you don't." Stopping in front of her desk, he said, "I guess you could say that he's kind of the opposite of you."

"Because I'm trying to be Amish, while he left for the English world?"

"Yes. Also that you have a clue in life and he doesn't. To say we don't usually see eye to eye is an understatement."

And . . . he'd said too much.

She stood up. "You know what? It just occurred to me that I could take some of these ledgers home and work on them there. Then you could have your privacy. I know it will probably not do any favors for my reputation around here, but you and I will know the truth."

"Please don't."

She studied his tense expression. Noticed how stiff his posture was. He was really on edge. "Are you sure you don't want to be alone? I promise, I could be out of here in just a few moments."

"Would you mind if I asked you not to do that?"

She put back down the ledger that she was holding in her arms. "Of course not. I mean, it's your company and your ledgers."

"Elizabeth. Beth. Please, don't take this the wrong way. It's not that I don't trust you. But . . . I could use a buffer right now between me and my brother."

"Oh." She was starting to get a little worried. What did

Junior think was going to happen? Were they likely to come to blows?

"See, I think if you're here, then I might be able to hold it together. Or Sam might not be quite as demanding."

She sat back down. "All right."

"Thanks." He walked to his desk and started organizing things into piles.

Watching him from the corner of her eye, Beth had a pretty good idea how his paperwork and invoices got so mixed up. He was truly just piling them in a big stack.

Two raps on the door brought both of their attention to the door.

"Come in," he said.

Cherry opened the door with a bit of a flourish. "Junior, look who came for a visit! Samuel!"

Beth barely refrained from rolling her eyes. Honestly, Cherry acted like she was announcing the Queen of England.

All thoughts froze when she spied Sam, however. He looked a lot like Junior, but the movie-star version of him. He was slick-looking. Movie-star handsome.

And had obviously been flirting with Cherry, which was just wrong.

Then, just before he focused on his brother, he glanced her way.

And then he somehow managed to look even more sleazy. His smile widened.

Junior had not been right about his brother. It wasn't that he didn't fit in, it was that he didn't seem nice.

He didn't seem nice at all.

But that was only a first impression.

CHAPTER 22

Junior hadn't expected his brother to be any different since the last time they'd seen each other. He wasn't. With a confidence that he didn't even try to hide, he'd walked through the door to Junior's office like he'd owned the place.

When Junior was in a bad mood, he'd sometimes be sure that Sam thought he did own a portion of Walden Wax Works. His brother often took on foolhardy notions that made no sense like other folks collected souvenirs at a truck stop. He'd done that once with a drinking problem that he'd blamed on their childhood, a gambling habit that he still couldn't seem to kick, and an assortment of other chips on his shoulders that he believed were the fault of Sam, his teachers, and their parents' deaths.

"Boy, it's been a long time, John," he said after they hugged hello. "How long? Two months?"

"Pretty sure it's more like four."

"Too long, then. How are you?"

"I've been well."

"Good." Something in Sam's eyes flickered, but Junior

wasn't sure if it was regret or relief. With Sam, one could never be sure. "Thanks for letting me come right over."

"You never need to worry about that. We're brothers."

"Right." Sam took a deep breath, then glanced Elizabeth. Again.

When he turned her way, Junior fought the urge to step in front of Elizabeth. It was shocking. He seemed to have had a dormant protective streak. He wanted to shield her from everything that his brother had become.

But Junior knew one thing that his brother did not—Sam Lambright was no match for Elizabeth Schrock. Curious to know more about her, he'd gotten on the internet the other day and looked her up. He'd spied her professional photo and saw more than a few photographs of her holding awards.

And, because he had been both impressed and amused, he'd gone ahead and read a bunch of her clients' words and recommendations. Almost every one of them mentioned how smart, assertive, and driven she was. Elizabeth was impressive in more ways than one.

Sam had no idea who he'd just set his sights on.

"Now who might you be?" he said with a smile.

Elizabeth smiled back at him. "I'm Beth. And you are Junior's brother."

"I am." He leaned closer and held out his hand. "My name is Sam. It's nice to meet you."

"Same." Elizabeth smiled. She did not hold out her hand.

Some of Sam's smile lost its shine. "Do you not shake hands?"

"I do. Just not all the time."

"Why? Are you Amish or English?" He blatantly looked over her hair, face, dress.

Junior was tempted to step in, but he feared he'd only make things worse. Instead, he focused on how smart people said she could be.

She didn't disappoint. After a few seconds, she lifted her chin. "I'm English, but I'm thinking about being Amish."

"No way. Really?"

"Really."

"Let me save you the trouble," he said in a much harder tone. "You do not want to be Amish. There are a ton of rules."

"Since we are strangers, I don't believe you know what I want."

Samual drew back in surprise. "Boy. There's some fire to ya, huh?"

"You have no idea."

Junior couldn't help it. He started laughing.

Obviously stung by both Beth's dismissal and Junior's laughter, Sam turned to him. At last. "What's so funny?"

"You are. After calling to say you need to come right over, you flirt with my receptionist and then focus on one of my employees. Then, after she holds her own against your questioning, you act shocked. All in all, I'd say that's pretty funny."

Sam looked down at his feet. "You might be right. But in my defense . . . Cherry flirts with everyone."

Since he wasn't wrong, Junior chuckled again. "It's good to see you, *bruder*. You're looking well."

"You are, too." He glanced in Elizabeth's direction. "It was a surprise to see another desk in here. What is Beth doing for you?"

"Beth is helping me out with some paperwork and my ledgers."

"Okay . . . but I don't understand why she's sharing your office. Wait, is she your girl?"

"*Nee.*" Glancing at Elizabeth, he grinned again. "And, just to let you know, she can both hear you and speak for herself."

Looking annoyed, Sam turned to her again. "Beth, would you mind taking a five- or ten-minute break outside of this room?" When she didn't rush to her feet, his voice hardened. "Please?"

Elizabeth glanced his way. When Junior shook his head, she replied, "Sorry, but I've got a lot to do. But don't mind me. I won't interrupt and I'll pretend I don't understand a word you say."

"She's very cheeky, Junior."

"I know. It takes some getting used to." He waved a hand. "Have a seat."

When Samuel sat down, he looked far less sure of himself. It was odd to see, but Junior wasn't going to complain about that. For too long he'd felt as if he'd been at his brother's beck and call while Samuel did whatever he wanted.

"What's going on?"

"Well, I've been having some difficulties."

"Of what sort? Are you ill?"

"*Nee.* No. Nothing like that." After glancing at Elizabeth yet again, his brother seemed to make up his mind. "They are of a financial nature."

"Oh."

"I need you to give me a loan, Junior."

"For what?"

Sam's eyes narrowed. "For living."

"I thought you were sharing an apartment with two other guys in Millersburg."

"Yeah, well, that didn't work out. I moved somewhere else, but it's nowhere that you would know. It's in the city, since I'm English now."

"What city are you talking about?" Elizabeth asked.

"That ain't none of your business."

"Samuel, don't snap at Elizabeth."

"I don't mind if he snaps," she said, almost looking amused.

"Especially since he is right. Your conversation is none of my business. But if the city is Cleveland, I would be interested. Until recently I was a Realtor there."

"You sold real estate?"

"Yes."

Junior smiled. "She was very successful."

Beth looked his way. "How did you know that?"

"I might have looked you up." When she flushed with happiness, he felt an answering response deep in his gut. It was a fact. He wasn't going to be able to deny it any longer. He liked Elizabeth. A lot.

Sam's scoff brought Junior's attention back to him. "If you did that well in real estate, I don't know why you're working here . . . or thinking about being Amish. No Amish woman is gonna be a real-estate agent."

"Well, I'm not so sure I want to sell real estate anymore. But, I will say that I know plenty of Amish women who would do just fine in the profession."

"Hmm." Turning back to Junior, he lowered his voice. "Listen, as entertaining as sparring with Beth is, I really just came for a favor."

"How much do you need?"

"Not much. Maybe a couple of grand?"

Junior was floored. Both by the amount and by the brazen way Sam had stopped by to ask for it. "You need several thousand dollars?"

"I do." All traces of any humor left his expression. "It's important."

"I'm not going to give you anything until I know why you need such a big sum."

"I don't know why that's the difference."

"You know why."

As they stared at each other, Junior knew that Sam was only going through the motions. He was waiting for him to bail him out. Just like always. And, because Sam usually irritated him and made him feel guilty at the same time, Junior knew he did it because he felt sorry for him. And so he would leave him alone.

But he could practically feel Beth's irritation with Sam through the room. She didn't want him to give his brother any help. Which made him realize that he'd been letting his brother off—and maybe himself—too easily. And for too long. "What are you doing now, *bruder*?"

"I . . . I'm between jobs at the moment."

"So you need work?"

"No. I'll find it. I just need something to get me through."

"Junior, wasn't Raymond just telling you that he was shorthanded on the line?" Beth asked.

"He was. Two of my men are out."

"Well, there you go." Beth smiled.

Sam erupted as he jumped to his feet. "Junior, no. I didn't come here to ask for a job."

"Why can't you work here?"

"Beyond the fact that I don't want to . . . I have obligations."

"Do you owe someone money?" he asked.

"Yes," he bit out.

"Who?"

"No one you know."

"I'm sure I don't. But if you're asking for funds, then I think I deserve to hear the truth."

"You've never asked for all the details before." Looking a little like a feral cat stuck in a corner, Sam's voice rose. "Where is this coming from? From her?"

"That is enough, Samuel. You may not come in here and disparage my employees. Now, do you want to go work on the line or not?"

"I can't believe you would make me do that. We're family."

"*Jah*, we are." Standing up, he made his decision. "And because we're family, I think it's time I made you grow up. Either ask Eli and Rhoda if you can move in with them and work here to replenish your bank account . . . or leave."

"I cannot go back without that money, Junior." Standing up, he walked to his side. "Come on. You know I wouldn't ask if it wasn't important."

"I'm pretty sure that's what you told me in the past. So, today I'm going to tell you the same thing. I wouldn't refuse you if I didn't think it was important as well."

He closed his eyes. "How about I live with you?"

"*Nee.*"

"Why? Is she living with you?"

An anger he didn't know he could feel threatened to overtake him. "Don't disrespect her like that."

"Oh, please. She's a grown woman. Not a scared, sheltered girl."

Before he could throw Samuel out, Elizabeth jumped in.

"I'm not living with your brother. But if I was, I sure wouldn't let you live there, too."

"You're mighty tough talking for an almost-Amish girl."

"First, I think there are plenty of Amish women who could hold their own with you. Secondly, you're going to have to try harder to put me down than ask if I'm living at your brother's *haus*." After a pause, she said, "But if you do decide to disparage me, let me warn you about something. I grew up with two brothers and a sister. I'm used to arguing with them." With a hint of a smile, she added, "I'm also used to winning."

Junior couldn't help it. He started laughing. "Remind me to have you by my side if I ever get in a bar fight."

Giggling as well, she reached out to fist-bump him. "Don't worry. I'll have your back."

Samuel, who'd been watching their interplay like he was

watching a tennis match, strode toward the door. "You've changed, Junior."

"If you think that I have because I've no longer been your carpet to walk on, then that's a good thing." Just as he was about to leave, his conscience prevailed. "Hey, Sam?"

"*Jah?*"

"If you decide to take me up on my offer, it's still good. It will be good whenever you need it."

"That's not an offer, John. It's blackmail. I don't need any more of that in my life."

When he walked down the hall, Junior sat down behind his desk. Instead of feeling triumphant, he was embarrassed and ashamed. He should have handled that better. He knew he should have.

"Sorry you had to witness that, Elizabeth."

"I'm sorry I got all bulldog-like and weighed in. Sam was right. Your conversation wasn't any of my business."

"Just curious. Why did you? Sam isn't the easiest person to be around on his best days."

"I don't know. Maybe because it felt like someone should? All my life I've had my brothers and Kelsey. My grandparents and parents, too, of course. But the four of us are close. Sometimes I feel that if Kelsey got a cut on her leg, I'd bleed, too. I hated the idea of you having to face your silly brother all by yourself."

"I guess Samuel is acting kind of silly."

"I think so. Maybe destructive, too? All I do know is that I'd rather he not bring you down with him in front of me."

"I appreciate that. Thanks."

"Like I said earlier, I've got your back."

He'd never thought that his future partner in life would be someone who would have his back. He'd assumed that she'd be one more person in his life that he needed to look after. To be his priority.

But now, when he thought about a companion . . . No, a wife. A partner.

Yes, he definitely needed someone like Beth.

No, he wanted Beth.

It seemed from time to time he needed to be taken care of, too.

CHAPTER 23

Martin had spent the last four hours in a coffee shop in Berlin. There, he'd sipped iced coffees, ate both a roast beef sandwich and two cookies, and worked. The internet was good there. Almost as good as in his office.

In between emails, video conference calls, and texts, he people-watched. There was a lot to see, and it was mildly entertaining to watch the dynamics of the people chatting nearby.

Every so often one of the workers would stop by to see if he wanted a refill or to collect his trash.

It was all very pleasant. He wasn't the only person camped out in a back table making use of it. Far from it.

However, Martin was pretty sure that he was the only one who'd been there three days in a row. Not only were his coffee bills beginning to edge out of control, working this way wasn't sustainable. He knew that.

But for some reason, he couldn't bear to drive back to Cleveland. Not yet.

Each day, when he finally loaded his laptop in his car, he was more than ready to go back to his grandparents' house.

He needed to have conversations in person with people he cared about. Or to be put to work in the barn. The first day, his grandfather obliged, and he'd spent two hours cleaning stalls. Yesterday, he'd played cards with Beth.

As he drove back to the farm, Martin wondered who he'd see that afternoon. Maybe Kesley and Richard would stop by. Or Jonny and Treva. He needed that interaction. He was used to working in an office and chatting with other guys about the latest ball game.

And, of course, he was trying very hard not to see Patti.

After stopping by the store for a couple of sodas for his *dawdi*, he felt dismayed when he walked inside. The kitchen was completely quiet.

Actually, the entire house was quiet. That was probably a welcome change for his grandparents but strange for him to get used to. Unless they were gone, too? Dismay filled him. Now what was he going to do? "Mommi? Dawdi?" he called out. "Is anyone home?"

"We're in here, Martin."

Glad to hear his grandfather's voice, he strode to the living room. They were both sitting in their matching recliners in front of the fireplace. His grandfather had a library book on his lap, and his grandmother was looking at a magazine. They both had cups of coffee on the table positioned in between their chairs. They looked completely at ease and at peace.

Kind of the opposite of how he was feeling.

His grandmother was the first to remove her reading glasses. "Martin, you're back a little early today."

"Am I? I didn't notice."

"Hmm. How was your day? Did you get a lot of work done?"

"Yes. I was at the Big Chill in Berlin again." He sat down on the couch. "Where is Beth?"

"She went over to see Treva and Jonny this afternoon. She mentioned she might stay there for supper."

"Really? I didn't know she was going over there." He would have tagged along.

"She came home from Walden Wax Works looking as if she had a bee in her bonnet. I think she was hoping the two of them could give her both a willing ear and a bit of advice."

"What was wrong?"

"I couldn't say." Mommi's eyes were bright with amusement. "If I had to guess, I'd say her prickly mood had a lot to do with Junior Lambright."

"Why? Is he not treating her well? I hope she told him that she doesn't need to put up with an attitude."

Dawdi chuckled. "Come now, Martin. When has your sister ever been shy about telling people what she thinks?"

"Never."

"She'll be fine. Don't worry."

"I won't." When his grandfather continued to stare, he added, "I'm a little surprised that Beth didn't reach out to me. I could have taken her to Jonny's *haus*. Or talked to her about this Junior guy."

"Or tagged along to see Jonny and Treva?" Mommi murmured.

"Yes." Embarrassment washed over him. He was being both needy and selfish. Two attributes he wasn't proud of.

To his surprise, neither of his grandparents appeared ready to chastise him.

"Just because you are the oldest doesn't mean you have all the answers, true?" Dawdi murmured in a mild tone.

"True. Sorry. I'm trying to act as if I'm needed, but the truth is I think I might be the needy one."

"If it helps, I think Beth needed to hear some relationship advice," Mommi said. "Since both Jonny and Kelsey are happily married, it seems reasonable to reach out to them."

"That is true. Wait. About who? Kiran?"

"No, dear. I think it might be her new boss."

"So this Junior guy means something to her?" When his grandparents exchanged looks again, he sighed. "Wow. I hope she knows what she's doing."

"I wouldn't worry about Beth too much," Mommi said. "She is stronger than you think and has a way of figuring things out in the end."

"I hope so."

"You are a good and faithful brother. You've looked after Jonny, Kelsey, and Beth most of your entire life."

"I tried my best, but we all helped each other." That wasn't modesty talking, either. They all had helped each other in multiple ways.

"I agree, but all three of them have shared about how much they appreciate you."

"That's good to hear."

"Which means, son, that it's time for you to focus on yourself."

"I feel like that's all I've been doing lately. I mean, I moved back to Cleveland. I think I might be the only one who doesn't become Amish. That was pretty selfish, too."

"No, it isn't," Mommi said.

"Making the best decision for your future isn't a failure, son. That is being true to yourself."

"I suppose, but it still feels as if I've crossed a boundary that didn't used to be there."

"Only if you see it as one," Dawdi said. "Don't forget that your grandmother and I loved you just as much when we were positive you would remain in Cleveland."

"Love has a way of overlooking problems, doesn't it?"

Mommi frowned. "I'd say that love has a way of accepting each other's problems and quirks."

"Yes. That's a much better way of looking at love."

"Which brings us to Patti," Dawdi announced.

Martin was tempted to roll his eyes. Nothing had brought Patti into the conversation except his grandparents. And he really didn't want to discuss Patti with them.

"You guys . . ."

"It's time to talk about it, Martin. Past time."

Mommi's focus on him felt laser sharp. Or, maybe it was more the case of him feeling vulnerable. He was so very vulnerable where Patti was concerned. "There's not much to say about Patti."

"Of course there is."

"We know you love her, Martin," his grandfather chided. "That's no secret."

"I do love her."

"How does Patti feel?" Mommi asked.

"She loves me, too." Before either of them could say a word, he rushed on. "But it doesn't really matter if we're in love, because a relationship isn't possible for us." He shook his head. "No, that's not quite true. The relationship that I want to have with her isn't possible."

Looking pained, his grandmother said, "Forgive me, but I think you're overlooking the fact that you two are *already* in a relationship."

"You're right, but it's not a good one." Not for her, anyway. Taking a deep breath, he said. "It's all my fault, too."

"You sure about that?" Dawdi asked.

"I'm positive." He got to his feet. "Dawdi, I put Patti in a terrible position. An impossible one."

"Because she's already been baptized."

"Yes. I can't believe I've been so selfish."

His grandmother sighed. "What did Patti say?"

"Not much. Even though she loves me, but she also doesn't want to break her vow." Unable to remain seated, he jumped to his feet. "And the problem is that I knew she would feel torn, but I fell in love with her, anyway."

"I don't think your heart is any stronger than the rest of the population, Martin," Mommi chided. "One can't help falling in love."

"I agree, but I could have kept my feelings to myself."

His grandfather grunted. "Do you really think it would have helped for her to not know how you felt?"

"I don't know." He ran his hands through his short hair, fighting the urge to tug on the strands. Maybe if he felt a little bit of pain in his scalp it would make his heartache easier to bear. "We came to an agreement of sorts." Remembering how their conversation had eased some of the tension but hadn't exactly alleviated their pain, he added, "I don't know if it helped all that much, though."

"Poor Patti."

"Yeah." Fighting back the urge to pull on his hair again, Martin turned to face them. "I wanted to stay here for a while to check on Beth. I didn't want her to doubt that I supported her. But with everything that's going on with Patti, it might be best if I leave." And . . . here he was again. Pretending that he was looking out for everyone else when what he was really doing was looking out for himself.

"I don't know if you leaving here is going to make Patti feel better, Martin," Dawdi replied after a moment. "Since you've been able to work at the coffee shops, I think it might be a better choice to stay here until the two of you talk some more."

He wished he could see life as clearly as his grandparents, but the fact of the matter was that he knew that life was complicated. "Dawdi, as much as I want to move here and be Amish for Patti, I . . . I just can't."

"You're right, son. You can't change who you are. I don't think you should, either. The man you've become is a good one. All of us are proud of you. Your grandmother and me, your sisters and Jonny, and your parents."

Both relieved and touched by his grandfather's words, Martin felt a lump form in his throat. "Thanks, Dawdi."

Mommi leaned forward. "I think that Patti is proud of you, too."

His grandmother's expression was kind. Gentle and loving. But that didn't make sense.

They were supposed to be reminding him of how important their baptismal vows were.

They were supposed to be upset. Maybe even reminding him that everything would be okay if he would change his life like Jonny and Kelsey had done.

Even though he was filled with hurt and confusion, he forced himself to speak the truth. "Patti can't be proud of me if I'm breaking her heart and making her upset."

"Perhaps it's time to let her make the next move," Mommi said. "And yes, I do think that there is another move to make."

Dawdi nodded. "Just like in a game of chess, sometimes a player is blind to the best option."

"Or they lose," Martin said.

His grandfather smiled. "*Jah.* But it's time you started looking at the bright side of things, ain't so? The Lord has your best interests at heart. Let Him bear the load for a spell."

"I fear that will be easier said than done."

"Of course it will be," Dawdi said with a touch of impatience in his voice.

Martin sat up a little bit straighter. What had he just said wrong? "Okay."

"Don't stress, child. You're misunderstanding what your grandfather means." Mommi waited a beat, then continued. "Everything in life is easy when it's only talked about. That's why it's so easy to dispense advice to other people." Getting to her feet, she stared at him. "It's the doing that matters, Martin. It matters more because it's difficult. Doing some-

thing right and meaningful is much, much harder than simply talking about it."

The words were hard to hear, but ironically, even though
his mind wanted to ignore his grandparents' advice, his heart
was urging him to rush over to Patti's side.

He knew right then and there that there was only one
thing to do.

"I get it now. I need to do some praying and figure out
how I can make things work out with Patti." Swallowing
hard, he added, "Or come to terms with the fact that she and
I might be headed toward a happily ever after one day, but it
might not be with each other."

When his grandparents only gazed at him with sad, understanding eyes, he relaxed at last.

They didn't have all the answers.

But they did have the things he'd needed—hope, love,
and advice. They had those in spades. He'd gotten what he
came for.

CHAPTER 24

Had she ever felt more alone? Patti couldn't remember. She probably had. The days after her aunt died and she'd moved into the house she'd inherited had been awfully lonely. Unable to sleep at night, she would wander the empty halls, half expecting to hear her aunt's voice filtering through a doorway. Of course, it never came. Instead, she'd been surrounded by her aunt's belongings, knowing that it was time to put them up for auction but being reluctant to give away those last pieces of her family.

Now, as she sat next to the firepit in her backyard, soaking in the heat and gazing into the flames, Patti compared her current mood with the way she'd felt all those years ago.

They weren't the same.

Not even close.

When she was mourning for her aunt, when it was sometimes difficult to get out of bed, she'd done a lot of soul searching.

No, that wasn't true. She'd been struggling to find herself and where she fit in her life—and where her future was headed. When her head had finally cleared and she was productive again, she'd made a great number of lists.

She took note of what made her happy. And what did not.

She contemplated what she was good at, and came to terms with what she wasn't.

She talked to God a lot, and He'd seemed happy to listen. She'd been grateful for that. However, He hadn't been in a hurry to give her a sign of His wishes. She'd been so frustrated. Sometimes she'd even sat in this very spot and asked him to let her know what to do.

Which, now that she thought about it, was all very silly. Even the greatest of Christ's disciples had to fumble about on their own from time to time.

But one thing she had learned during that period was that it was possible to become content. She'd mostly found peace with her port-wine stain on her neck. She'd been filled with hope for her new opportunities, too. She'd felt a lot of satisfaction about her business.

Yes, that was the big difference between now and then. In those days, she'd been so pleased to have her talent for math and organization. And when she'd begun to gain clients—all from word of mouth—she'd felt very proud. Every night when she said her prayers, she thanked the Lord for giving her so many gifts.

She still was grateful. Her job was flourishing, and she had a wide circle of friends now. People who enjoyed her skills and help and her company. She was rarely lonely anymore, and the halls of the house now felt comfortable and familiar.

But now Patti was kind of starting to think that the Lord hadn't had her back, after all. Maybe she'd made some mistakes and He'd decided to give her some repercussions.

How else could she explain why He'd gone and done something that she didn't know how to handle?

Why had He allowed her to fall in love with the wrong person? Patti had no earthly idea.

All she did know was that the feeling was everything she'd ever dreamed it would be. She felt giddy and attractive and tentative and scared. Sometimes, she was pretty sure she felt all those things at the same time! Why, it was a wonder she didn't feel sick to her stomach all day long.

Now she understood what so many of her friends had talked about when they'd shared stories about their husband or wife. Now she understood that lovesick expression Kelsey had worn whenever she spied Preacher Richard.

Kelsey had been so in love that she didn't care how silly or moonstruck she'd looked. And no wonder everyone who witnessed it had only smiled. They'd known. They'd known that addictive feeling.

So, she was grateful for that.

But she wasn't able to understand why the Lord had blessed her with such an experience if it was wrong. Why did He give her something so beautiful just to take it all away?

Staring into the flames, she felt a lump form in her throat.

Determined not to cry, she allowed anger to fuel her words. "Why, Gott?" she whispered into the night. "Why did you let me fall in love just to make it be the wrong person? Haven't I been through enough heartache?"

And that was what was hardest, Patti decided. She'd already lost both her parents and her favorite person in the world. She lived alone and had been forced to do care for the land and a house with little help. He'd already given her a birthmark that had made her a target for bullies.

Weren't those things enough?

She blinked.

But if she hadn't lost her family, she would have never had such a cozy, wonderful place to live. The Lord had also given her a fine mind and a talent for numbers. And because of those gifts, she'd been able to have a wonderful career. It made her feel fulfilled and enabled her to pay men to come out and help with the mowing and heavy yardwork.

Finally, she'd also realized that her birthmark wasn't all

that "terrible," after all. So many other people had diseases or ailments that ruined their bodies. What was an unsightly mark compared to that?

"I'm sorry, Lord. I guess I have been given more than enough. I shouldn't be so greedy."

"Patti? Who are you talking to?"

She looked up to see Martin himself walking her way. Glad for the dark skies, at least he wouldn't be able to see her blush.

"Martin, I didn't expect to see you."

"I was out for a walk and spied your fire. I came over to make sure it wasn't unattended." He stopped. Scanned the area. Peeked at her back door. "Do you have a guest over?"

"Hmm?"

"Your conversation." He was beginning to appear a bit impatient. Like he thought she was playing a game or something with him.

She was not. "Nope. No one is here. Just me."

"Oh. It sounded as if you were conversing with something."

"I was. I was chatting with God."

His expression, lit by firelight, eased as he sat down on the chair across from her. "How's it going?"

She waved a hand. "About like you'd expect. I've been doing a lot of talking and He's doing a lot of listening."

"That's not a surprise. Is it?"

"*Nee.*" She poked at the firepit with the end of a stick. "But I would be lying if I said I wasn't disappointed."

She poked one of the smoldering logs. When it didn't catch, she stepped closer and gave it another jab.

"Hey, how about I give you a hand with that?"

"I don't need a hand."

"Of course not." His voice was even, but his lips were pursed. Like he was forcing himself not to say anything more.

196 Shelley Shepard Gray

Studying his expression, she realized that Martin was truly worried that she was going to burn herself. "I'm worrying you, aren't I?"

"Yes."

Patti didn't bother hiding her amusement. Not at him—at herself. "I guess I look like a fool?"

"Not at all." Before she could protest, he took the stick out of her hand. "It's more like you maybe don't have your mind on the fire as much as some other things."

"I can't deny that that is the case."

"Want to talk about it?"

And admit that he was the focus of all her thoughts and prayers? "It's probably best we didn't talk about it."

"Why not?"

She literally almost ached to lie. To tell him a fabricated story, one that he would believe. Something mundane and boring. Something that he would soon forget.

But it felt as if that was what she'd been doing for most of her life. Whenever she'd felt things that might make another person uncomfortable, she'd bury them inside of her.

She used to tell herself it was because she didn't like confrontation, but now she knew better. She'd been too afraid of losing another person whom she'd wanted to like her.

"If you really want to hear, it might be best for you to sit down."

The mild curiosity that had been shining in his eyes faded into worry. Martin walked to the opposite chair and sat down. Faced her.

They stared at each other for a long moment. Or, maybe it was actually a short one. Or, maybe she wasn't even sure? Whenever she was around him, nothing in her orderly life seemed to make sense.

She took a deep breath, remembered the promise she'd just made to herself, and forced herself to continue.

"I used to think I was falling in love with you, Martin Schrock."

She could practically see every muscle in his body tense. "Used to?"

"*Jah.*" Forcing herself to admit the rest, she averted her eyes. "Now I know that I am."

"So you're saying that you love me?"

It was still too hard to meet his eyes. "Yes. I love you so much that I can't do anything about it. It's done."

"Patti, you know I love you, too."

She turned her head. Met his gaze. "Martin, you came to Walden to learn how to be Amish. You've tried to farm, you've helped with horses, you've attempted to drive a buggy."

"Buggies." He grimaced. "I never could figure out how to tell a horse what to do."

"Oh, I know. I think everyone in Walden knows." She smiled at him. "You tried different jobs and you tried to be happy. I know you did."

"Everything you're saying is true."

"I've tried to help you."

"You did help."

"And I certainly talked to your sisters and your grand-parents about your struggles. But I still think I failed you."

He shook his head slowly. "You didn't. Patti, you could never fail me."

"But I did, Martin. You shared your feelings for me, but I was too afraid to admit mine. I mean, not completely. You tried so hard to fit into my world, but I did little in yours. All I did was visit you for a few days."

"You've done more than that."

"Maybe. Maybe not. But the outcome is still the same."

He looked at the fire. Lifted his head to study her. In the distance the wind rustled through the trees. In the summer, fireflies lit the sky, twinkling like old friends. Now, it felt like the only two people in the world were Martin and her.

Maybe that was the Lord's doing. After all, hadn't she just been praying for a sign? For some help? She wanted to feel like he was her world.

No, she realized. He already was.

"So . . . what are you thinking?" he asked.

It was time. It was time to tell both him and herself the truth—and then face the consequences. "I think giving up a life with you would be unbearable."

He inhaled sharply. His entire body seemed to tense. Every muscle poised to spring, but whether it was forward toward her or away from everything they were . . . she didn't know. "Patti, I can't afford to misunderstand you." Every word sounded as if it were being yanked out of him. Inch by painful inch.

Seeming like he was attempting to collect himself, Martin swallowed. Sounding a little stronger, he continued. "I don't want to misunderstand what you're saying."

"Misunderstand?"

"Yes. What does a life with me look like to you?"

It was time. It was time to just say the words. To jump in with both feet. "A life with you looks like an English one, Martin. In Cleveland."

His entire expression froze. "You'd be willing to give this up for me?"

"I'd be willing to give up almost anything for you. I love you."

Martin stared at her. Closed his eyes. Seemed to say a prayer. Or, maybe he was coaching himself?

Nerves began to take hold of her. Doubts set in. Maybe she'd been wrong. Maybe she should've waited to tell him her thoughts a lot longer.

But then he stood up. Walked around the firepit. Reached for her hand. Pulled her to her feet.

When she opened her mouth to protest. To ask what he was doing . . .

It turned out that no explanation was needed. Because he was kissing the life out of her, holding her so close to him that she was pretty sure she could feel his heartbeat against her own.

Her arms snaked around his neck. She somehow managed a way to press even closer and kissed him with everything she was.

It was unseemly. Maybe even too passionate and reckless for two people not even engaged.

But her heart didn't seem to care. And honestly, neither did the rest of her. For so long, she'd put everything and everyone above her own selfish wants. Usually, that was fine. Patti liked being needed.

So, as for tonight? It seemed tonight was the exception.

CHAPTER 25

Over the last three weeks, they'd developed a routine of sorts. Junior would arrive for work at his usual time, walk through the plant, and talk to some of the earliest employees on shift. Then, after pouring himself another cup of coffee, he would retreat to his desk, where he would open the computer and begin to respond to the most urgent emails. He found the quiet soothing and was able to get a lot accomplished.

Then, around a quarter to nine, he'd begin to start watching the clock. As each minute ticked by, his insides would begin to churn a bit and his mood would lift. All because he was impatiently waiting for Elizabeth to arrive.

Unlike everyone else at Walden Wax Works, Beth never arrived or left at the same exact time. Though this habit bothered Cherry—and she had no qualms about relaying this fact—Junior found Beth's nonconformity amusing. He sometimes got the feeling that Beth was maintaining this erratic schedule on purpose, like maybe she was trying to gain some control in her life since pretty much everything else was up in the air.

Or maybe she just didn't care when she showed up.

Regardless of the reason, Elizabeth's comings and goings didn't affect the company's success. Her work was appreciated, but not time sensitive. Besides, her arrival and departure times weren't too chaotic. She always arrived sometime between nine and ten in the morning and left between four and five in the afternoon.

To Junior's shame, he was always aware of the exact times.

Sometimes she would simply walk in, wish him good morning, and then get to work. Other times she'd fly in like a fierce wind. She'd be talking a mile a minute, each sentence filled with apologies, and often blaming her tardiness on her pregnancy. She was either nauseous, exhausted, or hungry. Since he'd never had much contact with an expectant mother before, Junior had no idea if her reasons were valid or simply part of a game she was playing.

Whatever the reason, Junior would simply wish her a good morning and continue what he was doing.

Then, about ten days ago, he'd started playing a game with himself every morning. He'd make a guess about what time Elizabeth would walk through his office door. It amused him so much, he'd even devised a prize for himself when his guess was within three minutes of her arrival: lunch out.

That was why, when Beth walked into his office at 9:08, he felt like he'd won the lottery.

"Good morning," she said as she slipped off her coat. "How are you?"

He couldn't resist grinning. "I'm very well. You made my day, Elizabeth."

She stopped fussing with her backpack and looked his way. "Do I even want to know why?"

"It's because you arrived at 9:08 on the dot."

Suspicion mixed with an additional dose of irritation brightened her blue eyes. "Junior, I told you from the start that I wasn't going to adhere to a time clock."

"I know. I didn't forget."

"Then why are you looking so pleased about 9:08? Because it doesn't make much sense, especially since Cherry was her usual harpy self when I walked in the door."

"I'm pleased because that was today's guess."

She tossed the backpack on the ground and then crossed her arms across her chest. "I think you're going to have to explain yourself."

"I've begun to make a guessing game about your arrival time." He laughed, fully intending to tell her why he was so pleased: he was going to take her out to lunch.

But he didn't get the chance because her eyes filled with tears. Those amazing blue eyes that he couldn't seem to stop marveling over. Not quite understanding what was wrong but eager to fix it, he strode to her side. "Elizabeth, what in the world? What's wrong?" It seemed to be the wrong thing to say. A tear escaped and landed on her cheek. "Hey," he murmured as he reached out to wipe it off with the pad of his thumb.

She recoiled as if he'd burned her. "Don't."

"Don't wipe your tears?" He smiled. "Elizabeth."

"I can't believe you," she snapped as she picked back up her tote bag. "I thought we were friends."

"We are," he said quickly. Dismay filled him as he began to realize that he might be making things worse instead of better.

"That's doubtful." She turned.

To walk out!

Unable to help himself, he reached for her arm in order to force her to a stop.

She flinched before turning on her heel. "Don't touch me!"

Against his better judgment, he curved his fingers around her elbow. "Sorry, but I'm not going to let you leave until you tell me what I did that you're so upset about."

"You told me that my arrival and departure times weren't an issue. You've told me that the work I have done for you made a difference to you. But obviously you lied."

"I didn't lie."

"What do you call a betting pool, then? How did you think I would feel when I learned that everyone in here was fixated on when I came in?"

"*Nee*, Elizabeth."

Either she was ignoring him or she didn't hear, because she continued to talk as the tears continued to fall. "I'm not lazy and I'm not the type to take advantage of others. I can't believe that's who you decided I was."

"I didn't think that. I don't think that." He ran his hand down her arm, then pulled her close into a loose hug. "I've never said a word about my game to anyone else. Never."

"What do you mean?"

Giving in to temptation, he brushed his lips against her cheek. Seeking to dry her tears with kisses, it seemed. "It means that it's been my own silly game. That's all."

"Only yours?"

"Only mine. No one else's."

She sniffed. "I don't understand."

Feeling foolish—and maybe far too vulnerable—he said, "Elizabeth, the truth is that I like seeing you every morning. Whenever you walk in the door, my day feels like it starts. And because of that, I'm guilty of looking forward to you walking through the door far too eagerly. So, about two weeks ago, I developed a little game. I took to guessing about when you might get here. And, because I've never liked a challenge without an accompanying surprise, I decided to give myself a prize for guesstimating your arrival within three minutes."

Her eyebrows rose. "Three minutes?"

"*Jah*. Give or take."

"Has that ever happened?"

"Twice before."

"Hmm."

Glad that she no longer was crying—or contemplating a place and time to kill him—he pushed back a lock of her hair. It had fallen across her temple. "Today was special, though."

"How so?"

"I guessed 9:08, and that was the exact time you walked through the door. That's why I was so pleased with myself."

She shook her head. "You are something else, Junior Lambright."

"I reckon that's true, but don't be mad, okay? My childish game had nothing to do with your choices and everything to do with my fixation with my new employee."

"Almost-new employee." Even though her eyes still looked a bit damp, she was smiling.

Which allowed him to catch his breath. He didn't want to make her cry ever again.

"That's true," he agreed, playing on their long-running joke that she wasn't actually an employee since he wasn't paying her a dime.

"So, what is your prize?"

"Lunch out. Want to come?"

"That hardly seems fair. I can't partake in the celebration for your win."

"Of course you can. I made the rules."

"But someone could accuse you of making it rigged. If I get to partake in the spoils, then I could have planned it with you."

"No one else knows, Elizabeth. Besides, anyone knows that sitting in a restaurant by oneself isn't all that fun. It will be far more enjoyable to share it with you."

She closed her eyes and chuckled. "You really are too much."

"So, is that a yes to a lunch date?"

"I suppose so." She smiled at him. At last. It was bright and sweet and perfect.

And irresistible.

He leaned close, cupped the back of her head, and finally gave in to temptation. He brushed his lips across hers.

It went so well, he did it again.

Elizabeth kissed him back. Smiled.

Then frowned when the door swung open and someone inhaled sharply.

No, not someone. He knew that gasp. "Close the door, Cherry," he barked. Still keeping his attention where he needed it to belong.

Elizabeth pressed her forehead to his chest. Glad she wasn't pulling away, he wrapped an arm around her. Held her close. "Now, if you please," he bit out.

Cherry muttered something under her breath before speaking his name far more loudly. "Junior—"

No. No way was she going to ruin this moment any more than she already had. "I don't care if the building is on fire. Close the door."

When the door slammed, Elizabeth broke away.

"I'm so sorry about that," he murmured as he reached out to touch her. "I can't believe Cherry didn't knock. Are you okay?"

"Yeah."

Scanning her face, he thought she looked a little more mad than upset, but he didn't want to take any chances. "You sure?"

"Yeah. I've been just thinking that there's a silver lining to her barging in on our first kiss."

"Which is?"

"Well, at least I won't have to worry anymore about everyone taking bets on my arrival. They've got something far more interesting to talk about now."

Junior reckoned she had a point. It was just too bad he didn't know whether to laugh or cry.

CHAPTER 26

Way too many things were spinning around in Beth's head. The kiss. Cherry's outraged tone. The fact that she'd walked in late yet again, and that her inability to adhere to a set schedule was 180 degrees from the way things used to be.

No, with the person who she used to be.

Mixed in all of that was Junior's embarrassed, almost-adorable explanation of his "game." She had been upset with him about it . . . until she realized his clock watching meant he'd been looking for her every day. Eagerly.

Then, of course, there was the kiss. No, it hadn't been just a kiss. As kisses went, it had been a doozy. At the very least, she should be thinking of it in all capital letters, like the symbol of bad decision-making it was.

Though . . . it hadn't felt like a bad decision. It had not only been a great kiss, but it had also felt right. Almost as if everything in her life had just clicked into place at long last.

She blinked. Met Junior's eyes. And realized that she should be concentrating on all of the new feelings that were zipping between them. It was positively electric.

What was she going to do about that?

Junior's hand brushing back the hair from her face felt like another caress. Just like the soft, concerned expression he was wearing. "Hey. Are you okay?" he murmured.

"Yes, of course." The response was automatic. Her usual response to life. No matter how hard or confusing the situation was, she'd never given herself the option to be any other way. Not when she was a child. Not when she was a teenager looking after Jonny and Kelsey, and not when she was working in real estate.

Or, say, when she got unexpectedly pregnant and was living in her Amish grandparents' house while she attempted to figure out the rest of her life.

Usually, everyone accepted that response. She was never questioned. It wasn't a surprise. After all, no one really wanted to hear about someone else's problems.

She lifted her chin and smiled.

Junior didn't budge. "Let's try this again. Are you okay, Elizabeth?"

He was worried about her, and he wasn't going to accept either a pasted-on smile or a fib. Just as importantly, Beth knew that if she told him she wasn't okay, he would try to fix it.

She swallowed. Gathered her courage.

And finally decided to tell him the truth. "I don't know."

"What's upsetting you?" He ran his fingers along her cheek again. Reached for her hand. And when their fingers were linked, he tugged her even closer. Beth didn't even try to fight it.

She was surrounded by him. His scent. His warmth. His concern.

But he wasn't her boyfriend. "What isn't?" she said with a half smile.

He didn't respond. Instead, he kept her hand tightly enclosed in his while he continued to wait.

"I guess you want something more than a sarcastic quip, huh?"

"What I want is a real answer."

"Okay." He deserved that, and maybe she deserved to acknowledge her feelings, too. She was so tired of handling life by herself. Not only was it exhausting, but she wasn't doing a very good job of it. Here, she'd left a good job and good life in order to hide out at her grandparents' house. But she still wasn't wholeheartedly embracing the Amish faith. Only kind of, sort of doing that. Even though both her brother-in-law, Richard, and the bishop had told her that such things took time, she ached to feel certain about one thing in her life.

"If you're talking about that kiss . . . yes, I'm okay about that." She averted her eyes. "It's everything else that I'm having trouble with." She took a deep breath. "At the moment, I think I'm slowly ruining my whole life and I don't seem to be able to put the brakes on it."

"Are you talking about your baby?"

"Yes. I mean, no." Flustered, she continued. "I mean, I want this baby and I don't look at it as anything but a blessing. But I didn't plan on it, and I sure didn't plan on . . ." Her voice drifted off, because how many times was she going to feel obligated to divulge her lapse in judgment?

Beth tensed. Waiting for him to remind her of it. For Junior to put it out there for both of them. So it could sit there in the air. In between them, like one of those awful flies that flew into her grandparents' kitchen and zipped around too quickly to kill.

But he didn't. "If not the babe, then what?"

"Oh, I don't know. The fact that instead of staying put and keeping the rest of my life on course, I decided to leave my really good job and become Amish."

He raised his eyebrows. "And . . ."

"And, what?" Hadn't she told him enough?

"And you're now working for me and it feels awkward."

"Well, yes. I like the lack of stress, but I think I'm acting a bit too relaxed now."

"Are you sure about that?"

"Pretty sure." Feeling more and more awkward, she tugged on her fingers and tried to joke. "Besides, I'm only half working. Remember?"

His hand tightened, trapping her fingers. "I'd never forget that." He smiled then. A flash of pure-white teeth and the hint of a dimple that never seemed to be completely at home on his face.

Which reminded her that she'd been awfully judgmental when he shared his "what time is Beth going to show up?" game. He wasn't the only person in the room who liked to play games.

Junior tilted his head to one side. "So, is that it?"

"It?"

"Is your list complete?"

"Yes." And that was the truth, if one discounted the fact that she'd just kissed and was currently holding the hand of her not-boss.

And the fact that she had secretly enjoyed getting the upper hand with Cherry. Maybe she should feel bad about that, but Beth didn't. She didn't care if Cherry was Amish. The fact of the matter was that she was a mean girl, and mean girls could pop up anywhere at any time. Bonnets and *kapps* didn't change a thing.

"You might feel like you're ruining your life, but I'm beginning to wonder if you're really just putting things in order."

"Really?"

He nodded. "Everyone faces challenges and changes in plans. Everyone also gets older and changes their priorities from time to time."

1

"You think that is what's happening with me?"

"I don't know. But I'd guess that most anyone would find everything you're going through to be a lot." Finally releasing her hand, he added, "And, uh, as far as the kiss went . . ."

"Yes?"

"I don't regret a thing."

Happiness surged through her . . . before reality hit again. This wasn't the time or the place to discuss the attraction that was sizzling between them. "I think it's time I got to work."

"All right."

"Good. Thank you." Heading to her desk, she scanned the top. Noticed that the usual pile of papers for her to set to rights was nowhere to be found. "Where is everything?"

He approached. "What are you looking for?"

"The receipts. The paperwork. My job."

"Oh. I, ah, took care of everything already."

"When?" Last night when she left, there had easily been four hours of work to do.

"This morning." Looking a little sheepish, he said, "I couldn't sleep, so I came in here early. But everything was in order . . ."

"So you did all my work?"

"*Jah.*"

He looked puzzled, which was a shame. Because she felt like shaking him. "Junior Lambright, I think it's time we did a quick recap."

"Recap?"

Ignoring both the sarcasm in his voice and the narrowing of his eyes, Beth held up a finger. "First, we had to have a whole discussion about what time I arrived, and this was after I got a talking-to by your mean-girl receptionist." She took a deep breath. "Then, we got to have a review of my life, which you felt comfortable commenting on. And now,

212 Shelley Shepard Gray

after all of that, it turns out that I didn't even need to show up, after all." She waved her hands in the air. "Oh my gosh! We could have saved ourselves from this last hour."

"Elizabeth, you should calm down."

"Why? Because it's not good for the baby?"

"*Nee*," he snapped. "Because your rant is as annoying as all get out. It's also unnecessary."

Hurt, mixed with a healthy dose of anger and irritation, made tears threaten. Which made her even more upset. "I can't believe you." Reaching for her purse, she started for the door. "I'm out of here."

"Have supper with me tonight."

"What?"

"You heard me."

"Okay, then. Why?"

"Because I want to take you out for a meal. I want to sit across from you and not talk about work."

She couldn't help but turn back around to face him. "Are you serious right now?"

"Stop asking me questions you already know the answers to."

"You're asking me out on a date."

"Absolutely."

And . . . man. There was that dimple again. That real smile. That genuine smile. The one she was starting to crave, even though there were a hundred reasons not to.

She felt as if she was at another precipice. She could either say no, walk out, and sit at her grandparents' house, or do what she wanted.

"Okay."

An almost smug look formed on his face. "I'll pick you up at six."

"That's it?"

"*Nee*. I'll be happy to walk you out, if you'd like. Or, if you've a mind of being patient for a spell, you could have a seat and wait for some more work to show up. I have a feeling I've probably received ten or twelve emails that you could deal with in the last hour."

Maybe waiting for work and sitting near him while pretending that she wasn't thinking about their date was the right thing to do, but she wasn't up for it. "I think I'll head on home."

"You sure?"

"Positive. I'm also positive that I don't need to be walked out."

"Okay, then. See you tonight."

She grabbed her sweater, tightened her grip on her purse, and opened his office door. After that, it wasn't difficult to ignore everyone's curious expressions as she walked out the way she'd come in.

Just forty minutes ago.

Only when the door to Walden Wax Works shut behind her and the cool breeze cooled her cheeks did she bother smiling.

And then she couldn't help but smile the whole way back home. Junior had forced her to talk, listened to everything she said, and offered advice.

He'd also sparred with her, hadn't taken a bit of her attitude, and had kissed her like he was a starving man and she was the main course.

He was everything.

It seemed she'd met her match.

CHAPTER 27

Junior had a date in two hours and he had no idea what he was doing. He felt restless, anxious, and confused. None were emotions he welcomed. The trio of unwanted emotions had sprung up the moment Elizabeth walked out of his office, and had persisted long after she'd gone home. If anything, they'd intensified whenever he spied the questioning looks of his employees.

There had been a lot of those.

There was no doubt that Cherry had happily shared what she'd seen in his office. There was also no doubt that pretty much everyone in the company had an opinion on the matter.

He didn't appreciate that.

But did he blame everyone for gossiping about their boss? Nope. If the positions had been reversed, he would have done the same.

It would have been much better if he could avoid everyone, but since that wasn't possible, he sidestepped every question or comment that had to do with Beth and redirected the attention back where it belonged: around all things candles.

After he got home and greeted his old dogs, he walked with them in the fields and attempted to push his mind off Beth. No, off of the way he felt whenever he was around her. She made him feel foolish and reckless. He didn't like that.

It wasn't him. Not even a little bit.

"What is going on with me, Clyde?" he asked. "I'm usually all about being forthright and careful. Now, here I am, mooning over a woman who's not only English, but she's expecting another man's baby."

His infatuation with her was firmly ripped from the pages of one of those tawdry books his mother liked to read.

Not that she'd ever said they were tawdry. She'd simply called the books romances and explained that they were all about people facing difficult circumstances in their lives but somehow still found love. She had always liked them.

Come to think of it, his *daed* had never complained about Mamm reading those books. Once, he'd even admitted that he'd read one when he'd been sick in bed and bored. He'd said it was good and had made the hours fly by.

Maybe Junior was the only one who seemed to feel that falling in love was a bad thing.

Looking down at the Labrador closest to him, he said, "What do you think, Honor? Is what I'm feeling normal and I'm just late to the party?"

Honor whined a bit, leaned close for a pat, then trotted off to Clyde's side. Her mate. Her best friend.

"There's your answer, you fool," he muttered to himself. "Even your dogs know how to fall in love. What's wrong with you?"

"You talking to yourself again, Junior?" Samuel asked.

And now his evening was complete. If he wasn't dealing with enough confusing emotions, he now had to add his brother into the mix. He felt like throwing his hands up in the air and yelling.

But since that wasn't possible, he settled with something a whole lot more direct. "What are you doing here, Sam?"

His brother stopped. For a second he looked hurt, but then he blinked and that hint of insecurity was gone. As he started forward, his usual cocky expression was in full force.

"If it ain't obvious to you, then I reckon you've got more problems than I already imagined." He knelt on the ground as both dogs rushed toward him, tails wagging. As both Honor and Clyde leaned close for pets, even circling him in an attempt to get closer, Junior watched with a somewhat bemused feeling.

It wasn't directed toward Sam or the dogs, either. Instead, he was bemused with himself. He'd always believed that his two Labs were the best judges of character he knew.

They avoided some folks like the plague, and no manner of coaxing could get them to change their mind about them.

Then, just as he was getting fed up with apologizing for his pets' behavior, the person who they were avoiding would show his or her true colors and he'd be feeling justified all over again.

There had never been a day that Clyde and Honor had shied away from Sam. He'd been the only one to do that.

"You're awfully quiet, brother," Sam said as he fell into step by his side.

"I guess I am. I was just thinking about how much the *hunds* enjoy your company."

He looked down at them again. "That's because they're smart."

Unable to help himself, he laughed. "Maybe smarter than me."

Most of the smirk that had been staining Sam's expression evaporated. "What's going on with you?"

He opened his mouth to tell him nothing. After all, his relationship with Elizabeth was his own business and no one else's. But keeping all his feelings to himself wasn't helping him any. Worse, it wasn't helping things with Elizabeth. Sure, he'd told her some of his feelings, but he hadn't given her any promises.

Women needed promises. More importantly, Elizabeth deserved for him to give some to her.

Taking a deep breath, he said, "I think I'm in love."

Sam straightened. "Yep, I reckon you are."

"Wait. You're not going to ask who I'm in love with?"

"It's Beth. Of course it's Beth. I'm sure anyone who's seen you with her thinks it's obvious."

"You think so?"

"I know so." As they continued to walk, Samuel waved a hand. "Fact of the matter is . . . you're different, Brother. You're wearing a look on your face that says your focus has changed, and that focus has nothing to do with candles and everything to do with a pretty blond woman who's much younger."

"You're right."

Sam's smirk widened into a true grin. "If I wasn't feeling so sorry for you, I'd ask you to repeat yourself. I don't remember you ever saying that I was right about anything before."

"Yeah, well . . . Enjoy your fun. It's right awkward and I don't know what to do."

"That's because there ain't anything you can do. Your heart has already made up its mind."

"You sound almost poetic. How is that?"

With a shrug, Sam strode closer. "I don't know. I guess I'm just remembering what being in love felt like."

He'd been in love? His screw-up brother had already felt this way and Junior had had no memory of it? "I didn't know that. When?"

Sam darted a look his way before staring directly in front

of himself again. "I fell in love when I was sixteen." His voice was monotone and his expression was blank.

As if even remembering the girl brought him almost too much pain to bear.

Shocked, Junior tried to remember that far back. When Samuel was sixteen, he'd been twenty.

Fifteen years ago.

Junior had been consumed with growing his company and helping with the farm. He'd been frustrated with his brother because he hadn't done either of those things. He'd always been away from the house. With Alison.

His girlfriend.

"Ally," he whispered.

"*Jah*. Don't you remember that I was courting her seriously? Practically every evening I showed up at her *haus* with a bouquet of flowers and a bunch of sweet words."

"I remember you courting. And I vaguely remember Ally, but I don't remember what happened." It was right around the time their parents died and their lives had upended.

"What happened is I proposed to Ally, John. I got down on one knee, bared my heart, and promised not only to get baptized, but to work hard and make her proud of me. I promised that we could be engaged for years, if she wanted. That I wouldn't push her to marriage or . . . or anything. We could take everything as slowly as she wanted. I promised a ton of things."

"Sam . . ." He was at a loss for words. How had he forgotten this?

Still not looking at him, Sam shook his head. "I can't believe I said so much. I pretty much pulled my heart out and laid it at her feet. I would have done anything to win her hand. Anything." Sounding hoarse, he grunted. "I was such a fool. And naïve. So naïve."

"So, she refused?"

"Not at first."

"What happened?"

"It was her parents who refused me. They called me a charmer and a fool, and then made sure Ally soon felt that way, too. Two days later, she refused me. Just days after . . ."

"After our parents died." Junior said as they came to a stop.

"*Jah.*" He swallowed. "Her parents not only believed that I was too young and a charmer, but I had no support system, either. They said she could do so much better."

"She wouldn't consider waiting?"

"Nope. Even though we were young, she didn't want to give me more of her time. She didn't want to give me time to prove myself."

"She didn't believe in you."

Looking at him directly in the eye, Sam nodded. "She didn't believe in me enough."

"What happened to her?"

"A year later, she believed in her second cousin a whole lot more and married him. They live on some farm in Indiana now."

Suddenly, a memory surfaced. One that he'd firmly tucked away. "You came home one night crushed and told me about it. But I didn't listen."

"You did more than that, John."

He was right. It had been a bad night after a worse day. He'd discovered that his father owed money to a lot of people and they were going to lose the farm. He'd felt so alone and scared, both for his future and for Sam's.

He'd also been exhausted, because he'd been caring for the animals and trying to get food and cook something that wasn't burned.

He'd been resentful of Samuel never being much help and was even guilty of being resentful of his brother's young age. He hadn't wanted to raise him.

He'd been feeling so many terrible, shameful things, when

Sam had come home with tears in his eyes, he'd lashed out at Sam. He'd told his little brother that Ally's parents had been right not to believe in him because he was lazy. Then he'd said that he hadn't believed in him, either.

"That's when you left."

"Yeah." He shrugged. "I mean, what else could I do? Mom and Dad were gone, you were angry, and everything inside of me was breaking."

"I'm sorry." Inwardly, he cringed. He sounded trite. Ineffectual. Even though he was sincere, what did it matter? What mattered was that he hadn't been there for his brother years ago, and he hadn't been there for him yesterday.

If he wanted things to change, he was going to have to be different. Starting this minute. "You want something to eat?"

"When? Like now?"

"Well, yeah. Are you hungry?"

He shrugged. "I could eat."

Those three words were straight from the past. Straight out from their childhood, when their mother had always teased Sam, saying that if she wasn't careful, he would eat her out of house and home. Junior couldn't remember a time when Sam had ever refused a meal, snack, or treat.

"You are giving me the oddest look," Sam said. "Like you're trying not to laugh. What did I say?"

"Nothing." When he saw the hurt flare in his brother's eyes, he knew that he was going to have to explain himself. "It's just you used to say that same thing when we were growing up. Mamm would ask if you were hungry or wanted a snack and you always said that."

He looked away. "I'd forgotten."

"Until just now, I had, too." Getting chilled, he led the way inside. "Come on. I'll make you a roast beef sandwich."

"You going to make one for yourself, too?"

"No. I'm taking Beth out tonight."

"When? In a little over an hour."

Sam's eyebrows rose. "Hey, how about I leave?"

"Please don't. I . . . I think I need to sit with you for a while. Besides, while we are sitting, you can tell me what's going on."

"Maybe I stopped by just because I wanted to say hello and see how you were doing."

"Since you know I'm in love, we've got that covered. I'm more than happy to talk about you now," he added as he opened the refrigerator and took out a brown paper package with a pound of roast beef inside.

"You might regret that."

"Doubt it," he replied as he pulled out a package of cheese, a loaf of rye bread, and a jar of refrigerator pickles. "Help yourself. There's mustard and mayo in the fridge."

He sipped water while Samuel put together his meal. Sam might be different from him, but it seemed that their choice in sandwiches was exactly the same.

Junior thought about that while Sam poured himself a glass of milk, sat down, and finally bowed his head in silent prayer. He realized that there was an ease between them that hadn't been there in a long while.

Maybe not ever.

When he finished the meal, Samuel leaned back in his chair. "To finally answer your question, the reason I came over was because I wanted to see you."

Junior nodded. Prepared himself to hear the reason why. Maybe he wanted to work at Walden Wax Works, after all? "Whatever you have to say, I promise to listen."

"All right." He shifted. "I wanted to get to know you again."

Junior held his breath, waiting for the rest of the words. None were forthcoming.

"Wait, that's it?"

"That's it." His younger brother's brows lowered. Reminded him of the way he used to ask him to do things when he couldn't. Open jars. Reach items on a top shelf.

Spell words. Solve math homework.

Lift a shovel filled with fresh dirt.

"Is that all right with you?"

Sam's voice penetrated the memories. Pulled on his heart. "Yes," he said at last. "Yeah. I'd like that, too."

A pleased smile appeared on his face. "That's good, right?"

"It's real good." As he returned his brother's smile, Junior reckoned that there wasn't another thing that needed to be said.

CHAPTER 28

For the first time in months Beth had a date. A real date, and one that she was excited about, a guy she was excited about. But instead of being able to focus completely on that, her younger brother was making a nuisance of himself. Just like when they were teenagers.

"Do you really think that this is a smart idea?" Jonny asked from his perch on the end of Beth's bed.

Beth was a little taken aback by his comment. Jonny was rarely critical about anything she did. Taking another look at her reflection in the mirror that hung over her dresser, she shrugged. "I know I shouldn't want to wear any makeup, but this is just a little bit of mascara." Feeling his judgmental gaze on her back, she added, "I might have brushed a little bit of bronzer on my cheeks, too, but I'm so pale. It's not the end of the world, Jon. I'm not Amish yet."

Leaning back on his hands—which were positioned behind him on her neatly made twin bed—her brother snorted. "I could care less how much makeup you're wearing."

"Are you sure? Because you've been kind of glaring at my reflection."

"I haven't been glaring. Don't be so dramatic."

"Sorry, but you kind of have been shooting disproving looks at my back." After smoothing back her hair, which she'd left long, she decided she was as ready as she'd ever be for her date.

Well, she would be if she could get her brother to leave her room.

Turning to him, she smiled. "What do you think?"

"I think you look fine."

"Fine? That's it?"

"What else do you want me to say? You're my sister, not my wife."

She supposed he had a point. "How about this, then? Do I look really pregnant?"

Jonny sat up and studied her. "I think women look pregnant or they don't. There aren't varying degrees."

"You're wrong about that." When he frowned, she exhaled. "I don't even know why I'm talking to you about makeup and my baby bump, anyway." She snapped her fingers. "Oh yeah. Because you were asking if I thought wearing mascara on my pale-blond eyelashes was smart."

"I wasn't talking about your eyelashes, Bethy. I was talking about this date." He sounded annoyed.

"Why would you think going out to supper with Junior Lambright wouldn't be smart?"

"There are about three good reasons to start with."

Boy, she hated it when her younger brother tried to act like he was the boss of her. Feeling like they were kids again, she turned to face him. "Like what?"

"One, you're pregnant."

Oh! He'd had the gall to hold up a finger. "Junior's already figured that out, Jon."

"Still."

She folded her arms across her chest. "Is that reason number two?" she asked with false sweetness.

"No." He got off the bed. "Reason number two is that he's thirty-five years old."

"That's not a surprise, either."

"He's too old for you, Beth."

"He's not. I'm twenty-eight. Seven years isn't a big deal."

"It is when you're older."

"It would've been a problem if he was eighteen and I was eleven, too. But it isn't a problem now." She rolled her eyes. "I cannot even believe you."

"Just because you don't want to hear what I have to say doesn't mean I'm wrong."

He looked so smug. "I agree, but in this case, you *are* wrong!"

"Beth, stop yelling!" Mommi called up the stairs.

She winced. "Sorry!" she called out. Lowering her voice, she said, "Well, don't stop now. Tell me the third reason."

"Why should I? You're not even listening to me."

"I have been listening. I just haven't been agreeing with you. Now just tell me your third reason so I can get you out of my room."

He strode toward the door. "Fine. You work for him. You can't date your boss."

"He's not my boss." He was her almost-boss.

"He owns Walden Wax Works, Beth!"

"I know that!"

"Jonny and Elizabeth Schrock!" Mommi called. "What are you two doing?"

"We're arguing, Mommi!"

"Well, stop it now. You two are too old for this."

"We aren't!" Beth yelled. When they heard boots stomp on the stairs, she pointed to the door. "Good for you, Jonny. You've brought Dawdi up here."

Jonny paled slightly. "He canna blame me—Oh. Hey, Martin."

"Hi." Looking like he was trying not to smile, he turned to face Beth. "Having fun?"

Beyond frustrated, she grabbed her purse. "No. I cannot even believe that my baby brother is dispensing words of wisdom. Sorry you had to get involved."

"I didn't care. Though I admit that this is a first. Way to go, Jon."

"Stop. I'm already baptized and happily married. I might be younger than the two of you, but I think I'm doing something right."

"Please. You have Treva to thank for all of your good fortune," Martin countered. "And don't say a word because your wife is here and we've all been listening to the two of you act like you are fifteen years younger."

Jonny groaned. "Treva is never going to let me live this down. Why didn't you tell me that before?"

"Mainly because I couldn't get a word in edgewise." While Jonny muttered something under his breath and strode down the hall, Martin grinned. "It was also kind of fun listening to the two of you embarrass yourselves."

Beth was hurt. "Martin, that is kind of mean. All I was doing was defending myself."

"Maybe. Or . . . maybe you were having a good time acting like a kid again."

Exchanging glances with Jonny, Beth felt all her irritation with him fade away. "It was kind of fun, but I'm sorry that I got so mad."

"Don't worry about it. Richard told me that Kelsey got real emotional over every little thing he said when she was pregnant. I shouldn't have egged you on."

Martin chuckled. "When we were kids, I would have given anything for the two of you to apologize and move on so easily."

"Whatever, Martin."

"Don't get annoyed with me now. Listening was fun. Plus, Junior looked a little stunned."

"Junior is here, too? Why didn't anyone tell me?"

"I came up here to tell you."

"Oh, stop!" she blurted. "You know you could've come up earlier."

"Sorry, Bethy. But, for the record, I think your eyelashes look great."

He'd been listening that long? "I hate you right now."

He threw an arm over her shoulder as they headed to the stairs. "I know you don't."

"I don't. I love you. But, oh my gosh." And then she didn't have anything to say, because there was Junior, standing next to Treva, Jonny, her grandparents, and Patti. "Hey, Junior," she said weakly. "Sorry to keep you waiting."

"I didn't mind," he said as he moved to her side. Lowering his voice, he added, "Besides, we both know I'm kind of used to it."

Her embarrassment was now complete.

Two hours later, after they'd demolished half a pizza, she was smiling at him. "This was a fun night. Thank you for taking me out."

"I hope we do it again."

"I hope so, too."

Leaning back against the fake leather red seat in the booth, Junior said, "Hey, Beth, may I ask you something?"

"Of course."

"Did you agree with any of those things that Jonny was saying?"

"No."

"Are you sure?"

"Junior, I don't know what the 'right' thing to do is anymore. All I know is that I want to worry less about what other people think and more about what I want."

He leaned forward. "What do you want?"

"I want to be around you," she admitted. "I don't care that I'm pregnant and you're seven years older and that I still can't quite give up my mascara. When I'm with you, none of that matters."

"That's all I needed to hear."

"Are you sure?"

He nodded. "Beth, I know we need to spend more time together, and I'm willing to do that. But even now, I know a couple of things, too."

"What?"

"One, I don't care about our ages because I want you in my life. Two, I want to be a part of your life and your baby's life. And three, I could care less if you work for me or sell real estate or don't want to work ever again. I just want you."

"I just want you, too."

"Then let's get out of here so I can kiss you again."

She smiled when he signaled for the check.

CHAPTER 29

Almost two weeks after Beth's first "real" date with Junior, Martin asked for all of them to get together. All of them had meant the four of them, plus Treva and Richard. And Patti, too.

After much discussion, they'd ended up going to the Trailside Café. The restaurant had a large oak community table near the back. A dozen people could sit there easily, which meant their group had plenty of space to arrange their coffee cups and assorted pastries.

Even though it was after hours and past time for Treva to be working, she still was manning the counter and making everyone's favorite coffee drinks—all in decaf so none of them would be up all night.

Sitting next to Patti, he shared a smile with her. When the group of them all got together, it got pretty loud. They all chatted like it had been weeks since they'd all seen each other.

Patti was always a bit taken aback by the chatter, but it was as comforting to him as the faint chirps of crickets in late summer. Both things were familiar.

"Anyone need anything else?" Treva called out over the

low din. When no one answered immediately, she raised her voice. "Last call!"

"We're good, Trev!" Jonny yelled to his wife. "Come sit down."

"Okay, but I'm serious. It's now or never, gang."

Beth chuckled. "In another life, Treva would have been a fantastic bartender."

"I've thought the same thing," Jonny said with a laugh. Looking down the row at the lot of them, he said, "Treva might disagree, but for my sake, please say you're good. She's been serving people all day."

"I think we're good, Jonny," Patti said.

"Richard and I are fine, too," said Kelsey.

"I'm fine, too. Come join us," Beth half shouted.

Treva placed her elbows on the countertop. "Are you sure, Beth? You looked pretty tired when you came in. Feel free to ask for something." When Jonny looked ready to interrupt, she shot him an impatient look. "Don't start. You know this is different."

Beth smiled. "Thanks, but I really am fine."

"We're all good, Treva," Martin said. "Come sit down."

"Yes," Kelsey added. "Plus, before we leave, we'll help you wash all the dishes and set you up for the morning."

"That isn't necessary."

"Of course it is," she retorted. "We're family, right?"

Treva smiled, transforming her already pretty features into something really lovely. "Right."

Five minutes later, after she took the vacant chair next to her husband, Kelsey's husband, Richard, cast a sympathetic glance toward Patti, who'd been appearing more and more apprehensive as each minute passed. "I'm happy to hang out with all of you as long as you'd like, but if there's a specific reason you asked us all to join you, maybe it's time to do that, Martin."

"Richard's right," Beth said. "Patti, at first I thought all our noise was making you uncomfortable, but it's something more, isn't it?"

She nodded.

Kelsey cleared her throat. "Say something, Martin. Please put Patti out of her misery."

Wishing that he'd thought things through a bit more, Martin wrapped an arm around Patti's shoulders. "What do you think? Are you ready?"

"*Nee*, but I don't think I'll ever be ready," she whispered.

He hated to hear that. Starting to fear that he'd rushed her into a big announcement before she was truly ready, he said, "Do you want me to do it?"

"*Nee*. I'll be okay."

She didn't sound close to being "okay," though. Beth, who was sitting across from her, studied her carefully.

"You're starting to worry me," Kelsey said. "Are you okay?"

"*Jah*. I mean, I think so."

"You think?" Kelsey, never one to sit around and wait for an answer when she could take charge, frowned. "What is wrong? Are you sick? Martin—"

Richard covered one of her hands with his own. "Patience, love."

"I'm trying."

Kelsey and Richard's exchange seemed to give Patti the burst of bravery that she'd been trying to summon. "I'm ready, and *nee*, I'm not sick." When she looked his way again, Martin nodded. "All right, then." She leaned closer to Martin's side, took a fortifying breath, and then finally lifted her chin. "I'm in love."

One second passed. Two. Then, like the appearance of fireflies on a hot July night, bright grins and laughter surrounded them.

"Tell me that you've finally put Martin out of his misery," Jonny teased.

"I have. I mean, I'm hoping I have."

"You have," he whispered. Turning back to everyone else, Martin grinned. "Absolutely."

Treva beamed at them. "This is wonderful news. *Wunderbar!* Right, Jonny?"

"Very much so."

Martin wrapped his arm around Patti. "We have even better news. We're going to get married."

Looking shy, Patti reached into the pocket of her dress and pulled out a ring.

The ring he'd handed her just the night before.

A small gasp was heard, just seconds before applause, whistles, and a chorus of "congratulations" rang out.

Richard and Kelsey stood up and hugged them, followed by Treva and Jonny, and then Beth.

"*Now* you tell us?" Beth teased as she finally got her turn to hug them. "One day someone needs to teach you how to break good news. The way you both were dragging your feet made us all afraid that something was wrong."

"I concur," Kelsey said as they all returned to their seats. "Wait. Patti, you don't look relieved."

"Patience, Kels," Richard murmured.

When Martin met his eyes, he realized his preacher brother-in-law knew exactly what that ring signified. "That's because we haven't finished telling you what we need to," he said. "We have something more to share."

"I know," Jonny said. "The two of you are going to live on Patti's beautiful farm, right next to Mommi and Dawdi?"

"No, that's not what's going to happen," Martin admitted.

"What is?"

"Yeah, what are you going to do? Where are you going to live?"

"In Cleveland," Patti said in a rush. She'd spoken a bit loudly. She'd needed to because of the way his family couldn't stop interrupting each other.

But those two words seemed to echo in the room and reverberate.

And little by little, all the meaning behind her statement permeated the room.

And with it, the happy, excited smiles faded.

As well as the lighthearted teasing.

Richard, most especially, looked somber. "You've decided to leave the faith, Patti."

His voice had no doubt been carefully judgmental, but the way Patti's eyes filled with tears made Martin want to lash out at him. Yes, he was a preacher, but couldn't he have simply acted like a future brother-in-law for a moment first? Didn't Richard see how nervous and scared Patti was already?

"Yes."

Concern filled his features as he turned to Martin. "I'm assuming you understand what this means?"

"Of course I do. You don't honestly think I don't, do you?" Looking at each member of the family, Martin wasn't afraid to let his feelings show. "Look, I think each of you understand what Patti and I have been going through. Especially Beth, Jonny, and Kelsey."

"We do," Kelsey said.

"If you do, then you might remember a specific conversation the four of us had in the car on the way to our grandparents' house several years ago."

"Of course we do," Jonny added. "We all agreed to give this decision a try but to understand and support every one of our choices."

"Each one of you has made one. Each one of you has upended your life. And I'm talking about Richard and Treva

here, too. The Lord knows I tried my hardest to leave everything behind. I just couldn't. I couldn't."

"And I didn't want him to," Patti blurted.

When they all turned to face her, her voice grew stronger.
More determined and confident. "I didn't make this decision
lightly, but I love Martin with all my heart. I'm going to be
able to make a life by his side. I'm going to be just fine, because he loves me just as much." Her voice turned strained,
but she continued. "Please. I know a lot of people in this
community aren't going to support my decision. Maybe they
never will. But I'm hoping that you will. Please put your
love for Martin ahead of your personal opinions."

"No, Patti," Beth said. "I'm sorry, but I can't do that."

The collective group inhaled sharply.

As Patti stared at her with a wide-eyed expression, Martin
felt his temper flare. "Do you hear yourself, Beth?" he bit
out. "I suggest you apologize now."

"Just listen, will you?"

Jonny groaned. "Sorry, but you're off track, Sister."

"Yes, the guys are right, Beth. You're out of line," Kelsey
said. "What has gotten into you?"

Just as Martin was about to heap on more criticism,
Richard cleared his throat. "Let's allow Beth to speak."

"*Danke*, Richard." Turning back to Patti, Beth said, "What
I've been trying to say is that we all love you, too, Patti. I
don't want to only think of Martin. We want to put our love
for you and Martin first."

"Thank you," Patti said. "I'm very touched."

"And I apologize," Martin said. "I guess —"

"That you want to protect your girl from hurt? I get it."

"What's going to happen now?"

"Well, since I've already spoken to the bishop and my ex-
tended family, I'm going to put my house on the market."

"When is the wedding?"

They exchanged glances again. "We were thinking sooner than later," Martin said. "Something private and small. Maybe at the courthouse."

Kelsey gasped. "Martin."

"I know it's not ideal, but I also know that any service is going to be filled with some hurt feelings." Reaching for Patti's hand, he said, "I intend to spare her that."

"What about Pastor Donovan in Cleveland?" Jonny said. "I always liked him. He might be able to give you some ideas about your ceremony."

"Who is he?" Treva asked.

"He was the pastor of the nondenominational church near my university," Martin said. "Now he's head of a church in Wooster."

Beth nodded. "That's a good idea. Hmm. Or I could see if the chaplain from my college might officiate. Maybe you should think—"

Martin interrupted. "Everyone, I love you, but it needs to be our choice. Especially Patti's choice. I want her to be comfortable."

"What do you think, Patti?" Jonny asked in a soft voice.

"I think that I'd like to visit with your pastor. Your family is right. There are a lot of ways to involve the Lord in our wedding. We should investigate that." Turning to look into his eyes, she added, "That is, if you think so, too, Martin."

"I want whatever you want." Unable to help himself, he pressed a kiss on her brow. "As long as you're happy, I'll be happy."

When Patti's smile lit up the room, everything in his world finally felt right.

CHAPTER 30

One week later, Patti was staring out the passenger's side window of Martin's car as he exited the highway in Cleveland. They were going to spend the next week in the city, and she was both nervous and excited about getting a preview of her new life.

Martin had handled all the arrangements with care. He'd be staying in his condominium while she stayed with Martin's father, Matt, and his wife, Kennedy. Matt had taken off a few days of work to help answer any questions she might have, and Kennedy had offered to take her shopping for some "English" clothes.

In addition, she was going on two interviews with small companies in need of a bookkeeper. After much debate, she'd decided to go that route instead of continuing to run her own business. Working for someone else five days a week sounded easier than doing contract work for multiple people. At least, she hoped so. She figured the interviews would help make that decision.

They had lots of other things planned, too. Most importantly, she and Martin would be meeting with a chaplain and finalizing their simple wedding plans. They also planned to have dinner with some of Martin's longtime friends, go for long walks, and simply spend time together in the English world.

They'd both agreed that they needed these few days out of Walden, where they could be supported by his parents but also allowed to blend into the general population and simply "be." Patti was excited for that. Yes, they needed to talk a lot more about how they each envisioned their married life was going to be, but she also wanted some time to get used to all the technology that would soon be part of her daily routine.

But most of all, she and Martin just wanted to be in each other's company. They were in love and engaged to be married. Patti reckoned she was no different from most other brides-to-be. Stars were in her eyes when it came to Martin Schrock.

When Martin stopped at a light, he glanced her way. "How are you feeling, Patti?"

"I'm all right." She shifted, looking down at her legs. They still looked unfamiliar to her. She was wearing a pair of loose jeans, tennis shoes, and a sweatshirt. Her hair was in a long braid down her back. "I still feel a little strange, if you want to know the truth."

A line formed between his brows. "You brought a couple of dresses from Sammi, right?" Sammi was Patti's Mennonite friend back in Walden. When Patti had run into her at the store, she'd filled in Sammi on her big decision. Sammi had been supportive and so kind. She'd also lent Patti a couple of her loose dresses, saying that she might want to ease into dressing English.

But Patti hadn't wanted to go that route. She had a vision for how she wanted to live her life as Martin's wife, and it wasn't as a Mennonite woman. It was as a confident, strong

English woman. And though being "English" didn't mean jeans, there had always been a part of her that thought wearing jeans, a sweatshirt, and tennis shoes would be comfortable.

She hadn't been wrong.

They were comfortable. But they didn't feel familiar, either. More than once, she'd pulled at her sweatshirt and stared at her jeans in confusion.

Returning to Martin's question, Patti said, "I did bring those dresses."

"When we get to my place, you can change if you'd rather."

"Thanks, but I think I'll be fine. Like I said, I'm not uncomfortable, I . . . I just feel a little bit exposed."

"Would you get mad if I told you that I love seeing your hair down?"

"I won't get mad." Pulling her braid over one shoulder, she added, "I do enjoy it being in a braid instead of pinned up on the back of my head."

"I bet," he said as he drove ahead.

Picking up the end of the braid, she frowned. "Do you think I should cut it?"

"Your hair?"

"Of course, my hair."

"No."

"Are you sure? I don't think too many women have hair that reaches the middle of their back."

"If they don't, it's because they don't have pretty hair like you do."

"Martin."

"Sorry, but that's my opinion. I like your hair that length." As he clicked on a turning signal, he frowned. "Of course, it's your hair. You should do whatever you want with it."

She couldn't help but giggle. "Thanks for giving me permission," she teased.

"You're right. You don't need my permission. But you did ask my opinion."

"True."

"At least we're here at last," he said, as he scanned some kind of card and then they entered a vast, dark parking garage.

Ten minutes later, Martin was opening the door to their future home.

It looked the same as it had almost two years previously. Pristine and modern, with big, bright windows and comfortable, casual furniture.

She walked to the kitchen while Martin deposited his backpack and suitcase on the floor next to the front door.

"Does it look like you remember?"

"It does," she murmured before changing her mind. "I mean, it almost does."

"Almost?" Walking farther into the space, which was really just a galley kitchen against the back wall of the large living area, Martin frowned. "I'm trying to think what could be different. I don't think I changed anything."

"Maybe it's just me." Turning to face him, Patti said, "Before, I was trying to get an appreciation for everything that you would be giving up to live Amish. Now . . ." She allowed her voice to drift off. She didn't want to make things more awkward than they already were.

"Now, you're checking out your new home."

"Yes." She smiled, though she suddenly felt like tearing up. She didn't want to cry because she was marrying Martin, it was that she was going to be adopting a different life.

Martin strode to her side. "Hey," he murmured as he pulled her into his arms for a hug. "We're spending a week here so you can really get a feel for living in the city and being English."

"I know. I know." She swallowed. More doubts settled in, but she pushed them away. The last thing she wanted to do was throw them both into a doubtful limbo again—straddling two worlds.

"Hey, nothing is set in stone, Patti. If you want a longer engagement, we'll do that. If you want to come up to Cleveland four more times, I'll make it happen."

"You'd do that?"

"I'd do just about anything for you."

His words were the stuff of daydreams and romance novels. Sweet, gentle, heartfelt promises that made her believe in the future she always wanted—to be loved for herself, flaws and all.

"I'd do just about anything for you, too," she said.

"Patti, I know you would. You came here." Stepping away, he opened up his refrigerator. With the exception of a few lonely looking condiments, it was empty. "I'll head to the grocery store tonight after I drop you off."

"We can go first thing."

"Nope." He pointed to the digital clock shining white numbers on the front of his oven. "We need to meet Matt and Kennedy for lunch in an hour. Let's get cleaned up and then go."

Three hours later, Patti was feeling far more optimistic. She and Martin had eaten soup and sandwiches with his father and Kennedy at a crowded restaurant near his house. Then, by mutual agreement, they split up. Kennedy took her shopping for more clothes, while Matt went with Martin to the grocery store, the bank, and who knew where else. They had plans to all meet at Matt and Kennedy's house around five. Then, Martin would pick Patti up for a date, then drop her off in time to get a good night's sleep before her interviews the next day.

Walking out of the dressing room in a surprisingly comfortable pair of black slacks, a lavender sweater, and black flats, she looked for Kennedy. She was still on the chair where Patti had left her ten minutes before. "What do you think?" she asked.

"I think you look professional and pretty," Kennedy said.

"Really?"

"Really." When Patti continued to look at herself in the mirror, feeling more and more like an imposter, Kennedy walked closer. With a puzzled smile, the older woman continued. "The slacks fit you well, the sweater looks comfortable, but not too chunky, and the shoes are just fine, too."

"What do you think Martin will say?"

"I think he's going to think the same thing." She took a breath. "Patti, you know you're pretty, right?" When Patti shrugged, Kennedy added, "You have a nice, trim figure, pretty features, and really lovely brown hair."

Unable to help herself, Patti ran a finger along the port-wine stain on her neck. "I hope the folks interviewing me won't think this looks too bad."

"First of all, I barely notice it. And secondly, they're going to want to hire you for your bookkeeping skills, not your looks." Lowering her voice, she added, "You are going to be fine, Patti. I just know it."

"Thanks. Thanks for taking me shopping, too."

Kennedy smiled. "It's been my pleasure. Plus, I wanted to get us off on the right foot. After all, I'm about to be your stepmother-in-law."

The title sounded as silly as Kennedy's worry that Patti wouldn't immediately be comfortable with her. "I don't think you have a thing to worry about."

Reaching out, Kennedy gave her a quick hug. "Good. Now, how about you go try on those other outfits?"

"Okay. I hope we'll have enough time."

"If we run late, I'll text Matt and let him know."

"He won't get mad?"

"Nope. None of us will, honey." Lowering her voice, she added, "Both Matt and Martin warned me that this might be a hard couple of hours for you. You can take all the time that you need to buy your new wardrobe."

"It is hard, but not as hard as I imagined," Patti admitted before heading back into the dressing room.

As she changed clothes yet again, she realized that she was no longer looking at her flaws but her attributes. And was almost looking forward to showing Martin her new look.

Everything was going to be okay.

CHAPTER 31

It was impossible to ignore everything that Elizabeth was saying on the phone. Junior had tried, too. But two things made it hard to do. The first was that she was talking at her desk, which was right across from him. The second reason had more to do with the subject matter. She was talking to a nurse about her baby.

When she'd first started, he would have likely ignored the conversation the best he could. Now, though?

Now they were not only friends, but now they were something more. A lot more. She had his heart.

Life with Elizabeth in it was better. He'd become extremely interested in everything about Elizabeth.

As the conversation continued and her voice turned tense, Junior knew he should leave the room. Or, at the very least, encourage her to do so in order to have privacy.

Not that she ever looked for permission to do much around the office.

However, Junior had long since come to terms with the fact that his entire body had a sixth sense when it came to anything that had to do with Elizabeth. Whenever she was near, half of his head concentrated on her. He now knew when she was tired and needed a break. He knew how much water she should be drinking. He even could tell when she was uncomfortable and needed to take a walk.

Even more perplexing was that she listened to him. He'd watched her shrug off her brothers attempting to help her. He'd even seen her flat out lie to her grandparents and tell them that she felt good and didn't mind helping to wash dishes or sweep the floor.

But whenever he suggested she sit down or take a rest, Elizabeth did.

Even more disturbing than his connection with her was the fact that he wanted to be the person who took care of everything for her. He wanted to be the man who encouraged her to take a ten-minute walk. Or to get her a fresh bottle of water.

Or to fetch her a snack.

Elizabeth Schrock, who appeared to be able to organize entire businesses in hours. Who could probably manage a small country if needed. Whenever he rested a hand on her back, she leaned closer. Whenever he held out his hand, she took it.

No doubt she wasn't sure how to deal with him.

But maybe she did know, after all. Every time he brought her a drink, she'd smile at him in such a way that made him wonder if she'd ever had anyone go out of their way to take care of her.

That was why he knew she was speaking to the doctor and he knew she was worried about whatever she was hearing.

"Okay, thank you," she said quietly. "Yes, I will. No, you're right. This sounds like the right thing to do." She turned and stared at the large calendar on the wall. "That day and time will work for me." She sighed. "Yes. Goodbye."

By the time she hung up, his curiosity—and his obvious eavesdropping—got the best of him. "Was that your doctor?"

"Yes. Well, it was a nurse from the doctor's office." She seemed to take a cleansing breath before looking his way again. "I guess that was obvious, huh?"

"*Jah*. Just like it was obvious that I was trying not to listen but I still did."

She shrugged. "If I was worried about you listening, I would've gone outside or to the staff's room."

"You sounded pretty serious. Is everything all right?"

She shrugged. "I don't know."

Alarm bells went off inside him before he was able to shut them down. "What's wrong? Are you in pain?"

She shrugged again. "No. I mean, not really. I've been experiencing some cramping and numbness in one of my legs. The nurse said the babe might be positioned in a funny way against my spine or something."

"Is that normal?"

"I don't know. I haven't been through this before."

"What did your grandmother say? Or Kelsey? She has a new baby."

"I haven't told them."

"Why not?"

She averted her eyes. "I don't know."

Everything he knew about her was forthright. This uncertainty was both a little disconcerting and endearing. "What is going to happen next?"

"They want me to go to the doctor tomorrow. They're going to take some blood and do an ultrasound."

"Are you worried about going?"

"Maybe . . . but I'll be fine." She smiled, but it didn't reach her eyes. "Don't worry, though. When I get done I'll come back here and catch up on the work I missed."

"I'm not going to worry."

"Oh. Good."

"I'm not going to worry because I'm coming with you."

Her eyes widened in a way that was very un-Elizabeth-like. "Uh, no."

"Sorry, the decision's already been made."

"You can't, Junior."

"Why?"

She folded her arms over her chest. "Because it's private."

"If you don't want me in the room with you, I'll stay in the waiting room." And yes, he was making things up as he went along because he had no idea what he was talking about.

"Do you really think that I'd allow you to be in the room while I'm getting a sonogram?"

"Obviously . . . yes. I mean, unless you were naked or something."

"You and I are not that close."

"Okay. Like I said, I'll wait for you in the waiting room."

"I'd rather I went by myself."

"That ain't going to happen." When she opened her mouth to argue, he stood up and walked to stand in front of her. "And the reason is because I don't want you to have to face anything by yourself."

"Maybe I should just call my mother or something."

"Maybe. Or, maybe you should accept that I'm your friend."

"If you go with me, the staff is going to think you're the baby's father."

"You can tell them I'm not."

"If I tell them that, they're going to think I'm in a relationship with someone else."

Her blue eyes were wide. She looked scandalized, which he thought was hysterical. "I didn't know you cared so much about what strangers thought."

"It's hard not to when I'm lying on a table and those strangers are examining my stomach."

"Understood." Though he knew the right thing to do would be to leave it at that, Junior couldn't help but speak frankly. "Elizabeth, take it from me. People are going to judge you even when you're thinking you do everything right. It's natural to judge each other. I'd worry less about what doctors and nurses think about your lifestyle and more about your health and the baby's well-being. And that includes your mental health, too."

Tears formed in her eyes. "You . . ."

"I know. I'm wading into things that aren't my business."

She shook her head. "No, I was going to say that you are filled with surprises. Thanks for offering to come with me."

"Does that mean you'll take me up on my offer?"

"Yes."

"Good. Now, stand up so I can give you a hug."

She stood up but couldn't help gesturing toward the door. "What if Cherry walks in on us again?"

"Then I reckon she'll have a lot to say about it. But we'll survive. Ain't so?"

Swiping another runaway tear from her face, she nodded.

"*Gut*. Now, come here, Elizabeth. Please."

Because she wanted to be in his arms again, Beth did what he asked. In no time, she was leaning against him, he was holding her close, and it felt like there was nowhere else on earth where she should be.

She relaxed against him and didn't protest once when he began to rub her back. She smiled when he pressed a kiss to the top of her head. Didn't protest when he whispered that everything was going to be okay.

It was almost easy to control her tears when he asked her to stop crying, especially since he'd whispered that he hated it when she cried.

And then, when she glared at him for telling her what to do, he leaned down and kissed her.

And she kissed him back. Eagerly responded when he deepened the kiss.

Enjoyed the moment.

Okay, maybe she enjoyed it all too much. Because now she was pretty sure that there was no way she was going to willingly give him up, no matter what was in store for them in the future.

As she thought about the consequences of that decision, and the possible obstacles they would one day face together, Beth realized her heart was in big trouble. There was no doubt about that.

She'd fallen in love.

CHAPTER 32

Beth had fully expected to be uncomfortable. Junior's determination to accompany her to the doctor had taken her off guard. So had the way he'd acted so relaxed when he'd sat beside her in the waiting room.

She was pretty sure that only Junior Lambright could walk into the middle of an obstetrician's office as nonchalantly as if he was in a feed supply store. While she'd checked in with the receptionist, he'd nodded to the pair of women sitting across the room. Then, ignoring their stares, had started reading a magazine.

When she'd sat down beside him, he'd studied her expression. "You okay?"

"Yes. We might have to wait a couple of minutes, though."

He shrugged. "We got time."

"Thanks for coming with me."

His eyes warmed. "I wanted to be here."

Everything inside of Beth seemed to shift when his words registered. Junior wasn't giving her a line. He meant what he said. He wanted to go to this appointment because she mattered to him.

Just like she'd wanted him to be there because he was important to her.

Still processing that truth, when the waiting room door opened and the nurse called her name, then asked if Beth would like Junior to come back with her, she nodded.

As they walked down the hall, Junior chatted with the nurse about the weather. He stepped to the side when she was weighed, and waited in the hall when she had to run into the bathroom.

Next, she was sent down the hall for a blood draw, her least favorite part of any doctor's appointment.

"Right or left arm?" the tech asked.

"I don't care which arm. I just don't want to see it."

"Let's do your right, then."

As the tech efficiently poked and prodded, she averted her eyes. Inhaled.

"Breathe," Junior murmured. "Yeah?"

At last she exhaled. When she eased, he leaned a little closer and reached for her free hand.

To Beth's amazement, Junior had managed to do everything for her in a quiet, unobtrusive way. He hadn't looked uncomfortable, but it had also been obvious that he didn't want to get in anyone's way.

Not as surprising was the fact that nearly every nurse and tech they saw had smiled at him. Beth didn't blame them. Junior was handsome. The light green shirt he was wearing accentuated his hazel eyes. Plus, there was something about his personality that was so giving and warm. Within five minutes of meeting him, it seemed almost everyone wanted to be his friend.

Beth was starting to feel a little like an odd duck, since she'd had quite a different reaction to Junior the first time they'd talked. Then, too, was the memory of him driving her to her grandparents' house and she being so surly. Back then, she'd judged him unfairly and had barely listened to a word he'd said.

Looking back, she realized that so much of her crossness had been based on how she'd felt inside. She'd been so scared and unsure and wanted to lash out at anything and anyone she could.

Now Beth was beginning to think that their rocky beginning had forged a stronger connection. After all these weeks of working together, they were embedded in each other's lives. Whenever they didn't see each other on the weekends, she missed him terribly. Sometimes she even tried to tell herself that she should stop thinking about him so much.

But that didn't seem possible.

After Junior had stayed out in the hall for the beginning of her doctor's appointment, she'd wanted him by her side when they did the sonogram. For every other one she'd been by herself, even though Kelsey, Treva, Patti, and Mommi had offered to come. She'd refused because she'd felt so alone.

No longer.

"Let's see how this little one is doing," Dr. Summers said, interrupting her thoughts.

After they'd listened to the heartbeat and the doctor explained the numbers she was recording, she turned to Beth. "Are you ready to find out the sex of your baby, Beth?" Dr. Summers asked. "Or have you elected to wait?"

Did she want to know? Discovering that she was going to have either a son or a daughter somehow made everything suddenly seem too real.

She turned to Junior. "What do you think?"

"I think it's your decision, Elizabeth."

"I know. But do you want to know?"

"Yes, but I'm a planner by nature." He looked a bit sheepish. "But more than that, I want you to be happy most of all."

His words meant everything. And, just like the way his presence eased her in the waiting room, his calm acceptance of her decision helped to erase all the doubts she had.

"All right, then." Fortifying herself, she turned back to Dr. Summers. "Yes, we want to know."

The doctor smiled. "You're going to have a boy."

"A boy, Junior."

Eyes on the screen, Junior stepped closer. Linked his hand with the one closest to him. Squeezed gently. "That's wonderful. Nee, *wunderbar*." Turning back to Dr. Summers, he added, "How . . . how is he? Healthy?"

"I believe so. Now, this is his head, obviously. Here's the spine . . ." As she continued, she pointed to the various body parts, sometimes pausing to explain something.

Junior listened intently. Beth had a feeling if she quizzed him about the doctor's explanation, he'd be able to recite all sorts of things right back to her.

For her part, she felt dreamy. And, well, a bit shocked, too. Since Kiran wasn't in the picture, she'd begun to only think of the baby as hers. And because of that, she'd latched on to the baby looking just like her. Her very own mini-me.

But now the reality was shifting things a bit. Instead, she was having a boy. Would he look like Kiran? What would she do if he did? How awkward would that be?

And . . . he'd said he didn't want to be a father. But what would he do if he actually saw his son? Would he change his mind and suddenly try to take him from her?

"Elizabeth?"

"Hmm?" She was startled to discover that Junior had crouched down and was gazing at her in concern. "What's wrong?"

"You started looking a little pale."

"Are you feeling all right, Beth?" Dr. Summers asked.

"I'm fine. It . . . well, I guess reality just hit me hard." She attempted to smile. "I'm good now."

After wiping her stomach, Dr. Summers helped Beth pull back down her dress and pull up her tights. Then Junior on her other side helped her sit up and finally get to her feet.

"Thanks, guys, but I'm good now."

"I printed a few pictures for you to take with you," the doctor said. "Here you go."

Moments later, Dr. Summers left and Junior was helping her put on her cloak. "You know what? I've heard a lot of good things about the diner that's around the corner. How about we go get something to eat."

Eat? She kind of felt like she was on the verge of throwing up. "I don't know . . ."

"Elizabeth, this is a pretty big day. It would be a shame not to celebrate it. Don't you think? I heard the pancakes are fantastic."

"You're right. Pancakes sound like a good way to celebrate this boy."

"Good. Come on, then." After retrieving everything, he walked her out to the reception area, double-checked the date of the next appointment, and then he guided her to the elevator.

When they were alone, he said, "What's gotten you so rattled?"

"I always imagined that this baby was a girl. It's caught me off guard."

"Do you really not want a boy?"

"Oh no. It's not that at all. I think a little boy would be adorable. It's more . . . well, it makes me wonder if the boy will look like his dad."

"I reckon he might."

"But . . . what if that makes Kiran change his mind about being involved?" She knew she was focusing on her greatest fears, but what could she do?

Junior shrugged. "If this man wants to be involved in your boy's life, I reckon that is a good thing. That means he loves him."

254 Shelley Shepard Gray

"Maybe," she said as the elevator doors opened and they stepped out.

As they passed two nurses in the hall, Junior motioned her to one side. "What are you thinking?"

"I'm worried that Kiran will suddenly want more rights or try to take this baby from me . . . or, I don't know." Tears started to fill her eyes as all her worries compounded, strengthened, and seemed to threaten to take her breath away.

Reaching for her hand, Junior whispered, "I thought you told me that you and Kiran were friends."

"We were."

"Did you think he was a terrible or unreasonable person when you were friends?"

"No, of course not."

"And didn't he agree to get a lawyer involved and sign paperwork?"

"He did. But I also promised to let him know if anything important happened or if I needed his help."

"I think it's best you focus on the positive, then. When you get back home, give this Kiran a call and tell him that your babe is a boy."

"And then what?"

"Listen to what he has to say. But I reckon he won't be all that surprised. I mean, there was a fifty percent chance that was going to happen, ain't so?"

"I suppose."

Lowering his voice, Junior added, "Please stop worrying. No matter what happens, you're not alone. We'll handle the future together. Okay?" After she nodded, he exhaled. "*Gut.* Now, let's go eat."

"You make everything seem so easy."

"Life ain't easy, but you can't be borrowing trouble, Elizabeth. Let's choose to think good things. I feel certain that a great many good things are coming our way."

As they walked to their table in the diner, Beth sat down across from him with a big smile.

"Aren't the two of you cute?" the server asked as she came to take their order. "I haven't seen a couple look so happy together in ages. And . . . are you expecting?"

Elizabeth's cheeks were pink, but it was obvious that her flush was from happiness, not embarrassment. "I am."

"Do you know what you're having?"

Turning to Junior, she shared a smile with him. "We're having a boy," she said.

"A boy! Congratulations!"

"Thank you," Junior said. "We're very happy."

EPILOGUE

It was June again. On this month, five years ago, the four of them had piled in Martin's vehicle and driven down to Walden to speak to their grandparents about becoming Amish.

While he drove, Beth directed—and Kelsey and Jonny had both tried to tell each of them what to do—and the four of them had weighed the pros and cons about becoming Amish. It hadn't been the first time they'd discussed it. It hadn't even been the tenth.

No, after their first, eye-opening discussion, they'd talked, texted, and emailed each other over and over again. Each of them had been excited to announce their plans to their grandparents.

They'd each been worried about their grandparents' reaction. Martin had tried to pretend that everything was fine. It had been what he did all his life—take care of his brother and sisters no matter what happened.

But inside? Well, inside, he'd been a nervous wreck.

No, they'd all been nervous wrecks.

Remembering their grandparents' expressions when they'd

shared their plans, he had to smile. He was pretty sure that they'd been nervous wrecks, too.

That hadn't stopped them from moving forward, though.

Now that that day was so far in the past, Martin often found himself wondering how they'd ever been so brave in the first place.

But then, of course, he knew. God had been in charge. Martin might have been behind the wheel of his vehicle and Beth might have been trying to keep the four of them organized and calm . . . but in actuality, the four of them had merely been along for the ride. All they'd had to do was trust in what He was directing them to do and hold on tight.

Martin shook his head. He'd always thought that he'd had a strong faith. He'd believed in God and he attended church when he could. But it wasn't until they'd pushed themselves and tested the boundaries of their lives that things had changed. He'd stopped imagining that the Lord was kind of, sort of looking after him, and started believing that deep in his very soul.

Three years ago, after a series of events had caused Treva and Jonny to miss spending Thanksgiving with them, and Beth and Junior had been forced to stay home for Christmas, Kelsey had decided to make June fourth "their" day. No matter if kids were sick, or there was an important project at work due, or even a torrential thunderstorm, the four of them promised to meet at their grandparents' house for supper.

And now, here they were again.

Well, he, Beth, and Kelsey were. Jonny was running late. Again.

Standing on the front porch, Beth crossed her arms over her chest. "I swear. Next year, I'm going to pick him up."

"If you stop by his *haus* to get him, you'll end up being late, too," Kelsey pointed out. "Jonny gets sidetracked like no one else on earth. I used to think Treva was to blame, but now I realize that he makes her late, too."

"I don't know why we thought he'd change. Remember how he'd poke around eating breakfast before school?"

"Or take the longest showers?" Martin added.

"I heard that!" Jonny called out as he sauntered toward them.

Martin felt like rolling his eyes. His younger brother was tan, fit, and looking far too much like an Amish romance cover model. But maybe that was because he was wearing a broad grin.

"Glad you could make it, Jon," Beth said sarcastically.

He didn't miss a beat. "Thanks, Sis. I wouldn't miss our annual get-together for the world. And I'm not that late. Only five minutes."

"The rest of us managed to get here early." Kelsey sniffed.

Jonny raised his eyebrows. "Kelsey, if you start saying stuff like that, I'm going to call you Beth Junior."

As they'd all expected, Beth narrowed her eyes. "I take exception to that."

"Come on. You've played that card from the time we were small. Showing up early and then looking down your nose at the rest of us for actually taking the clock—and the schedule—at face value."

"I might have done that."

"You did, Bethy," Kelsey blurted.

"Well, I don't anymore."

"I'll ask Junior."

When Beth inhaled sharply, Martin blurted, "I did not leave Patti's side to listen to the three of you argue."

"I'm surprised you left her side at all," Jonny teased.

Feeling his cheeks heat, he glared at his brother. Then he realized that Beth and Kelsey were grinning as much as Jonny was. "There's nothing wrong with liking my wife's company."

Beth looked down at her feet, but he was sure she was smiling.

"Come on, guys."

"All I'm saying is that you two have been married for a

while now. Things have got to be settled down by now, Martin," Kelsey said.

He kept his mouth shut but as far as he was concerned, he hoped nothing would ever settle down between him and Patti. They'd both overcome so many things in order to make their relationship happen. And then to become husband and wife.

"Now that you've all given me grief, should we go on inside? At last? It's time."

"I suppose," Beth said.

He knew why she hesitated. Their grandparents weren't home. After he and Patti had returned from their honeymoon, Mommi and Dawdi had announced that they were going to spend the next couple of years traveling. Without looking all that apologetic, they'd declared that as much as they'd enjoyed shepherding three of them into the Amish faith and counseling them as they each fell in love and got engaged, they wanted a break. A long break.

They were big fans of taking long bus trips around the country. Dawdi even confided that they were considering a cruise.

This week Martin was pretty sure they were in Oregon, but he wasn't sure. All he did know was that being in the big farmhouse without their guiding presence would always feel strange.

After they went inside at last, Kelsey opened a few of the windows and screened doors to let in fresh air. Jonny and Beth brought in the coolers filled with lunch and drinks. While he went to the kitchen to pull out dishes and silverware.

When they sat down together, their plates piled high with sandwiches, chips, fruit, and pickles, Martin realized that Beth, Kelsey, and Jonny looked as stunned as he did.

"Let us bow our heads in silent prayer," Kelsey murmured.

And so each of them did.

When the prayers were completed, Beth raised her glass of lemonade.

"Five years ago, I felt like something was missing. It made no sense to me, because I'd gone to college on scholarships that I'd worked hard to earn and I'd obtained a good job that I'd done my best to obtain. I was making good money, and I had a good circle of friends. All I knew was that it wasn't enough. Never did I imagine what would happen."

"You and Martin had it harder than Jonny and me," Kelsey said. "I'd just finished college and felt guilty because I couldn't find a job."

"I was only two years in, but I felt like a failure," Jonny said. "All of you did so much more. I couldn't understand what was wrong with me."

"I was at a crossroads, too," Martin said. "I was working hard, successful, and completely confused." He took a breath. "In some ways, I felt like I was being pulled in two different directions. I wanted to keep my life the way it was, but I wasn't happy and couldn't figure out why. Then, when I realized that the three of you weren't all that happy, either, I felt so guilty."

"You should have never felt guilty," Beth said.

"I know, but for so long I wanted to take care of the three of you. Then, I had to come to terms with the fact that you guys didn't need me anymore. You were grown adults."

"We did need you, Martin. I might be married and have kids of my own, but I still need you," Kelsey added. "I think I always will."

"She's right," Beth added. "I might have tried to mother everyone, but you always made it seem like no burden was too big for you to handle."

As Martin shook his head, Jonny interrupted. "Beth is right. And for the record, that isn't a bad thing. You were our rock. Always. Whenever we needed you, you were there. Just like you made sure that we all made it here."

Feeling embarrassed at receiving so much praise, he said, "Each of us is important to the others. How about that?"

Kelsey smiled. "I'll take that." Then she leaned back in her chair and crossed her arms. "Now all we have to do is figure out what's next."

"What are you talking about?" Jonny asked. "We're all married, two of you have kids, Mom and Dad are happy, and our grandparents are hiking around Crater Lake today. For today, at least, the Schrock family is well."

Kelsey blinked. "So that's it? We're all set?"

She sounded so appalled, Martin chuckled. "Don't worry, Kels. You know that sooner or later something's going to happen and we'll all have to get involved."

She sighed. "I suppose you're right."

"I know I am," Beth said. Gazing at the open screen door, she smiled. "Just like I had an idea that maybe we didn't need to hang out with only the four of us today."

Martin turned his head to see what she was talking about, and then grinned. "You invited everyone else?"

"It felt right."

Jonny was already walking toward Treva with a delighted smile on his face. Kesley was kneeling on the ground to pick up their toddler while Richard was holding their three-year-old's hand.

Beth couldn't seem to look anywhere but at Junior and their son in his arms.

At first, he didn't see Patti. Remembered that she'd told him she was going to go to a garden club meeting or something with some ladies in the neighborhood.

But then, there she was. Walking toward him in a pair of loose khakis, a pale-green T-shirt, and her beautiful hair curled and hanging loose on her back.

He couldn't get to her side fast enough. "What are you doing here?"

"Surprising you."

"But I thought you were going to go to a garden club meeting."

She wrinkled her nose. "Martin Schrock. I can safely say that I've grown more flowers and vegetables than anyone in that club. I just made that up to fool you."

"Well, you succeeded. Hey, how did you get here?" Patti still had no interest in learning to drive.

"I called your dad. He and Kennedy drove me down."

"Are they coming, too?"

Kelsey answered. "Nope. They're staying at our house. Richard and I are going away for the night. His parents are going to watch the kids."

"You look a little perplexed, Martin," Patti said. "Is something wrong? Do you wish we would have stayed away?"

"Never." Looking around at the ten other people, seven adults and three children, he reached for her hand. "You know me. I love a good plan."

"You always have," Jonny said.

"Even though this wasn't how I thought today was going to turn out, it's better than I expected."

"I was thinking the same thing," Beth said as Junior handed her Joe. "But I guess that's how our big decision turned out, right?"

Kelsey nodded. "Our plan to convince our grandparents to take us in was the best thing we ever did."

"Absolutely," Jonny said. "I wanted to be happy. I wanted to feel fulfilled. I wanted to live Plain, but I never imagined that this journey would eventually lead me to so much more."

Looking around at their group, Martin felt a sense of peace he'd once thought would always be out of his grasp. "This feels right, you know?"

"Yeah," said Beth. "I know, exactly."

ACKNOWLEDGMENTS

I wrote most of *C Is for Courting* on my laptop last summer. I began the story just a few weeks before my grandson August was born in California, and finished the novel two weeks after my granddaughter Sloane was born in Tennessee. I wrote lots of this book when I was on a plane, in guest bedrooms, and at my daughter's kitchen table.

Now, looking back, I guess it was rather fitting that the heroine of this novel was expecting a baby of her own. Babies were certainly on my mind!

Because of all that, I have many people to thank for their help with this book. First and most importantly is my husband, Tom. It's not always easy having a wife who's constantly on deadline. Thank you, Tom, for understanding when I needed "just an hour" every day to get my pages done, and for also being the person to tell me to stop typing and pick up a baby!

Big thanks also go out to my friend Lynne, who read this book one chapter at a time. She also kept such good notes about all the Schrock siblings. Thank you again, Lynne!

I'm also very grateful to my editor, Elizabeth Trout. Her kindness and patience are very appreciated. She—and the entire Kensington team—work so hard to make the covers shine and my stories polished. It's a pleasure to write novels for them.

Last but not least, I'd like to thank my readers. It's because of them that we'll continue on this alphabet journey. Readers, thank you so much for embracing this series and my stories. It's because of you that I wake up every morning excited to go to work. I'm blessed.